Clare R.

Clare R.

R. K. Blessing

Book Design and Production
Columbus Publishing Lab
www.ColumbusPublishingLab.com

Copyright © 2014 by Ryan K. Blessing
LCCN 2014950535

All rights reserved. This book, or parts thereof, may not be reproduced in any form without permission.

Print ISBN 978-1-63337-011-1
E-book ISBN 978-1-63337-012-8

Printed in the United States of America
1 3 5 7 9 10 8 6 4 2

To my beautiful muse who time and time again makes me smile.
Thank you.

Foreword

When I started writing this book, I couldn't decide if I wanted to include a foreword or not. A foreword seems very sophisticated and I wasn't sure if it belonged in my goofy attempt at a romantic comedy. However, in the year it took to put this story together, I was privy to some wonderful experiences and it seemed like a foreword would be a great place to share a few of them.

There was also a great deal of unplanned time spent pondering topics that I hadn't ever really thought about before in any measurable detail; life, death, and religion to name a few. But I definitely didn't want to fill a foreword with stuffy hubbub that readers would find boring and just skip. Then before publishing, I read some rather unsettling news on the Internet that kind of ruined my day, so I decided to scrap what I had written for the following.

I always thought it would be fun to write a book but it never seemed possible. The ideas came and went along with my motivation. Never was there anything of substance to keep me going. Then there was the issue of actual publication, which was elusive and daunting. How are you supposed to publish a book if you don't have a killer idea or a good portion of money to get a manu-

Clare R.

script to a reputable publisher?

But last year, I realized it had nothing to do with those things. The reason for not being able to write a book was because I lacked true inspiration, and last year I found that inspiration. It came to me as a complete surprise in the form a person. This person has a personality unlike anything I've ever seen before. This person made me feel like I could do anything, and although we haven't actually met yet, I thank this person every day for helping me to realize what I really want out of life.

As mentioned above, I don't want this to get too stuffy. If you are at all interested in writing, or passionate about anything for that matter, and if you find your inspiration, take the chance and go for it! It will most assuredly be an interesting ride. And to the person who inspired me, if you get the chance to read this I hope you enjoy the story. It would be awesome to meet you in person someday.

Thank you for reading the foreword.

RKB

Chapter 1

Clare was definitely someone you could call a multi-tasker. She had the energy of a marathon athlete, but hated running, so Clare focused that energy into her job. When the alarm on her nightstand went off bright and early, she hustled around the house getting dressed, packing a few leftover items, made a small breakfast, and then hopped into a cab that would take her to the airport. Nothing unpredictable or unexpected happened at the airport and soon she was aboard a short regional flight, enjoying her new book. When the plane landed, Clare wheeled her small carry-on back to the front of the airport and then took another taxi to a hotel her company had booked for her.

After getting settled in, Clare relaxed on the bed and continued reading. Before getting off the plane, the main character in the novel had been in quite a bind and the suspense had been absolutely killing her. By the time Clare reached a good stopping point, she had put a significant dent in the book. The clock on the nightstand burned with a digital glow and to her surprise it was already early in the evening.

Clare grabbed her phone and looked up one of her friends who lived in the area, and sent her a message to see if she was

Clare R.

interested in having dinner. Clare's friend did indeed want to have dinner and they met up at a quaint little place that her friend had wanted to try for some time. They had a great time and Clare returned to her hotel that night feeling content and full. After a hot shower, she climbed into bed and continued reading until she fell asleep.

Early the next morning, with her bag packed once again, Clare checked out of the hotel and took a cab to the conference center that the movie company had reserved for their late morning meeting. Upon arrival, there were several introductions to people Clare hadn't met before and reintroductions to the acquaintances she'd met in meetings past.

Then, with a calm and collected air about her, Clare broke down everything that would need to be done for the movie production to begin. It was a one woman show and she made it look easy. She had spent the past two weeks organizing information and schedules and today was presentation day.

By the end of her presentation, Clare felt that everyone was satisfied and only had to answer a few questions. A couple of the meeting's attendees asked her to lunch but she politely declined. All Clare wanted to do was get back on the plane and read more of her book.

It started to rain during the taxi ride back across town and large, fat drops of rain pounded the pavement as Clare hurried into the airport with her luggage in tow, trying not to get too wet. Usually Clare didn't mind heavy rainstorms but something about this one in particular felt ominous and no matter how hard she tried, she couldn't pinpoint the source of the strange feeling.

The line of travelers waiting to get through security that

snaked through the maze of metal posts and fabric straps appeared very lengthy, but moved along at a good pace. Just before getting to the security gate, her phone jingled and Clare let go of her luggage to check the message. A grim expression crossed her face when she saw that it was a message from a guy, Mike, whom she'd gone on a couple dates with.

Hey. Sorry I haven't called...Been busy.

Instantly Clare knew it was the typical bullshit, cliché cop out that she had heard or read far too many times. Clare did her best to keep a frustrated scowl off her face as she shoved the phone back in her purse and placed her carry-on items in the bins denoted for the x-ray machine. At the direction of a security agent, she stepped into a metal detector and after getting re-situated, Clare walked down the terminal toward her gate.

Like many people, Clare had a habit of always checking the flight boards before doing anything else just to make sure her flight was still in order. That was where she met Steve. Rather, that was where she noticed Steve.

Steve was busy perusing the flight board as well and Clare, to her immense displeasure, immediately noticed that every flight was delayed. It only added to the annoyance of being dumped by text because the last few times she'd been delayed the flights ended up being canceled causing her to spend another night away from home. But before her annoyance could reach a level where she would verbally complain to herself, Clare caught sight of the expression on Steve's face. It was unmistakable. He was smiling. Her annoyance was immediately replaced with curiosity.

How is someone happy about a delayed flight? she wondered. Steve turned away without noticing her and sat down a

Clare R.

short distance away. Clare noticed that the boots he was wearing were worn but his jeans, shirt, and jacket were fairly nice looking, although the jeans were a bit muddy on the bottoms. Since Clare frequently attended fancy functions and formal meetings for work, she was no stranger to dress clothes and often noticed people's shoes.

Maybe he works outside, she guessed. Clare looked back to the board for a moment hoping by some miracle her flight was reinstated. It wasn't and she knew it wouldn't be. Clare bit her lip and stole another glance in Steve's direction.

A pale, olive green baseball cap sat atop his head and she could see sprigs of hair poking out the sides and from under the brim. He removed the cap and ran a hand through his hair. Clare hid a titter behind her hand and turned away again. The hair above his forehead was sticking up because he'd had the hat on for such a long time. It looked sort of silly but Clare happened to like silly.

Steve leaned forward in his chair and she watched as he started digging in his bag. When he pulled out a very *familiar* looking book, Clare couldn't help but smile. Curiosity got the better of her and she decided to go say hello.

~~~~

That morning, Steve woke before his alarm and stared moodily at the ceiling wishing desperately that he could stay in bed. It wasn't long though before his alarm went off and he grumpily got up. It never failed that on days when he had to get up, these were more often than not the exact same days he seemed to sleep the best. It was one of life's conundrums that had always perplexed him. But once Steve was out of bed, he showered and got dressed.

While a bagel cooked in the toaster, Steve shoved the remaining items required for work that day in his bag. Then he paused for a moment to decide which book he wanted to take on the trip. One was a well-worn, travel stained text called, *Coping with Death*. The other was much less depressing and titled *Lunar Chronicles: The Fall of Castle Cerasus*. In the end, Steve opted for the latter and placed the fantasy novel in his carry-on bag. Then he made a final pass around the house to make sure nothing important had been forgotten.

Steve preferred to leave early for his flights and today was no exception. It was before six in the morning and the stars were still twinkling in the sky when the taxi arrived. Since this would only be a long day trip, Steve had decided not to drive and simply brought along his carry-on bag that had some work gear he needed. He sat comfortably in the back seat and talked on and off with the cab driver while eating his bagel.

A few hours later, Steve was walking around the project site discussing engineering matters with various members of the on-site contracting companies as well as taking a great deal of pictures. The notepad from his bag was steadily filling with notes that he scribbled throughout the day and by the time he left later that afternoon, Steve was hungry, tired, and anything regarding engineering was the last thing on his mind.

Now, on the occasions Steve had to travel for work, he more often than not ended up stranded in the airport due to a delay of one kind or another. Most people found this to be quite taxing and aggravating, but in all honesty, Steve rather enjoyed it. The airports were like their own sovereign nations and it was sort of

Clare R.

enjoyable to watch the comings and goings of all the travelers, maintenance personnel, and airport staff.

On past trips, Steve had the opportunity to meet some interesting people and he'd even seen a few celebrities. But no trip before had prepared him for the encounter he was about to have on this quiet, rainy evening. Steve was standing at the departure board after getting through security, searching for his flight. A smile crossed his face when he saw that the flight he was supposed to be on had been replaced with a red label.

Delayed.

Steve turned, not noticing the woman staring at him, found a seat in the gate, and sat down. Steve was in the process of pulling the book from his bag when he noticed the shoes of a lady walking up next to him and then a voice followed.

"Excuse me, but is this seat taken?" she asked. When Steve lifted his head, he looked into the face of a beautiful woman. She had long, wavy, auburn hair, very inviting blue eyes, and a smile that could make any man go weak in the knees.

"Um, no," Steve replied. Thankfully the spike in adrenaline was keeping his brain from losing touch with his vocabulary. "Go ahead."

"Thanks," she said and sat down next to him. Steve immediately caught the scent of her perfume and his senses went nuts. Resisting the urge to say a premature compliment, Steve found his mind racing to come up with some sort of conversation starter. But to his surprise, the woman continued talking. "OK, I have to ask... Was it just me or did I see you smile about a delayed flight?" Steve let loose a quick smile and lowered his head.

"Uh, yeah. You caught me," Steve said. "I kinda like the delays. I get to read a lot and I tend to meet a lot of cool people during them and I think it's fun watching all the stuff that happens in airports." Steve made a motion with his hand indicating all the travelers passing by.

"Do you ever make up stories for these people you watch?" she asked. "Assuming you're a people watcher."

"Oh, all the time," he replied.

"All right," she said. "How about him?" Clare subtly pointed to a gentleman at a nearby deli.

"Seriously? You're kinda putting me on the spot," he said.

"Yeah, sorry. But something tells me you don't mind," she replied. Steve didn't even answer. He just grinned and peered at the man across the concourse.

"His name is Jack and he's about to make a cross country flight. Flying makes him nervous, so he's going to order several sandwiches to eat during the flight to help distract him from the view out the window," Steve said and immediately Clare started grinning.

"OK, what about the guy next to him?" Clare asked. "The tall, thin one with glasses and big bug eyes who keeps glaring at Jack."

"That's Stewart and he's a vegetarian. He's appalled at Jack for ordering so many protein laden sandwiches. It's really stressing him out," Steve said. Just as the last words left his mouth, "Stewart" hit the counter awkwardly with his hand and walked away, causing both Clare and Steve to break out laughing.

"Wow, I guess so," Clare said. "All right. What about that group over there, a couple of gates down?"

"Oh, I don't know. I don't wanna push it," he said. "You try."

Clare R.

"OK," she said. Clare stared at Steve for a moment and he stared back. She did her best to ignore the tingling sensation that was spreading through her body and shifted her gaze to the group of teens. "That's Scarlet, Heather, Sarah, Nicole, Jacky, Tiffany, Erik and Brandon. There are a lot of duffel bags, so I'm going to say they're some sort of dance or cheer group. If you look close, you'll notice the guy to girl ratio is a *little* lopsided, so I'm thinking that those two muscle heads are hoping to get laid this weekend." When Clare looked back to Steve, he was shaking with silent laughter.

"That's pretty good. I like that," he said.

"Good," she said. "What about me?"

"Excuse me?" he said. She really was putting him on the spot now.

"What's my story?" Clare asked. Her lips formed a thin smile that Steve found immensely attractive.

"Well, clearly, you're a professional business woman of some sort. Your small amount of luggage suggests that you frequently make short day trips for meetings or whatever. But that could all just be a ruse because you're actually some sort of government agent wondering why I spend so much time people watching," Steve offered.

Clare racked her brain trying to think of a moment like this one but no memories of meeting someone like this guy came to mind. What was even more startling to Clare was that she found herself feeling rather fond of Steve despite the fact they had only just met. Stupid Mike was the furthest thing from her mind.

"That was awesome! I hope you can add me to your list of cool people then," she said enthusiastically. "I'm Clare. Agent

Clare." Steve laughed again. The tone of her voice was confident and her posture was perfect, but she still held on to the handle of her luggage, which gave Steve the impression that Clare didn't often strike up conversations with random travelers. If this was truly the case, then he was certainly glad she had made an exception.

Finally letting go of her luggage, she reached out a hand, which Steve gladly shook. Upon further inspection, Clare noticed more characteristics about this charming guy. He had beautiful green eyes that were very kind and his smile was sincere even though it was obvious that he was worn out. Freckles were popping out all over his face from being in the sun all day and there was also a shadow running along his jaw from stubble growing in.

"Nice to meet you. I'm Steve," he replied.

"Nice to meet you, Steve," Clare said. Everything about Clare made Steve wonder if he'd stepped into some sort of beautiful dream. They were only two among hundreds of grumpy travelers who were delayed and yet, her personality was radiant and cheery. A tinge of pink appeared on her cheeks above very pronounced dimples and a few locks of her hair were curling playfully under her chin. But best of all was her smile. It was charismatic and full of life and Steve had a hard time not staring.

Clare on the other hand was taken completely by the expression on Steve's face. It wasn't quite vacant but instead calm and serene. There was a deep sense of honesty that made her want to talk to him for hours. His smile was disarming and his eyes pierced her in such a way that she was sure he'd already slipped past years' worth of walls she had built up. When she was able to make eye contact with him, Clare swore his eyes dilated and she had to look away to hide another obvious grin.

Clare R.

"So, uh, what are you reading?" she asked. He turned the book over so she could see the cover.

"Oh, it's uh, one of those medieval, fantasy novels," Steve said. He was, admittedly, a bit of a nerd and he sincerely hoped she didn't think that was lame. But to his surprise, Clare nodded eagerly.

"That's a good book for flying," she replied. "I love the *Lunar Chronicles*."

"Really?" he asked. "I hope you're not kidding." Clare laughed and bent down to her own bag.

"You probably haven't read the new one then, have you?" she asked. Steve shook his head sideways and took the book when she handed it to him. The title gleamed in the bright lights of the airport: *Shadow of the Star Child.* "Oh, well it's really good so far. I just started it a couple nights ago."

ICE BROKEN! Steve thought. That was all it took and then they were off. Clare and Steve discussed the characters, who they favored and who they loved to hate. They also discussed which fictional city they would like to reside in if given the opportunity. Clare and Steve talked for at least half an hour about that book series alone before they transitioned to other books.

Steve had initially noticed that Clare carried herself with a strong sense of confidence and elegance that gave her the aura of a professional business person. But the more she talked and smiled, the faster Steve realized how much more Clare had to offer as a person. It had been a while since Steve had spent any measurable amount of time with a woman because with all the relocating he'd been doing, starting and ending relationships had seemed rather pointless. But as he listened to Clare talk, the notion of being a couple with her seemed plausible and enjoyable. That is, if she wasn't in a relationship already.

Clare's hands moved frequently as she talked, which he found quite amusing, and his face was actually getting a bit sore because he was smiling much more often than he usually did. When they stopped moving, Steve peered at her left hand and didn't see any ring.

Well that's good, he thought. *Maybe I have a chance.*

"Clare?" Steve said when they finally paused their book discussion.

"Yes?" she replied. It occurred to Clare that she'd been talking a great deal and sort of fast at that because she was kind of nervous, so for a second she worried that Steve found it annoying. Then he took her by surprise and she was grateful because she definitely wanted to keep talking.

"Would you like a coffee or tea?" he asked.

"Um, yeah. Sure. That sounds great. Breakfast tea if they have it," she said.

"All right, one sec," Steve replied. He got up and walked across the concourse to a coffee stand. A moment later he returned to their seats with two cups of hot tea.

"Thanks," she said. "This sounds so good on a night like tonight." Steve nodded in agreement and glanced out the window. Rain was still pounding down on the tarmac.

"No problem," he replied. "So, you've been delayed too, huh?"

"Yeah, but you are certainly making the experience much more enjoyable," she said before taking a sip of her tea. Steve smiled and shrugged.

Clare R.

"It's what I do," he said, and Clare chuckled.

"What do you do for real?" she asked. "If you don't mind me asking… Because your boots look like they've seen better days." Clare hoped that Steve didn't mind she was changing the subject, and apparently he didn't because Steve laughed as he leaned forward to stare at his boots.

The laces were starting to fray from being pulled tightly through the eyelets so many times and that new shoe sheen was long gone. It had been replaced by numerous scuffs and nicks from running into metal or concrete. But no matter how rough they looked on the outside, Steve loved them because this trusty pair of boots was still very comfortable.

"They have," Steve said. "I'm an engineer. Most of the time I sit at a computer doing design work, which doesn't really require work boots."

"Yeah, unless you work with some pretty dangerous computers?" Clare said from behind her cup of tea.

"Yeah, nothing screams dangerous like a cranky Dell computer," he replied, and Clare laughed again.

"I'm sorry," she said. "I didn't mean to interrupt..."

"No, you're fine. That was good," Steve said. "Umm… Once in a while I'll travel to job sites to make inspections and make sure everything is getting built correctly. That's how I end up stranded in the airports every so often. Well, more often than not." Clare realized that he must be fairly smart if he was an engineer. She hoped Steve was smart because she was tired of meeting dunces.

"That's pretty cool. Do you like it?" she asked.

Please don't mind that I'm asking so many questions, she

thought. Thankfully, Steve didn't seem to mind and he turned in his seat so he could talk to her easier.

"Yeah, it's all right. All the people I work with are really nice and we have a lot of projects right now, so I keep busy," Steve said. "Each project is always a bit different too, so it's always a new puzzle trying to get everything to fit on the site." Clare moved her head up and down but never did her eye contact falter and Steve found this incredibly intriguing.

"What do you do, Clare?" Steve asked.

"I work for movie production companies," Clare said, turning in her seat as well. "Well, actually I work for a logistics firm that gets hired by movie production companies. I handle a lot of the scheduling when it comes to getting movie personnel to sets if they have to travel." As she talked, Clare moved and shook her hands in a manner that made Steve smile. He found her mannerisms humorous and oddly soothing. It was refreshing to be in someone's company who had so much energy. Clare smiled when she saw Steve's eyes widen slightly.

"I imagine you keep pretty busy then," he said.

"Oh yes, very busy," she replied. "But it's fun, too. I really enjoy my job and I get to meet a lot of cool people and read a lot." She held up the book in her hand, indicating that she traveled often enough that it warranted reading such a large book.

"I bet," Steve said. "So, if I may...Does that mean you're a workaholic? I just mean, because movie schedules seem like they could be kinda nuts." Clare could tell that Steve was worried he might offend her and it made her laugh.

"My friend Amy would definitely say so. Schedules are definitely hectic and they can change in a moment's notice, which means I work at some strange times," Clare explained. "What about you? Do you ever do design work into the early morning hours?"

"I have pulled a few late nights and early mornings to meet deadlines, but not if I can help it. I do work a lot, but I try to keep a healthy balance. When I get home, I try to keep up with the hobbies I like or a few of the shows I enjoy watching."

"What are your hobbies?" she asked.

"Well, I really like to draw and I love reading," he said. "And on the weekends I like to go hiking or whatever. But I'm so tired from work usually that I just like to hang out at home." That was a feeling that Clare knew incredibly well.

This guy is awesome, Clare thought.

I don't care if we just met, Steve thought. *You are so cute and amazing.*

"OK, I have a serious question to ask you. Well, it's not that serious. I'm just curious I guess," Clare said. "How do you feel about sweatpants?" Somehow he managed to keep a straight face but on the inside Steve was coming undone. He had assumed she might ask about his relationship status or even something simple like a favorite food. But sweatpants were the last thing Steve had expected. Not only that, but Clare was dressed in her work attire and it took him a second to imagine what she would look like in comfortable clothes.

"Sweatpants?" he repeated.

"Yes, I mean, I know it's a strange question, but..." Clare said. Steve just smiled.

Gosh! What did I say that for? she thought. *So dumb!*

"No, no. It's just funny. I don't think I've ever been asked that by a beautiful lady in an airport before," he replied. "Um, I spend a lot of time outside, especially in the fall and winter, so when I get home I do like to put on warmer clothes. I have a stash of them back home."

"Wow, all right!" Clare replied. She could feel her cheeks reddening again because his passive compliment hadn't gone unnoticed.

"Why?" he replied. "Do you ask a lot of guys that question?" Steve was quickly coming to find that Clare had a humorous side to her. She was very clever and he was deeply fascinated by the playful banter that was developing between them.

"Oh, all the time," Clare said, also trying to keep a straight face. "I was going to ask what color socks you like next." Steve nearly burst at the seams. It had been so long since he'd met a girl with a good sense of humor.

"Awesome, good to know," Steve said. "Well if you must know, I prefer dark socks over white ones and definitely the occasional polka dot pair." The fact that he answered her question in such a casual manner made Clare break out laughing and she had to cover her mouth to subdue the sound. Her eyes were wide when she beamed at him and then they both sat back in their seats and took a sip of tea.

"I was just curious," she said. "Are you hungry?"

"I'm a little *peckish*," Steve said, and then he started laughing.

"Peckish? Really?" Clare said.

"Please, don't judge me," Steve said. "For some reason, that was the first word that came to mind."

"Oh, I'm not," she said. "I say knickers once in a while and

Clare R.

Amy teases me for it."

"You say *knickers*?" he asked.

"Yes," Clare said, giggling again. "Once in a while." He stared at her trying to remember the last time he heard someone say knickers.

"What?" Clare asked. "Are you going to make fun of me?"

"No way. You're just really cool. I'm glad you came to sit down," Steve said. Her face remained stoic for a moment and he knew she was going to say something humorous.

"*Really cool*...So, I'm definitely on the list then?" Clare said.

"Yes, Clare you're definitely on the list," Steve said. He pretended to look at something on his phone before continuing. "In fact, the tally is in. You have topped the list...Congratulations!"

"Aw, thank you. You don't know how hard I've worked for this," Clare said while pretending to accept some sort of imaginary award. Before she could finish, however, they both started laughing again.

How the hell did I manage to meet someone so amazing? Steve wondered.

"Come on," he said. "Let's go find something to eat." Clare caught his eye on purpose when they stood up.

"I'm glad I came to sit down, too, Steve," she said.

"Good. A little late on that reply though," he replied with a wink. Clare scoffed and batted at his arm playfully. It felt good to be teased that way. "What sounds good?"

She shrugged.

Everything sounds good, but I just want to keep talking, she thought. But then her stomach betrayed her and growled loud enough for Steve to hear. His eyes were raised when she looked at him.

"Everything. I'm so hungry," she said, grinning at him. Together, they walked down the terminal in search of something to eat. The airport was littered with all sorts of delicious smelling restaurants that catered to every type of hungry traveler and eventually, the pair settled on pizza. Once they got their order, they returned to their seats so they didn't have to stay in the crowded restaurant.

She was coming to find that Steve possessed several wonderful qualities and one of them she found out while they were eating. Despite being as careful as possible, Clare lost a couple of toppings when she laughed at a particularly humorous remark Steve made about jungle cats being majestic, and they landed right on her brand new dress pants.

"Oh darn," Steve said. But instead of laughing at her, he got up and went back to the coffee stand to get extra napkins to help wipe off the sauce before it soaked in. Clare smiled gratefully at him.

"Thanks," she said.

"No problem," he replied. "I hope it doesn't stain." Normally, something like this would have been frustrating, but tonight Clare just shrugged it off.

"I'm sure it will be fine," Clare said. "A little embarrassing though."

"I won't tell. I guess I'm just too damn funny," he said, and Clare started laughing again.

"Thank you for dinner," she said.

"You're very welcome," he said. "Maybe we can do this again sometime."

"I would like that very much," she replied. There was ab-

Clare R.

solutely no one else she wanted to spend a delay with. After dinner, Steve excused himself to use the bathroom and Clare gladly agreed to watch their belongings. When Steve disappeared into the bathroom, Clare exhaled a breath that she felt like she'd been holding since she first sat down.

Where in the world did you come from, Steve? Clare wondered. In all the time she traveled, Clare couldn't remember a more pleasant trip and there was no denying how she felt that rainy evening in the airport. Clare was completely taken by Steve. She ran her hands through her hair and sat back in her seat with a look of wonder upon her face. Then as her eyes glanced at a nearby book stand, she was struck with an idea. Clare wondered if it would be a little corny but she didn't care. She didn't want Steve to forget her.

Clare looked toward the bathroom to make sure she still had time. With no sign of Steve, Clare pulled the book from her bag and quickly unzipped a pocket on Steve's bag. The book fit inside perfectly and she zipped up the pocket and sat back in her chair, letting a mischievous grin spread across her face. She swallowed the last of her drink from dinner just as Steve came back from the bathroom, and with a handsome smile, he thanked her for watching their bags.

Clare also excused herself and when she returned from the restroom, they continued talking and at one point, their conversation switched to television shows. So far, Clare watched just about every show that Steve did and he was feeling more excited about this woman by the second.

"Have you ever watched *Sons of Anarchy*?" she asked.

"I haven't seen that one yet," he replied.

"Oh, you should. It's pretty good," Clare said. "A little rough...I mean if you're into that."

"I'll have to check it out then," he said.

"Did you hear that one of the main actors from that show is going to be in the *Fifty Shades of Grey* movie?" Clare asked. Steve had bent down to put his book away and without thinking the next words flew from his mouth.

"Nope, he pulled out." In a split second, the sexually explicit pun clicked in his brain and his eyes flew to Clare who had an equally surprised look on her face. Neither one could hold back their laughter for long. Steve leaned back in his seat while Clare was doubled over from laughing so hard.

"Pun intended," Steve finished. Her hand came to rest on his arm, and no matter how funny the pun had been, all Steve could think about was how wonderful it would be to hold her hand. Her slender fingers gently squeezed his arm and it felt amazing.

"Oh my God, Steve," Clare said. "That was so awesome!"

"Good. Wow. Um…" Steve replied. He hadn't exactly intended to say something so uncalled for to Clare, so he was unsure of how to proceed.

"How about another cup of tea? Next one is on me," Clare asked.

"Yeah sure," Steve replied. Clare walked across the concourse to the coffee stand. When she returned, she placed the warm cup in his hands and Steve felt himself blush again. Clare was shaking her head and still grinning.

"Thank you," he said. "What's so funny, Clare?"

"You, you dork," she said. "That was good. I needed that."

"Good. I'm glad," he replied. "Does that mean I get an award, too?" The ensuing giggles that escaped Clare made Steve's heart thump even harder and he had to look away even though all he wanted to do was watch her do the simplest things like dunk the tea bag up and down.

"So you enjoy tea then?" she asked.

"Oh yeah," Steve said. "Earl and I are best friends." Clare didn't say anything right away and Steve looked up, wondering if she'd missed his attempt at cleverness. She hadn't, and when Steve's eyes met hers, another bout of laughter escaped her.

"That's a good one," she finally said.

"Thanks," Steve replied. "I usually have a cup every morning at work."

"I do too, and sometimes after dinner I'll have a cup when I'm reading," Clare said. An image of Clare reading and drinking tea quickly formed in his mind. They continued talking, but it wasn't long after that an important announcement came over the airport intercom. It was a notice for both their flights that they were now boarding.

"Wow, has a couple of hours gone by already?" she asked. Steve nodded and looked at his watch.

"Gosh, I guess so," he replied. Neither one wanted to say goodbye because they'd been having such a wonderful time. Clare felt very warm and almost dizzy when she stood up. They had been going at such a good pace but now she felt rushed because she certainly didn't want to miss her flight. Even with so many people hustling and bustling around them, it sounded quiet to her. The whole night she had been grinning and smiling every time Steve had said something to her, and it was about to end.

Please don't think I'm too awkward or something, Clare thought, and without thinking, she raised her hand, ever so slightly.

"It was really great to meet you, Steve," she said. Clare

couldn't remember a time she'd felt more torn in her life. All she wanted to do was give him a hug and her phone number, but then another announcement for her flight came over the speaker.

"You too, Clare," Steve said as sincerely as possible. "I really hope we can see each other again sometime, maybe have another date in the airport."

"Anything is possible," she said, grinning. In truth, Clare couldn't have agreed more. Steve seemed like such a great guy and she definitely wanted to keep talking and drinking tea together. They stood smiling at each other and Clare hoped that he would like the surprise she left in his bag.

Steve had also raised his hand and for a brief moment, their hands touched. Both of them felt a very distinct tingle shoot up their arm, which caused them both to chuckle. Time seemed to slow down and as Clare stood there with Steve's fingers intertwined with her own, she was overcome by a strong desire to reach up with her free hand and run her fingers through his hair. But instead, she did something that even took herself by surprise.

Since Clare had her high heeled boots on, she didn't have to get up on her tip toes when she leaned in to give Steve a kiss on the cheek. A fresh wave of her perfume washed over him and the resulting tingling became so intense that he could no longer feel his feet. She was pleased to see red spots appear on his cheeks and they both laughed again. Her beautiful, fair skin looked as if it was almost glowing and all Steve wanted was to kiss her in return.

"Clare..." Steve said. All he wanted was more time. There was so much more to say but he also knew they both had to go.

"Just make sure I stay on the top of the list, OK?" she said, unleashing another dazzling smile as she reached for the handle

Clare R.

of her luggage. Clare knew Steve had more to say but she didn't want it to be rushed.

"I will," Steve said. "You're gorgeous, you know."

"Thanks and you're very handsome," Clare said. "You dork." Rarely did Clare experience anything that was memorable enough to make her cheeks actually feel hot, but they did that night in the airport. Steve stood in the middle of the terminal and watched her walk away. The beautiful smile never left her face as she turned into her gate. Steve gave her one last wave before falling into the hustle and bustle of people trying to get on his flight.

Chapter 2

Nope, he pulled out, Clare thought. The simple play on words kept replaying in her head causing her to giggle every few minutes. She had taken her seat on the plane and for the last several minutes, she'd been shaking with giddiness. Out of all the guys Clare dated in the past couple years, she couldn't have imagined she would meet the greatest one in an airport during a delay. She couldn't stop smiling.

But it was more than just the dirty joke. It was Steve's last comment about her being gorgeous. The combination of his smile and the kind expressions on his face. The passive compliments and goofy jokes. It was enough to make her wish they were still delayed. There was also no way she would forget the way it felt when their hands had touched. Clare could still feel her heart beating rapidly in her chest as she looked out the window of the plane.

My goodness. I'm crushing big time, Clare thought. But she didn't care. It was refreshing and exhilarating and as she watched several other planes taxiing across the runways, Clare wondered which one Steve was on.

~~~~

Clare R.

Everything was moving in slow motion as Steve handed his boarding pass to the gate officer and found his seat on the plane. Never in his life could he remember a moment when he was so warm; like there was a fire inside of him. Steve was so warm in fact, that he didn't even notice the drastic temperature change as he walked down the tunnel to board the plane.

Part of him felt like he was still standing in the terminal, amidst all the other travelers, staring at Clare's beaming face, with her fingers wrapped around his, and her soft lips on his cheek. Talking to Clare had been so invigorating and amazing that another part of him wished that he'd gone after her and got a seat on her plane. It didn't matter where she was headed. But for the most part, Steve wished he would have at least got her number and he silently cursed to himself for not being more proactive.

Shortly after taking his seat, the captain and stewardesses made the familiar announcements about flight procedures and the engines roared to life. A few passengers around him drifted off to sleep while others plugged into their various devices to listen to music or watch a movie. But Steve's mind was racing. Despite being frustrated with himself, he knew that there was so much more to be positive about.

Delayed flights are the absolute best! he yelled in his head. To him, Clare was so stunning and the kiss goodbye had taken him completely by surprise. He put his finger to his cheek where her lips had touched his face.

She kissed me! The nerdy engineer! Steve mused. The dirty pun came to the front of his mind again and he started chuckling to himself.

Then his thoughts came full circle, and once again, Steve stewed over how he should have asked for her number. But Clare's smiling face played across his mind's eye and all Steve could hear was her joking about being at the top of the list. Steve felt his heart beat faster and he knew for certain that there was no way Clare was ever falling from the top of that list.

~~~~

There was no rain by the time Steve made it home that evening and he couldn't help but stare at the neighbor's jack-o'-lantern as he pushed his key into the lock. A chilly gust of wind came up and the glowing eyes flickered which made the hauntingly crooked smile that much more eerie.

He finally tore his eyes away and went inside. Steve's body felt drained as he climbed the stairs to his room, but the soothing warmth of a long, hot shower eased his muscles that were stiff from hiking around the job site all day and sitting in the cramped seat on the plane.

Afterward, when he pulled on a pair of sweats, he immediately started laughing while recalling thoughts of Clare asking about socks and sweatpants. By the time he climbed into bed it was well after midnight and Steve knew that he should have been tired, but his mind was still racing while he relived the events of the day. After an hour of lying on his bed, grinning at the ceiling, sleep still eluded him and Steve decided to read, hoping that would help him fall asleep. He reached over the side of the bed to dig in his bag and to Steve's immense surprise, there were two books.

One was his and the other was the next book in the series that Clare had shown him. But there was something else. Coming from the bag was a distinct smell that Steve had grown to love in the time he had spent with Clare. As Steve gently lifted the book from the bag and brought it closer to his face, the smell grew stronger. It was definitely the smell of Clare and her perfume.

For a while Steve just stared at the book and when he finally

Clare R.

opened the cover, he saw her name written in very beautiful handwriting — *Clare R.* The blue ink shone like her smile, which had become such a welcome sight that evening.

So much for reading, he thought, and that night Steve fell asleep staring at her signature and picturing her smiling face in his mind.

~~~~

Keys clattered softly in the bowl that rested next to the door as Clare walked into her house later that evening. Leaving her luggage in the entryway, she walked around the house and turned on a few lights. Clare was so excited to reminisce about her time at the airport with Steve without the distraction of other people and overly talkative taxi drivers.

She also wanted to put on a pair of sweatpants and every time the thought crossed her mind during the trip home, a grin would spread across her face. By the time she got into bed one question was bouncing persistently around her brain.

Did you find my book yet, Steve? Clare knew there was absolutely no way she would forget Steve. He was the only engineer she'd ever met before and he was by far the dorkiest nerd she'd ever met. Yet, he was also the nicest guy she could remember meeting. Clare hoped the book would help him to not forget her and she gave herself a mental pat on the back for pulling off the sneaky maneuver.

It would be so cool to talk to him more though, she thought. But they hadn't exchanged numbers or emails or anything.

"Ughh, so dumb," she groaned. "I easily could have written my number in the book." Clare was also staring at the ceiling and her head was sunk comfortably into her pillow.

You're gorgeous, you know, Steve had said. The words floated around and around in her head like beautiful, fluffy clouds in a bright, blue sky and the minor frustration she felt floated away as well. The smile on Steve's face stayed with her as she finally drifted off to sleep later that night.

~~~

Clare spent much of the following day working from her couch, filling out forms for visas, organizing transportation for crews, and setting up lodging. It wasn't the ideal Saturday and by the time she was done it left her time at the airport with Steve feeling like an amazing dream more than anything else. When Clare's phone went off that afternoon due to a text from her best friend Amy, Clare gladly typed a reply.

Come over tonight! Have news!
All right, let's go out tonight! Amy replied.
Yeah okay. That could be fun. Clare typed.

Clare relished in the fact that she had three glorious, action-packed episodes of the *Lunar Chronicles* to watch and she had been hoping to enjoy at least one before Amy showed up. But before she was ten minutes into the first episode, Clare heard the front door open and she watched the entryway, waiting for Amy to appear.

Delayed again, she thought, and her finger pressed the pause button on the remote. *If only it was you delaying me Steve!* Amy walked in with a bounce in her step and her black wavy hair was bouncing along as well. Her well-proportioned body was hidden beneath her overcoat and gum smacked behind her bright red lips.

Clare R.

"Good, you're here," Amy said.

"Yeah. I live here," Clare replied. "I've got to start locking that door more often." Clare's dry sense of humor had always made Amy laugh.

"Yeah right," she said. "You love when I come over." That much was true, because ever since they were little, Amy had been there for her through thick and thin. Amy was the more boisterous half of Clare, or at least that's how she always thought of it. When Clare was feeling a little more serious about something, Amy would be the one who felt a little sillier. It was something that Clare had always enjoyed about their relationship because she thought it balanced them out nicely. It helped to make them the best of friends.

"It looks like someone really wants to go out tonight," Clare said.

"Well, yeah! It's Saturday night! Are we going or what?" Amy said. Clare had been planning on relaxing, chatting with Amy for a while and then immersing herself into her show. But that idea appeared to be floating out the window because often times, her suggestions were usually more of a statement.

"Eh, I don't know," she said, walking past Amy into the kitchen.

"Oh, come on, Clare," Amy said. She was very persistent and after a few more head shakes, Clare finally gave in.

"Fine, but I want to go shopping first. I need a few things," Clare said. She wasn't particularly excited about dealing with a fast talking business man at the bar. She'd dealt with enough duds to last her for a lifetime and after meeting Steve, putting up with guys at the bar seemed like nothing more than a chore.

But if she was going to go out, Clare would make sure it was productive in some fashion and provide moral support for Amy who was always on the lookout for that special someone. A little while later, they left Clare's house and arrived at a store where they both liked to shop. The two friends wandered through the aisles and laughed and joked like so many times before.

"Clare, you need a guy," Amy said. It was an abrupt change from their in-depth conversation about favorite cartoon characters. Clare laughed because she was still waiting for just the right moment to tell Amy about Steve.

"Why?" she said, pulling a bottle of shampoo off the shelf to see how it smelled.

"I don't know. I just think you do," Amy replied. "You need something else to look forward to besides work the next day." Her gum smacked loudly while she talked.

"I mean, like a good one!" Amy said. Clare nodded and let her eyebrows rise on her forehead.

"Well if you find one, let me know," she replied, and put the shampoo in her basket. Amy paused while Clare migrated to another aisle and tried to think of another angle to approach the topic. She knew that Clare could be very closed off about certain subjects and lately this was one of them.

When Amy found Clare, she was staring intently at the wall of boxed macaroni and cheese. When Clare found her favorite one, she put several boxes in her basket. It was a childhood meal that would never grow tiresome.

Amy, however, did not share the love for box macaroni and cheese like Clare did, so often times Amy would make a clever remark or two.

Clare R.

"Don't you ever get tired of that stuff?" Amy said.

"No way! It's the simple things in life, Amy!" Clare said.

"Well, I think they should give you a discount or something since you get so much of it. Least of all, you should win some sort of award," she said.

"I should..." she mumbled. "Come on, Amy. I'm good if you are. Let's get something to drink."

Chapter 3

Amy knew that Clare had changed the subject on purpose but she didn't mind at the moment because she was excited to have a girl's night with her best friend. They paid for their items and then drove down the street to the bar they liked. It was a fun place that they had found the week after moving to town several years before.

The typical neon lights were plastered around the entryway, but it didn't have that grungy feel that some bars had. The staff were all very nice and the atmosphere was always enjoyable. When they walked in, Clare surveyed the crowd and found it was fairly light, but she was sure it would fill up shortly.

On the bright side, their bartender friend Jenny was working. She was much taller than Clare with long, brown hair that she usually held back in a ponytail. Jenny had been in a college program similar to Amy and Clare's and that's how they had initially met. After graduation, Jenny had taken a job as a bartender while she continued job hunting. She conveniently mentioned that the local area around the bar was pleasant and Amy and Clare both ended up finding places nearby. Not long after Clare and Amy moved into town, Jenny was offered part ownership of the bar and she

Clare R.

quit searching for a job.

They moved past the tables and took a seat at the bar and a short bit later, Jenny stopped over.

"Hey, how's it going?" she asked.

"Good, how are you?" Clare asked.

"Pretty good," Jenny replied. "Just waiting for the rush to start. What are you two having?" Clare peeked at the menu, but got her usual drink, a Jack and Coke. Amy, on the other hand, tried something that she hadn't ever had before.

"I must say, Clare, you look thrilled to be out tonight," Jenny commented sarcastically while making their drinks. Before she could reply, Amy jumped in.

"She is," Amy said. "I had to drag her out tonight." Clare rolled her eyes and smiled, while Jenny laughed.

"Amy's exaggerating. I just made sure that we did something else productive tonight," Clare stated.

"Good thinking," Jenny said with a wink. "I'll be back in a bit, girls." She set their drinks down in front of them and moved off to help other new patrons.

"I hope you're having fun, Clare," Amy said. "Hmm, this is good." She slid the green grasshopper across the counter so Clare could try it. Clare rocked her head back and forth slightly, letting the drink play across her palette.

"It's good," she replied. "And I'm having fun." Having known her friend for so many years, Amy could practically read Clare like one of the many books she had at home.

"No luck, huh?" Amy asked. She was referring to the date with Mike the week before.

"Nope," Clare said sharply as she picked a kernel of popcorn from the bowl on the counter.

"And he really hasn't called you back?" Amy prodded.

"Nope. Another one bites the dust apparently," Clare replied.

"Well, a lot of guys are just idiots. Try not to let it bother you, OK?" Amy replied.

"Oh, I'm not," Clare said. Amy was a little surprised by her friend's sudden casualness but before she could reply, a guy walked up behind Amy, and Clare gave a quick nod to indicate she had a visitor. Amy made a sassy smile and turned to see who this fella was.

"Well, hello there," Amy said. Clare shook her head and turned on the swiveling barstool back to her drink. Jenny came back over shortly after.

"So, what's up?" she asked. "I haven't seen you in a while."

"Work," she said. "I was in L.A. a couple weeks ago and then New York last week."

"That's cool," Jenny replied. "Hopefully you don't mind traveling."

"Yeah, it's not so bad. I mean, I enjoy it," Clare replied with a shrug. "I get to read a lot of good books!"

"Well it's good to see you!" Jenny said. "Hang on." She walked down the bar again to help another new customer. Clare peered around and found that the bar had already filled up significantly since their arrival. Many of the empty tables were now full and several of the booths that lined the walls had couples sharing dinner or groups of friends laughing wildly. Clare took a sip of her drink and switched her attention to the pool area at the back of the bar.

Do you play pool, Steve? Clare wondered. She had never

Clare R.

played much pool but the dark green velvet and dim lighting looked so inviting, and in no time at all, Clare was imagining the best night ever.

She and Steve were together now. Amy had a boyfriend as well and they had all met up at the bar to play pool and have dinner. They were laughing and joking. Every once in a while Steve would tease her playfully and she would fire something back that would make him laugh.

Clare took a sip of her drink and her daydream took a very pleasant turn. *It was late now. Much of the bar had emptied out. She and Steve stayed to play one more round. Then he hoisted her onto the edge of the table and a very passionate make out session commenced—*

"Did I hear you say something about a guy not calling you back?" Jenny asked, and Clare jumped in her seat. Warmth radiated through her body and she turned back to Jenny hoping that her cheeks weren't too red.

"Yep, another dud," Clare said. "I don't really care though. No big deal."

"That's the spirit. Don't sweat it, Clare," Jenny replied. "You're a catch. You'll find a good one."

"Oh, I did," she replied. Clare had waited long enough and she was ready to tell someone about Steve.

"Excuse me?" Jenny said.

"Yeah, yesterday when I was delayed at the airport I met this really great guy named Steve," Clare said. Amy was like a fox and upon hearing this sentence, she dismissed the guy who was chatting her up with such speed that he didn't know what hit him. Clare and Jenny both started laughing.

"All right buddy. I'm sorry but you gotta beat it. My girl has news!" Amy said, and turned on the swivel chair to face Clare. "You were saying?"

"I was wondering when you were going to ask," Clare said.

"Well, I sorta forgot that you said you had news because I was excited to get out tonight. Sorry," Amy said.

"No biggie," she said.

"Come on, Clare. Out with it," Jenny said.

"I met someone," Clare repeated. "Well sort of..."

"What?" Amy said. "Who did you meet? You said his name was Steve?" Clare moved her head up and down as she finished chewing the popcorn she'd shoved in her mouth.

"Yep," she said.

"Well, how did you guys meet?" Jenny asked. An image of Steve grinning at the flight boards filled her mind.

"I went to check my flight at the departure board and he was there, too. When I looked at him he was smiling and I couldn't figure out why because all the flights were delayed."

"Why the hell would someone be happy their flight is delayed?" Amy asked.

"Exactly what I thought, so I went to ask him," Clare said.

"Oh, very outgoing of you," Amy said.

"I know, right? He said that he doesn't mind the delays because he likes watching everything that goes on in the airport and he really enjoys meeting cool, new people," Clare explained. Amy just shook her head and smiled. "So, then I took the opportunity to introduce myself."

"Of course you did," Jenny said with a laugh. "Then what happened?"

Clare R.

"Well, before I came to sit down he was pulling a book out of his bag, and get this, Steve is reading the same series I am! So, we talked about that for a while and then we started talking about other books, too."

"So nerdy! You two sound perfect for each other!" Amy said.

"Amy!" Jenny said. There were several things Clare loved about Amy and one of them was her direct personality, which led to many very humorous comments.

"What else?" Amy said.

"Well, like I said, we talked about books for a while, then he bought me a cup of tea and then we started talking about work and our jobs."

"What's this Steve guy do?" Jenny asked.

"He's an engineer," Clare said. "Then he asked about my job and when I told him about what I do, he seemed pretty impressed."

"Who wouldn't be? Do you even realize all the shit you have to keep straight?" Amy said. Clare laughed again and nodded. She was very proud of what she did because she was very good at her job.

"Apparently not all guys, Amy," Clare said, after taking a sip from her drink. She could name several guys who had chosen not to call her back for one reason or another.

"Forget those losers. Let's hear more about Steve. I can't believe this. You meet this goofy-sounding guy, at the airport of all places, and you two hit it off!" Amy said. Jenny nodded in agreement.

"Tell me about it," Clare said. "I don't know if I've ever had that much fun in the airport."

"Well...Keep going," Jenny said. Clare shrugged and rocked

back and forth on the bar stool.

"After talking for a while, we ended up getting dinner–" she started, but then Amy interrupted her again.

"Wait! How long were you delayed? You guys got dinner, too?" Amy exclaimed. "Clare! You are my inspiration. Picking up guys in the airport!"

"My goodness, Amy," Jenny said. "You're getting really excited. Let the woman talk!"

"Well are you listening to this? You couldn't make this stuff up! This is like the awesome, cheesy stuff you see in a movie," Amy replied. When she looked back to Clare, her cheeks had reddened but there was a subtle hint of uncertainty in her friend's eyes.

"Both our flights were delayed a couple hours, so we got something to eat. Oh, and Steve said *peckish*!"

"Oh, great! He really is a nerd if he has a vocabulary like yours, too," Jenny said. "What did you guys have?"

"We ended up getting pizza after checking out some of the restaurants," Clare replied. Then she laughed randomly.

"What?" Amy asked.

"Steve told a really funny joke, and when I was laughing, some of the toppings fell off my pizza and landed right on my pant leg and the first thing he did was go get me more napkins."

"Wow! That was nice of him," Jenny said. "Sounds like quite the gentleman."

Steve was definitely a gentleman, Clare thought.

"Yeah, it was awesome. Then he told me a dirty pun," she said. A mischievous grin spread across her face as she quickly rehashed the story of how she and Steve had begun talking about

Clare R.

television shows, and how that eventually led to Steve making a pun about *Fifty Shades of Grey*. Both Jenny and Amy were in disbelief.

"What the fuck. I can't believe you met a guy who told you a dirty pun," Amy said. "I want to meet a guy like that. I'm coming to the airport with you next time, Clare."

"Oh, yeah," Clare scoffed.

"I'll be right back. All this excitement makes me have to go to the bathroom," Amy said, and she headed off to the bathroom.

"Anything else?" Jenny asked.

"When Steve went to the bathroom after we finished eating I stuffed my book in his bag so he would remember me," Clare said.

"Girl, you sound determined," Jenny said.

"There was just something about him, Jenny. He was so awesome! Really great," Clare said.

"But?" Jenny asked.

"We didn't get to talk too much longer because the announcements for our flights came over the intercom and we had to get ready to leave," Clare began. "I'm pretty sure that Steve's into me, so I gave him a kiss on the cheek and he totally blushed. Then when I finally had to leave, I turned and Steve was waiting to give me one last wave."

"Oh, honey, I don't think he will forget you," she said.

"I hope not," Clare said. "The sucky part is that we didn't exchange numbers or emails or anything."

"Ah, so that's why you're not texting furiously with him. I'm sorry," Jenny said. Clare moved her head up and down and put on a defeated expression.

"Yeah, me too," Clare said.

"Well, Clare. If it's meant to be, it will be. Otherwise you've got an awesome memory to appreciate," Jenny said.

"Yep," she said. The only problem was that Clare didn't want it to be just a memory. But before she could dwell any more, Jenny nodded her head ever so subtly just as Clare had for Amy. A guy was approaching.

Clare would usually put up with the B.S. from one or two guys, which was usually the time it took for Amy to put down a couple drinks. Then Clare played one of her favorite games. Amy was still in the bathroom but Clare knew she would be returning shortly, so she put on a fake smile as she turned away from Jenny.

"Hey beautiful! What are you drinking?" the guy asked.

Really? This line again? I have lost track of the number of times that's been said to me. The drunk guy playbook must be pretty thin, Clare thought as she tried to maintain her knockoff smile.

"I'll have another one of these," she said, lifting her glass. The guy tapped the counter to get the bartender's attention.

"Another one for the pretty lady," he said. A minute later Jenny set a fresh drink next to Clare's first one, which she hadn't put much of a dent in.

"I'm Jack," the guy said.

"Clare," she replied. The guy was leaning coolly against the counter.

"So, what do you do?" Jack asked. He took a decent draw from his own drink, so Clare took the opportunity to see just how drunk this guy already was.

"I travel...*a lot*," was all she said. But Clare made sure to put extra emphasis on the words "a lot" to make it sound important.

"Whoa, that is so cool," he replied. Clare grinned when she

Clare R.

heard Jenny's quiet snort float across the counter.

"Yeah, it's pretty exciting," she replied.

Nearly gone, Clare thought on the inside. From the corner of her eye, she noticed Amy coming out of the bathroom.

"You know, my friend over there," Clare said, with a nod of her head. Her suitor nodded dumbly and again, she had to fight back a bout of laughter. When Clare was sure she had Jack's attention, she made a gesture with her finger for him to lean closer.

"She's a supermodel," Clare whispered. Despite Jack being nearly gone, his eyes dilated and he looked down the bar to see Amy.

"Really?" he asked.

"Yep," Clare said.

"Are you sure?" he asked.

Wow! Even when they are drunk, they can still manage to be shallow.

"Believe me," Clare said, trying to maintain her poker face. "She's got it where it counts." Clare made sure to add a very suggestive wink because she wanted to see the guy's reaction. Jack didn't even say goodbye. He just teetered on by, hoping to start a conversation with Amy. A moment later she heard the same pickup line Jack had used on her. Clare shook her head and raised her eyebrows. Jenny turned as well.

"So predictable," Clare said. Jenny just smiled and shrugged.

"Don't worry about it," she said.

"I'm not. Not anymore," Clare said. As she swirled the straw around the glass, the sound of clinking ice cubes jarred a particularly humorous bar memory.

Clare had been sitting in the very same seat when she had come out for drinks one night. Amy had been busy, so Clare was by herself. She and Jenny were having a good time chatting when a guy came up to the bar to chat with them. Since Jenny was busy tending to the other guests, it didn't take long for this guy to latch onto Clare. She played along for a few minutes, but before long, this guy's language became very crude. The drunken sex-talk was not attractive and he didn't quit or leave, even when Clare said she'd had enough. That's when Jenny stepped in.

Jenny happened to be standing nearby filling drink glasses and Clare knew she was listening. A moment later Jenny appeared beside her holding a glass of ice water.

"Excuse me, miss. Did you order this?" Jenny asked. Clare shook her head sideways, so Jenny turned to the guy who had been bothering her. His eyes were smoldering with drunken irritation at the fact that Jenny was destroying his "game."

"This must be yours then," Jenny said holding out the glass.

"I didn't order any water," he said.

"I think you did," she insisted. The expression on his face didn't change until Jenny used her free hand to yank on his belt and dump the entire glass of ice water down the front of his pants.

"Now keep it in your pants you pervert and get the hell out of my bar!" Jenny finished. Clare was shocked and amazed. But that was nothing compared to how the guy was feeling. Only moments before he'd been too drunk to protest, but now every eye in the bar was staring at him and the silence was deafening. The ice water running down his legs caused him to sober up faster than Clare knew was possible. He left not long after and they never saw him again.

The memory caused Clare to chuckle loudly.

"What's up?" Jenny asked.

Clare R.

"Do you remember the guy that you dumped water on?" Clare asked. The smirk on Jenny's face was a devious one.

"You mean ole' blue balls? The guy whose manhood shrunk under a waterfall of ice cubes?" Jenny clarified and Clare broke out laughing. "Yeah, I remember. It was one of my prouder moments as a bartender."

Jenny and Clare carried on a conversation in between the patrons who were coming to the bar. Then after an hour or so Amy tapped her shoulder.

"Hey, I'm gettin' outta here," she said with a wink. Clare saw the guy standing at the bar who had bought her a drink. She had thought for sure that Amy would have dismissed this Jack fellow as well.

"Really?" she asked.

"Yeah, I like this one," Amy replied. "He called me a supermodel." Clare put a hand to her face in an exasperated manner.

"Be careful, OK?" Clare said.

"I will, bestie," Amy replied after handing her the car keys. That was always what Amy tended to call Clare when she started getting tipsy. "Will you take the car back to my house?" Clare nodded and then let out a nervous laugh when Amy pinched the guy's butt.

"Oh my," Clare said. Once Amy had departed, she got back on her stool and paid for her first drink when Jenny returned.

"You want my other drink?" Clare asked. "Didn't even make it to the new one." Jenny nodded.

"Sure thing. I like these," Jenny replied. Then Clare said goodnight and headed for the door. The cold air felt good on her hot cheeks and she took several deep breaths trying to clear her head. Then her stomach grumbled and Clare actually laughed. She hadn't eaten anything since breakfast. So, before dropping Amy's car off, Clare stopped for dinner at her favorite fast food restaurant.

Whenever Clare made a late night fast food run, she usually sat in the parking lot and listened to music. The idea of driving and eating messy fast food wasn't that appealing, and the food never tasted as good if she took it home because no matter how fast she drove, it always cooled off.

She hummed along for a bit but after a while she was cruising down memory lane. At first, Clare reminisced about all the fun times they had shared in Amy's car. Stickers and assorted knick-knacks that were plastered around the car all had their own special memory, and when she found one of the oldest ones, Clare mused about the day she got her license.

Her father had handed her the keys to his little truck and told her to be safe and go have fun. Clare and Amy had gotten their favorite fast food for dinner that night. Then they drove around, savoring the feeling of their newfound freedom. Hours went by as the pair of friends talked about boys in a secluded park that they found on the edge of town. That park eventually became their go-to place throughout the rest of high school. Her thoughts continued to stray and soon Clare was thinking further into the past. The memories seemed so vivid.

Growing up had been far from easy for Clare. Although the relationship between Clare and her father had been wonderful, they often struggled to get by, which meant that Clare didn't have the assortment of new clothes and toys like many of the other children did. But after a while that didn't really matter to her because she was more curious about something else. Clare could remember

Clare R.

asking her father several times where her mother was or when she was coming home, and each time he would make up some story about her being gone for some reason or another.

It was many years before her father finally confessed that her mother had left them when Clare was only a couple years old. Being quite intuitive, Clare had come to this conclusion already, but she had been hopeful that it wasn't true. Many nights she fell asleep hoping that her mother would be home the next morning when she woke up.

However, once her father confessed the truth, the correlations to their struggling lifestyle suddenly became apparent. Clare realized that the reason things were difficult for her father was because he struggled so much with that loss.

This was made clear to her when she woke up one night during a thunderstorm and went to seek sanctuary with her father from the lightning and unsettling crashes of violent thunder. Before she even opened the door, Clare could hear hefty sobs coming from inside. After twisting the doorknob, Clare found her father sitting at the end of the bed and he looked up at her with a tear streaked face. She ran to him and gave him the biggest hug she could muster.

They never really talked about that night again and no matter how difficult life was for Clare and her father, he was always there for her. It was also around that time when Clare met Amy. Her would-be best friend lived a couple blocks down the street and they had met one day while waiting for the bus to school.

Amy's family had been much more put together and as her mother, Tracy, learned more about Clare, she tried to offer help as best she could. Sometimes Tracy would let the girls bake at their house and then would send Clare home with the extra desserts. Other times she would give Clare some of Amy's clothes that she didn't wear anymore.

At first Clare had been nervous to tell her father because she thought maybe he would be too proud for the help, so she would hide everything in her backpack. But to Clare's surprise, her father hadn't been mad or offended at all but instead very grateful.

"Clare," her father had said to her one night as she sat at the kitchen table doing homework, "I hope that you tell Amy's mom thank you every time she gives you something." Clare looked up at him and his expression was sad even though there was still a smile on his face.

"I do," she said. "Every time."

"Good, because you're very lucky to have found a friend like Amy," he said. "You two need to stick together."

"We will, daddy," Clare said. "She's my best friend." Then her father leaned over and kissed her forehead.

"Good," he said. "I need you to give this note to her mom, OK? It says that she can bring you home from school if I can't pick you up." Clare nodded and tucked it in her folder. Then he gave her a hug and went off to bed.

Many years later, Clare found out that the note had actually been a very long thank you note to Amy's mother and father for helping their family of two out all those years. Clare took a sip of her drink and let the cool soda soothe her throat from the spicy food she was eating. Then her thoughts switched back to Amy's comment about her needing a guy. Clare took several more sips of her drink while wondering if Steve could somehow be that guy who she had hoped to find. Someone who actually cared about her

Clare R.

and wanted to spend time with her. Someone who wasn't so predictable and definitely mature enough to call her back.

After dinner, Clare drove Amy's car back to her house and then toted her two bags of groceries the few blocks back to her own house. With each step Clare could hear Jenny's words crystal clear in her mind.

"...otherwise you've got an awesome memory to appreciate..." She was determined not to let their pseudo date become just a memory. By the time she made it home, Clare was relieved she hadn't over done it at the bar with Amy. She could make a fresh cup of tea and resume watching the *Lunar Chronicles* episodes she had recorded.

Chapter 4

The Monday following their chance meeting, Steve's emotions were still running rampant. That morning he'd stayed in bed much longer than usual, ignoring the alarm that was urging him to get up and go to work. All he wanted to do was let the beautiful smell of her perfume pull him back into a dream state.

By the time lunch came around, he was hungry and tired of sitting at his desk, so Steve was grateful when his coworker Jimmy asked if he wanted to grab some Chinese food. A brisk wind blew across the parking lot of a strip mall as the pair walked up to the restaurant. Steve held the door for Jimmy and let the cold air blow across his face. It felt incredibly refreshing after sitting inside all morning.

They grabbed a seat at one of the small, square tables that filled the little restaurant and Steve's eyes immediately began to wander between the intricate works of art that decorated the walls as he daydreamed about Clare. Jimmy laughed and rubbed a hand over his head. Steve had noticed that Jimmy tended to keep his hair short, and although he hadn't asked him, Steve was fairly sure he kept it short simply because he enjoyed running a hand over the bristly hairs.

Clare R.

"What?" Steve asked.

"Nothing," Jimmy replied. "You just look a little distracted."

"Hmm," he said. "Just tired I suppose. Busy weekend..." Steve shrugged it off and a few minutes later their meals were delivered. The savory, aromatic smells made his mouth water.

It's a wonderful day for Pad Thai, Steve thought, and he savored every bit of his meal. When they were done eating Steve reached for his fortune cookie while Jimmy went up to pay for his lunch.

"Why do you eat those?" Jimmy asked when he sat back down. It quickly became apparent to Steve that his coworker was overly practical and very logical. The fortunes were goofy to him. That's not to say that Steve wasn't practical or logical. He had to be for his job. However, Steve preferred to think that he had a much more open mind, which is why Jimmy's question made Steve chuckle. He shrugged his shoulders again.

"I like them," Steve replied, and pulled out the tiny slip of white paper. Jimmy just shook his head and took a few gulps of his drink while Steve read his fortune.

"OK seriously, who gets fortunes like these?" Steve asked. Jimmy scoffed.

"It's that bad, huh?" Jimmy guessed. "Just like the taste of those things, I'm sure."

"No, seriously! It says, *Your charms have not gone unnoticed by all the angels*," Steve read. Jimmy actually looked kind of surprised.

"That's...not bad at all," Jimmy commented as he pawed through his pile of used napkins. "That's awesome." It was enough to make Jimmy curious about his own fortune and he tore open the plastic package in earnest. Meanwhile, Steve sat and stared at the tiny slip of paper in his hands. It was a beautiful fortune and immediately it made him think of Clare. Then Jimmy swore across the table.

"Look at this," Jimmy exclaimed, and he handed Steve the piece of paper. The fortune read—*You're going to be very full come dinnertime.*

"No shit I'm going to be full," Jimmy said. "I just pounded a huge plate of Lo Mein. I probably won't have to eat for a week." Steve laughed and handed the fortune back to Jimmy when he got up to pay for his lunch. Steve buried his fortune deep in his pocket. A few minutes later, after saying goodbye to the owner, Steve and Jimmy were in the car again, heading back to the office.

"So, Erica and I are going out tonight if you want to join us," Jimmy said. Steve hadn't really been paying attention. But when Jimmy's invitation finally registered, he immediately got another feeling in his stomach and it wasn't a great one.

Since he'd moved to this new job Steve had gone out with Erica and Jimmy a few times, but by the end of each night, he ended up feeling like a third wheel and that was no fun at all. But of course, Steve never said anything when Jimmy asked if he wanted to join them. It only made him realize once again how alone he was.

"Thanks, but I think I'll have to pass," Steve said. "I already have plans for tonight." Jimmy shrugged.

"That's all right," Jimmy replied. "Maybe another time." Steve nodded and the two walked back inside with the brisk wind blowing at their backs. The afternoon was rather mind numbing and Steve left work excited to do something much more engaging. In fact, Steve was about to do something he never thought he would do again. He was going back to school, and it was all thanks to Clare. Well, Clare and his father.

The morning after Steve met Clare, he had stared at her book for a good hour before being overcome by a strange eagerness to do something. But he wasn't quite sure what that something was. He climbed out of bed and headed for the closet. From inside he pulled out boxes sealed shut with duct tape. After the past couple years of relocating he'd forgotten what was even in the boxes, but now the eagerness was mixing with excitement, so Steve ripped off the tape.

As he pawed through the box, Steve wondered if there was something in there that Clare would like. But it wasn't long before Steve found what he was looking for and it didn't exactly have to do with Clare. At the bottom of the box was a food-stained notebook full of recipes. It was his father's old cookbook. That was when he was struck by the idea of taking cooking classes. Not only would it be useful, but Steve thought it would be fun, relaxing, and if he and Clare did get to meet again, Steve knew he would have a way to impress her.

The rest of the morning was spent at the computer, searching for classes. In the end, Steve found a six week course at the local university that was three days a week; Monday, Tuesday, and Wednesday. His timing couldn't have been better either, since registration closed the next day and class began that Monday.

After work, he drove home to change, and then made his way out to the satellite campus where the class would be held. To Steve's delight, the class wasn't large. By the time the clock struck seven, there were fifteen people sitting at the various cooking stations spread around the classroom. He casually glanced at the students and silently wished Clare was there to make up stories with him.

Then their teacher appeared. He was tall, thin, and he strolled into the classroom wearing a pristine white apron. He had jet black hair pulled back in a ponytail, a meticulously groomed goatee, and a tan complexion that left Steve guessing he was from a foreign country. Everything about his demeanor signaled he meant business, so Steve sat up a little bit straighter on his stool. Their teacher walked with a certain grace that he assumed must come with working in a hectic kitchen for a number of years.

"My name is Gustaf Alero," he said. His voice carried a slight accent but it was nothing too distracting. "You can call me Mr. Alero, or Gus. Actually just call me Gus. It's too late to give a shit about formalities. We're here to cook! Yeah?" Several of the students laughed and most everyone nodded. For the next couple of minutes, Mr. Alero gave a brief rundown of his own prerequisites before telling the class the goals of the class.

"This is a six week course, so if you expect to walk out of here and join *Food Network*, you're sorely mistaken." Mr. Alero paused when one person actually stood and walked out. "And then there were fourteen." Steve continued to stare at Mr. Alero wondering what he would say next, but the teacher only clapped his hands.

"Too bad for him, should have stayed to listen. As I was saying, this is only a six week course but by the end you should have the ability to cook in any general restaurant in town or impress your friends and family with scrumptious dishes. Also, depending on your grades, you may receive my personal recommendation to a culinary school of your choice or continue with the program at this university. If you're serious, that is." Without another word, Mr. Alero turned to the board and began writing large letters.

LESSON 1: PANCAKES

Several people started laughing and even Gus turned with a smile.

"I expect you all to take notes, I hope you know," he said. The laughter subsided as people dug in their bags for notebooks and pens. It was several minutes after Steve started writing in his own book that he noticed his own muscles had relaxed and he felt at ease. Yes, he still missed Clare, but this felt right.

"Now many of you probably know how to make pancakes," Gus began. "However! One of the keys to good cooking is good technique. Cooking even the simplest things such as pancakes requires good technique to ensure consistent results."

Eventually, Gus gave the class a choice of five pancake recipes to choose from: standard, potato, pumpkin, apple cinnamon, and zucchini.

"After deciding what recipe you want to make, you may start mixing ingredients. I'm going to then talk to each of you, one on one," Gus said. Then with another clap of his hands, he gave his final sentiment. "Get cooking. You have one hour!"

After countless nights of eating alone, Steve had mastered making standard pancakes, so he decided to go for something new. By the time Gus reached Steve, he was just about ready to begin spreading the batter on the griddle.

"Well look at this. You're the only one who had the balls to use zucchini," said Gus. "What's your name kid?"

"Steve," he replied.

"And why are you here, Steve?" asked Gus. He stopped stirring and looked at Gus. Closer inspection revealed that Gus's eyes seemed to be searching him. Making something up seemed like the wrong route to take, so Steve went with the truth.

"I love cooking, I'm not a big fan of my current job and I want to impress a girl I like," Steve said. The hard expression on Gus's face faded and was replaced by an exuberant one.

"That's the most honest answer I've heard tonight! Cooking is all about the right emotions and I think you've got them. Don't let those burn. I want to try one later," Gus said. Then he walked away. At the end of class, once Mr. Alero gave each student a grade, they were allowed to place their food in takeout containers. As Steve thought he might, Gus saved him for last.

"So Steve, how did they turn out?" Gus asked. Steve could tell by the look on his face that he'd heard all sorts of bullshit, so once again, Steve spoke the truth.

"They're good with a sprinkle of salt," he said, before taking a bite. Gus nodded.

"Nothing like making good food bad for you," Gus said. "Cheers." He raised the salted hotcake like a drink and took a bite of his own.

"Not bad, Steve. Not bad at all," Gus said. To Steve's surprise, he picked up another pancake. While Gus ate, he watched Steve clean up his work area.

"So, what happened to you?" Gus asked. "Were you in the service?"

"Excuse me?" Steve said.

Clare R.

"You seem like you've experienced some shit. Not a lot of people are that honest," Gus said. Steve stared at Mr. Alero.

"You don't seem like someone who appreciates being lied to," Steve said.

"No, I don't. But that's not why you told the truth," Gus said. "Not really, anyway."

"What are you? The psychiatrist cook? I hardly know you," Steve laughed. Gus only shrugged and kept chewing.

"You don't have to tell me, Steve, and I'm not going to pry," he said. "But sometimes it's good to get that stuff out there. Otherwise it will eat at you." Steve didn't appreciate the way Gus seemed to make the issue feel trivial, but for some reason he felt like opening up.

"My dad died a couple years ago. He was a volunteer fireman," Steve said. That was all he could manage before numerous, terrible images flashed in his mind. Gus stopped chewing and Steve looked down at the plate of pancakes.

"I'm sorry," Gus said. "I bet your family was devastated." Steve nodded and then feelings of guilt welled inside of him like flood waters behind a dam.

"Yeah," he shrugged. "But I haven't seen them in a couple years. I left home after he passed away."

"Interesting," Gus said. "And don't you think that's a tad bit selfish? They're your family."

"Yeah maybe, but it was easier being gone. Home didn't feel the same anymore," Steve admitted.

"That may be so," Gus said. "But those same people may be counting on you. Who am I to say anything, though? I'm just the teacher slash cook."

"Yeah, I don't know," Steve said.

"Enough about that, though. What about the girl you mentioned? The one you want to impress." A smile spread across Steve's face and for the time being he forgot about the depressing thoughts regarding his father.

"She's this sweet girl I met while traveling for work," Steve offered.

"Like a *special* friend?" Gus teased. Steve laughed and shook his head no. When he glanced at Gus, there was the tiniest hint of a smile on the corners of his mouth.

"No, we just had a great time during a delay at the airport. You know the story. Guy meets girl. She's sweet, funny, and beautiful. Blah, blah, blah."

"Why are you making it seem so trivial?" Gus asked. "You're clearly taken by her."

"Because I might never see her again. We forgot to exchange numbers and stuff." Steve waited for a reply but all he got from Gus was a sigh and pensive stare.

"Well that was dumb," said Mr. Alero.

"Tell me about it," Steve replied. Once again, he found himself irritated at the casualness of Gus's response, but Steve tried to stay rational. It wasn't Mr. Alero's fault that he'd potentially missed a chance with Clare.

"Well, have you tried looking for her? I mean, all you young people are all connected on the Internet, aren't you? Or maybe try whatever company she works for?" Steve felt like an idiot. He'd been so happy go lucky and then skipped right to brooding teenager. He hadn't stopped to think that there could be a simple solution.

"That's not a bad idea," Steve admitted.

"Don't overthink things so much," Gus said.

"I'm an engineer. I get paid to overthink," Steve replied, and

Clare R.

Gus laughed.

"That may be. But this isn't engineering. This is your life. You gotta try something and if that doesn't work, then try something else. Not much different than cooking really," said Gus. The brief speech was followed by more silence while he chewed, and Steve pondered the cooking analogy.

"You want the rest of these?" Steve asked.

"No you take them. Enjoy them. They were good. I will see you tomorrow, yeah?" Gus said.

"Yeah," Steve replied. "Thanks for the, uh, chat."

"Anytime," Gus replied. "I hope everything works out."

"Thanks," Steve replied, and with a final wave, he headed for the door. Later that evening, Steve sat in front of the computer, mindlessly taking bites of zucchini pancakes while searching the social media site he was a member of. His account had been deactivated due to inactivity, but after getting the matter situated, he began his search for Clare.

It wasn't long though, before his feelings of excitement and anticipation began to deflate. There were countless Clares and a high percentage had "R" at the start of their last name. But none of the profile pictures were the girl he met. Sometime after midnight, Steve sat back in his chair and rubbed his eyes. His arms were crossed in frustration because his several hour search had yielded nothing. After a quick shower, Steve climbed into bed and fell asleep imagining him and Clare cooking something together.

~~~~

Nothing could stop the days from passing and soon it had already been a week since meeting Clare. He had attended the second and third sessions of his cooking class, which were *cooking with a wok* and *successful grilling,* respectively. Both had gone incredibly well. Before leaving on Wednesday night, Steve told Gus about his plan to head home for the weekend.

"I think that's a good idea, Steve," said Gus. "Make sure you give your mother an extra hug or two while you're visiting. I'm sure she could use it."

"I will," Steve said.

"Good. I'll see you next week then, yeah?" said Mr. Alero.

"You bet," Steve finished.

By Friday afternoon, Steve was staring blankly at his computer screen, bewildered by the thoughts floating around in his mind. Nobody Steve had met in the previous few years had come close to having this profound of an effect on him. No stranger, or any woman that he'd dated for that matter, stuck in his mind the way Clare did.

After being confined to the office most of the day, it was an incredible relief to turn up the music and amuse himself with more magnificent thoughts of Clare. Once Steve made it home, he quickly made a sandwich and gave the townhouse a once over to make sure he hadn't missed anything. Then after giving his neighbor a cheerful goodbye, Steve hopped back in the car and began his journey north.

Chapter 5

Patty was the senior administrative assistant at the local hospital where she had worked since before her children were born. It was a short jaunt from her home, perhaps ten minutes and maybe twenty if the traffic was bad. Every morning, while drinking a cup of tea, Patty toasted a slice of bread and made her lunch for the day.

When Patty was originally hired some thirty years before, she had been a brilliant nurse, fresh out of school with the bright spirit of anyone who had their whole life in front of them. Patty was newly married to a wonderful husband and she loved her job. Life was good. But as the years passed, Patty saw good friends pass away and enough gruesome injures to last a lifetime. It took a toll on her. It made her tired.

But Patty loved helping people and she loved the three people who were at home waiting for her each night when the shift ended. Those three people were her husband and their two sons. They made her appreciate life and gave her the strength to keep up with her job.

However, when her husband passed away unexpectedly, Patty was unable to continue with her duties as a nurse and moved off the floor to take up a desk position. It didn't help matters that shortly after her husband's passing, Patty's youngest son left home and she hadn't seen him in the last couple years. On rare occasions he would send a short letter or postcard, but that was it.

Some days were easier to handle than others. There might be a brightness in the sky or a sweet smell in the air that gave her a little more hope for the day. But today there was neither. It was cold and dreary. Winter was coming. She shuffled papers aimlessly and snatched up files that were put on the counter by attending nurses. Anything that could make her shift come to an end a little sooner was more than welcome.

It was late on Friday afternoon and Patty was anxious to get home. She turned to take yet another glance at the clock that rested on the wall behind the nurses' station. The hands hardly seemed to move, especially the second hand. It seemed like it took at least five seconds for that long, thin piece of plastic to move one tick.

Patty wanted to see the puppy that was waiting for her at home. But more so, Patty still held on to the hope that when she pulled into her driveway later that evening, Steve would finally be home. It pained her when people asked how her boys were because she knew everything about one and nothing of the other. Today, several people had asked her about her boys.

When Patty arrived home early that evening, there was no one to greet her except a dog that was ready to go pee. Like so many nights before this one, she buried her disappointment and tended to the dog. As darkness settled, she accepted the fact that she didn't have much of an appetite, so all Patty ate was a skimpy, frozen dinner. Then after a shower, she sat down in her husband's old recliner and picked up her knitting needles. It was a simple hobby that she found quite soothing. Currently, Patty was knitting a pair of warm, winter socks for her new grandson. It wasn't long, however, before the steady clicking of the needles caused her to doze off.

When the sound of a new television show woke her up, Patty decided to call it a night and she headed to bed and the puppy followed closely behind.

~~~

Steve reached over to the cup holder and took a sip from his steaming cup of coffee and breathed in the sweet aroma. It made him think of days gone by, growing up in a house where the smell of coffee pervaded every room because the pot was always going by ten after six every morning. However, as the cup emptied, the smell had faded some and Steve found himself wishing for a cup of tea instead because of the acrid taste left in his mouth.

Once the jam-packed streets of rush-hour were behind him, Steve and his car cruised down the nearly empty highway and he watched the bare farm fields pass by. Most of the fall harvest had been completed for the season and now the fields would rest until the following spring. But there were still plenty of wild animals making use of them and the farther north he drove, the more deer Steve saw picking through the pale, brown corn stalks.

The dreary, cold weather had finally blown off, leaving behind a pleasantly colorful sunset in its wake. Steve halfway paid attention to the road as he spied a contrail cutting across the orange-pink sky and thoughts of Clare swirled freshly in his mind. A warm feeling spread through his body as he pictured her smile and

Steve glanced at the phone in the empty passenger seat, wishing the screen would light up with a new message from Clare.

But no message came and he knew none would, so Steve kept on driving. The beautiful sunset soon faded to darker colors and the headlights from oncoming traffic burned through the growing darkness. Once the sun had set completely, Steve noticed a bright star shining through the passenger window and he couldn't help but make a wish.

~~~~

Steve wasn't surprised that his mother's house was dark when he arrived late that evening. The temperature had dropped significantly since departing that evening and Steve could see dense clouds of his breath mixing with a few snowflakes that had started to fall. His body ached as he lumbered up to the door of his mother's house and numbness was already setting in on his hands as he dug in his pockets. Steve cursed silently to himself for not being used to the cold weather any more.

Steve fished out a small clump of keys and found the right one. It was a dull, old key that his father had given him one afternoon before he had left to hang out with his friends. Apparently it was the original key to the house, at least that's what Steve's father had told him when he gave it to him. They had made a few copies but Steve held onto the trusty original and he had taken great care not to lose it.

Just like all the other nights he had come home late, Steve was greeted by a familiar sight when he opened the door. Although the rest of the house was dark, a soft glow could be seen coming from the kitchen because Steve's mother always left a light on in case anyone needed to get a glass of water late at night.

What astonished Steve, though, was the smell. It was like walking into a wall of memories and the distinct smell sent his mind reeling. In all the times he'd wondered about returning home, Steve never considered that the smell would have such a profound impact on him. But not long after he stepped in the door, a soft pitter patter of feet came rushing toward him out of the darkness, distracting him from his thoughts.

"Hi there," Steve said, bending over to pet his mother's newest addition to the family. "How you doing, boy? What's your name?" The dog was stocky and thick like a bratwurst with legs. Its long, floppy ears dangled almost to the floor and it had a welcoming toothy grin. By the light of his phone, Steve was able to read the tag- *Toby*. The dog responded to the attention by wagging his tail furiously and climbing up on Steve's knee after he knelt down. Steve was glad Toby was smart enough not to bark because the last thing he wanted to do was wake up his sleeping mother.

Eager for a glass of water before bed, Steve gave the puppy a few final pats before tiptoeing his way through the house and into the kitchen. His furry friend followed along as well, and sniffed around the kitchen while Steve sipped quietly from a glass.

No matter how quiet Steve tried to be, his mother's keen senses picked up on something different in the house and it wasn't long before she appeared in the kitchen, wrapped up in her bathrobe looking dreadfully tired.

"My God, Steve! Is that you? What are you doing here?" Patty asked, wondering if she was dreaming. She didn't expect her son to appear randomly like this, but nothing could have made Patty happier in that moment. Steve looked like he'd grown since she'd seen him last. His hair was about the same, but there was a very apparent shadow along his jawline that indicated the presence of facial hair. Her son was all grown up now. Steve had to clear his throat when he tried to talk.

"Hi ma," he finally said, and then with a shrug of his shoulders he continued. "I needed to get out of town for a couple days." Patty nodded and came over to give him a hug. It was indescribable how nice it felt to hug her son.

When she pulled away, Steve was able to see her face more in the dim light of the kitchen. He had expected to be greeted by the mother he'd left behind, and for the most part he was. But in the time that had passed since they'd last been together, Steve could see that the stress from her husband's passing had got to her as well. Her pretty brown hair was faded and flecked with gray. Her eyes looked sad and tired, like she didn't sleep well. But Steve wasn't surprised. It was hard to sleep when you felt so incredibly alone.

"OK, well you should get to bed. It's late," she said, and Steve nodded. "Toby is happy to see you." Toby had finally stopped sniffing everything in sight and was sitting patiently at Steve's feet. He was looking up at Steve with his brown eyes and the expression on his face was something like, *Yeah, we have a lot to talk about.* After saying goodnight to his mother, Steve headed for his bedroom with Toby hot on his tail.

Not much had changed in the years since Steve had moved out of his mother's house. Many of the posters he had growing up were still hanging on the walls and the closet still held an assortment of old clothes. Clearly, Steve's mother was still taking care of his room because as he looked around more, there wasn't much

Clare R.

in the way of dust accumulation and the bed was made up.

While Steve brushed his teeth, he surveyed the bookshelf that held many old books and movies he hadn't read or watched in several years. In fact, it was only recently that Steve had started reading frequently again.

I bet Clare has a bookshelf like this, Steve surmised. *I hope she does.* After a few more minutes of brushing and staring, Steve made a mental note to take a few along when he headed home.

Driving for several hours at a time always left Steve feeling gross, so he gladly shed the grungy clothes from his trip and jumped in the shower. Afterward, he hoisted Toby up onto the bed so that he could have some company while he slept. Toby playfully hopped around the bed and then busied himself with getting comfy near Steve's feet. All the while Steve watched because it was very amusing. He missed having a dog.

Do you like dogs? he wondered. Steve easily imagined her laughing while playing with a puppy and that thought alone eased his racing mind, but the aching feeling to see her again continued to grow evermore.

~~~~

When Steve woke the next morning, he could tell by the amount of light streaming through the window that he'd slept much later than he intended. Steve was laying on his back staring blankly at the ceiling contemplating the strange dream he had just before waking. It was incredibly vivid and he got to relive his time with Clare at the airport, which was amazing.

Her smile was so beautiful and it seemed like wherever she

was in the dream a brightness followed her. The dream progressed, and unlike what really transpired, Steve got the chance to walk Clare to her own gate and they continued laughing, joking, and holding hands. Only, when he tried to board the plane with her, the gate agent wouldn't let him. Then Clare was gone and his original flight was, too. Steve was stuck in the airport.

It had left him frustrated, seeing her so close and almost feeling the touch of her skin, only to wake in a mess of blankets. Steve shook his head and ran a hand through his hair in exasperation. It was hard not to smile, though, when he noticed that Toby was curled up under his arm.

Apparently Toby had come to sleep much closer at some point in the night. Steve scratched his back and the soft skin behind his ears. The result was immediate and the dog's tail quickly began to wag in excitement. When Steve stopped scratching, Toby would nuzzle his hand in hopes that the scratching would continue.

However, Toby didn't stay curled up for long because shortly after waking, they both noticed an awakening smell that was wafting through the partially open door. Toby scampered off the bed to investigate.

The house was quickly filling with the sweet smell of cinnamon and Steve gladly made his way to the kitchen to see what his mother was cooking. There were, in fact, cinnamon rolls cooking as well as scrambled eggs and sausage. Toby had learned well and was sitting patiently in the doorway waiting for his treat at the end of the meal.

"Morning, Steve," his mother said. Patty had been excited to get up this morning and woke feeling very refreshed. She couldn't remember the last time she'd slept that well.

Clare R.

"Mornin'," Steve replied. He went to a cupboard and reached for a mug so he could make some tea.

"I've already got the kettle going for you," she said, watching him dig in the cupboard. "You still like tea don't you?" Steve nodded and Patty smiled. It had been so long since she'd cooked for him, or anyone for that matter, and Patty was overjoyed to make one of Steve's favorite meals. In her excitement, she had cooked a whole pack of sausage links and scrambled half a dozen eggs.

I hope you're hungry, Steve, she thought.

"Thanks," he replied. "How have you been? What's new?"

"Good," his mother replied. Then she looked down at Toby. "Keeping busy. I've got this troublemaker to look after. How about yourself?" The kettle started whistling, so Steve didn't answer right away.

"I'm all right," he said. "Pretty good..." By the look in his eyes, Steve's mother could tell that he was distracted by something. Patty watched her son fill a glass with hot water and walk away into the living room. She could remember in great detail when Steve would come home from college, and during those visits he was so much more talkative. There was always something new and exciting that he would tell her about. But those days were gone now. He was like a locked up chest now, only giving up enough information to move conversations to their end.

Steve hadn't noticed it the night before, mostly because he was so tired, but after waking up feeling so empty, the solemn heaviness that he'd felt for so long was quickly filling him up. Steve knew it was because he was finally back home.

Pictures from many years past, all the way up to the previous Christmas, were scattered around much of the house and a large collection of them were in the living room. Various memories of his childhood took shape in his mind as Steve stared at pictures of himself and his brother playing in the snow when they were kids.

There were also a few pictures of their father throwing a baseball with them out in the yard after they had started little league. Steve turned suddenly, searching through the faces for one picture in particular. Sitting above his mother's fireplace was a beautifully framed photograph of Steve's entire family, smiling happily after his brother's wedding. This was the last family picture in which they were all together before his father had passed away. Steve felt his chest tighten as if some invisible force was squeezing his body, but he continued to stare at the picture.

Steve's mother had asked him to come home to visit several times when she wrote back to the occasional postcard or letter he sent, but he often declined the invitation using work as an excuse. In reality, it had been because he was too sad and frustrated to come home. It was easier to move and work than see evidence of memories that he would never again be able to share with his father.

The longer he stood there, Steve realized that the invisible vice was loosening and he didn't hurt as much. Ever since the accident had taken his father away from their family, it had felt like there was a gaping hole in his life with a bottom that stretched to infinity and edges that knew no bounds. But now he didn't feel so empty. The chasm that had opened in his life had shrunk dramatically and he knew it was because Clare was a brightness in his life that had brought him back into the world.

Then his mother interrupted his thoughts.

"Breakfast is ready, Steve," she said.

"All right," he replied.

Chapter 6

The hangers clattered together as Clare pawed through the rack of ladies underwear, and as she stood there amidst all the undergarments, the word *knickers* kept popping into her head and she kept smiling. She couldn't believe how much funnier everything seemed since meeting Steve.

It had been an interesting week for Clare. She had this newfound energy and stamina that allowed her to get even more work done than normal. At any given time, she was reliving some portion of the airport date in her head. When she was stopped for any length of time, Clare often found herself narrating the lives of the people around her and hoping that Steve was doing the same wherever he was.

For instance, Clare had been sitting at breakfast a few days earlier when a guy and his girlfriend sat down at the table next to her. It only took a brief glance for the gears to start turning in Clare's head.

My name's Derek. I have a super-hot girlfriend named Zoey and I love wearing my hat backward—

But before Clare could run the scenario any further, the boyfriend started talking to the waitress and his personality was completely different from what she'd imagined, which made it even funnier.

"How much breakfast food has anyone ever ordered?" asked the boyfriend.

"Um, I'm not sure. Why? What were you thinking?" replied the waitress.

"Well, I can't decide. Everything looks so good. I want to try the pancakes and the biscuits and gravy. How big is the order for that, by the way?"

"Um, it's two biscuits with a decent amount of sausage gravy," she said.

"Oh yeah, OK. Let's have that and the *Westgate*, too," continued the boyfriend. Clare scanned through the menu to find the *Westgate,* which turned out to be a huge scrambler dish with potatoes, chorizo, onions, eggs, and salsa.

How much food are you going to order? Clare wondered. She chanced a glance at the couple again and the boyfriend caught her eye and smiled. Then he continued to go back and forth with the waitress. By the time everything was said and done, the girlfriend had hardly said a word and it took a pair of waitresses to deliver all the food to their tiny table for two.

This was certainly one of those occasions, because even though there was nothing out of the ordinary about buying underwear, she was positive that if she and Steve were shopping together, he would make funny expressions and comments at her expense until she said the word *knickers*. When Clare looked up and noticed another woman staring at her because of her unprovoked giggling, she did her best to put on a serious face.

"Sorry," Clare mumbled. But nothing could stop another

Clare R.

smile from spreading across her face when the lady turned away. Eventually, after picking out a couple shirts and a pair of dress pants in another aisle, Clare made her way to the checkout line. She set her items on the belt and the clerk smiled brightly at her.

"Someone sure looks happy," the lady said. Clare laughed again.

"What? Oh, yeah. I am, I guess," she replied while digging in her wallet for some cash. Upon hearing the total, Clare tilted her head in confusion and looked into the bag the clerk had handed her.

"Oh, I'm sorry, miss. I got three pairs, not two," Clare said.

"I know, dear," said the clerk, returning a smile of her own. "It's your lucky day I guess. You get one pair free when you buy two."

"Oh," Clare said. "Well...Awesome!" She hadn't seen a sign anywhere on any of the racks. But with a happy shrug, she picked up her bags.

"Thanks," Clare said.

"You're welcome, sweetie," said the clerk. "Have a great day!" Clare walked through the doors and into the chilly, fall air. Suddenly, Steve's voice echoed crystal clear in her head.

Look at that, Clare! You got a pair of knickers for free. She burst out laughing as she opened the door on her car.

~~~~

After breakfast, Steve and Toby went for a walk around the block. The sun peeked out every now and again, but for the most part, it was another cloudy and blustery day. Toby didn't seem to mind though, and he pulled on the leash while prowling around the bases of trees and bushes.

When the pair got back to the house, Steve offered to help his mother with a few chores and repairs that needed to be done. Lately these items had fallen to Steve's uncle because his brother's life had become much busier after getting married and having a baby of his own. He busied himself most of the afternoon by raking leaves, cleaning out the gutters, doing some miscellaneous painting around the house, and a small amount of caulking in the bathroom.

Voices behind him caused Steve to turn away from the gutters, and from up on the ladder, he spotted a small gathering in the neighbor's driveway. While Steve was growing up, one of his good friends had lived across the street, but in the years since they graduated high school, Steve hadn't seen much of John. Yet, there he was with his family and as Steve looked closer, he noticed a pretty girl standing next to his old friend and she was carrying a little bundle in her arms.

Steve was hit with a strange range of emotions before his friend called out to him. There was excitement and wonder. But there was also a tinge of jealously. Steve knew that life wasn't a race by any means, but he couldn't help but think that in the time he'd been gone, he'd fallen behind his brother and now John, too. That feeling, however, only lingered for a moment before it was swept away by the breeze. In its wake, Steve simply felt empty again, wishing he could see Clare. Then he heard his name and it brought him back to reality.

"Steve! Is that you?" John called out. He turned, offering a simple wave, and began climbing down the ladder. John and his wife came across the street with their new baby. With a goofy grin

Clare R.

that Steve hadn't seen in many years, John reached out a hand. Steve tried to get the grime off his hands by wiping them on the backside of the ratty jeans he had on for outdoor work, and joined in the handshake. It was a firm grip from a strong man.

John and Steve had grown up doing many of the same things, but when they reached high school, their paths detoured slightly. John had bulked up after joining the football team whereas Steve had preferred running and played soccer and baseball, which left him much leaner. Steve noticed that John still held onto his wide frame and short haircuts. John's wife, whom his friend had met in college, was also athletic and about the same height as John. Her blond hair blew in the breeze as she cooed at the baby in her arms.

"It's been a while," Steve said, trying to recall his wife's name. He remembered getting an invitation for their wedding, but he'd been unable to attend because of his work schedule. Thankfully John cut in.

"You remember, Suzy?" John said. Steve nodded and reached out his hand again.

"Yeah, of course," he said. "And it looks like there is a new member in the family." Steve motioned to the soft, pink blanket in her arms and it was as if the little girl knew she was being talked about because the bundle started to squirm, causing Suzy to laugh.

"Yep, this is Anna," Suzy said. Steve leaned forward to peer into the blanket and the baby's wide eyes locked onto his. When Steve reached out, the baby wrapped a tiny hand around one of his fingers.

"She's beautiful," he said. "Congratulations."

"Thanks man," John said. Baby Anna held their attention for some time as she giggled and squirmed in the blanket. They didn't say much except for laugh. But finally Suzy decided that she should probably go inside and left the two friends on the sidewalk.

"So, what's new?" John asked. "What's been going on?" Steve let out a short sigh and kicked at a twig he'd missed while raking. Then he shrugged.

"Not much," Steve replied. "Work mostly." John nodded as Steve turned to look back at the ladder. He didn't really feel like working any more. He also felt sort of awkward about the current situation. Steve hadn't expected to run into many of his old friends, especially John.

"Yeah, I hear you there," John replied. "It never ends." Steve bowed his head in agreement.

"I'm sorry I couldn't make it to your wedding," he blurted out, feeling a pang of guilt.

"Hey, don't worry about it," John said. "It's great getting to see you now. Seriously, how's everything been? I know stuff was kind of rough there for a while." Steve nodded, knowing that John was referring to his father's passing. For an instant, he considered telling John that this was the first time he'd been home since the accident.

"It's been good. Better," he said instead. "I mean, I've got a good job now and a nice apartment south of here a few hours."

"Any ladies?" John asked. Steve caught his breath as more thoughts of Clare surfaced in his mind. He let out a funny sort of chuckle and turned to move the ladder farther down the roof. This just caused John to laugh.

"What's that about?" John said. "Come on, man!" Steve shook his head.

"I actually met a really sweet girl last week," he began. "But

Clare R.

I'm not sure if it will go anywhere."

"Why not?" John asked.

"We met in passing...Traveling for work," Steve said. "We didn't get to exchange any info."

"Ah," John said. "That's rough." Steve nodded and made a few final adjustments to the ladder.

"Yeah, so..." Steve said.

"Well you know, if it doesn't work out, I'm sure Suzy knows someone. She's got all sorts of friends from college she talks to still," John offered. "So, I guess...Let me know."

"Yeah, we'll see," Steve replied. He knew John meant well, but Steve didn't want to discuss Clare any more or any other *ladies,* and decided to change the subject. "Congratulations again with your new baby. Anna looks awesome. I can't believe you're a dad now."

"Thanks! She's great," John said with a grin. "I can't believe how tiny she is." John was clearly overcome with the exhilaration that Steve assumed most new dads felt and he nodded thinking about the feeling of Anna's little hand grabbing one of his fingers.

The miracle of life is pretty spectacular, Steve thought. After talking for a few more minutes, the two friends said their goodbyes and with a final wave John walked back across the street. Steve finished cleaning out the gutters before moving on to tasks in the house.

~~~

After dawdling around the house for several hours, Steve's mother decided to run a few errands and pick up some groceries.

She had expected to be nervous when she saw her son again, but it hadn't occurred to Patty that her ability to communicate with Steve would be so fragmented. Their breakfast conversation had been forced like when you see an acquaintance in a supermarket checkout line.

Maybe we were both nervous, Patty thought. The errand run was an excuse to collect her thoughts more than anything else. She didn't want a repeat of breakfast at their next meal.

Steve, on the other hand, was trying to take things one at a time and decided to make her dinner in hopes of breaking through the awkwardness associated with their breakfast that morning. He scoured the kitchen, looking through the cupboards, fridge, and the freezer before deciding on something that sounded good. Toby sat patiently in the kitchen and helped when he could by cleaning up food items that somehow managed to fall on the floor.

When Steve's mother stepped into her home early that evening, she was greeted by a very delightful smell that lifted even her dampest spirits. Patty gawked at the surprise dinner that was about finished in the kitchen.

"Wow, Steve. You've become quite the cook," she said. Steve smiled and motioned to the dog at his feet.

"I had a lot of good help," he said sarcastically. As she stood there admiring Steve and her puppy, it occurred to Patty that she hadn't laughed in a really long time.

"Good, Toby," she said while putting away the groceries. The dog wagged its tail happily. "That smells really good."

"Good, I hope you like it," Steve replied. "I've been taking cooking classes."

"Cooking classes? Really?" Patty said.

"Yeah," Steve said.

Clare R.

"Just for fun or..." she said.

"I don't know yet," he replied. "We'll see."

"Hmm, all right. Well, I'm going to go change and then we can eat," Patty said.

"Sounds good," Steve replied. A short while later, he set the table and dished up bowls of hot tomato soup with dill and garlic, gooey grilled cheese sandwiches, and a colorful tossed salad. Even the dressing was homemade, courtesy of Gus's large library of recipes.

Many years before, this would have been a very different setting. Most likely the television would have been on with either the news or some ball game playing, and there would have been four people sitting down at the table. But now there were only two and the television sat dark in the corner of the living room. The only other sound in the house came from a small radio that was sitting on the kitchen counter which Steve put on in order to break the silence that was lingering in his mother's home.

"So, how's everything going?" his mother asked, after Steve sat down. She surveyed him with a pensive expression because she was a bit unsure of where to start. "How's work?"

"Work's all right," Steve answered. "We're keeping really busy, so that's good. But I don't know...Everything else is...interesting." Patty slowly moved her head up and down and took a bite of dinner. It was delicious.

"Do you want any?" Steve asked after pouring a glass of milk.

"No. Thank you," his mother replied. "What does that mean? Interesting?" Steve had spent much of the afternoon wondering how much he wanted to divulge to his mother. A lot had happened in the last two years.

"Is everything OK? Is your car OK?" She asked. Steve answered with a shrug and was otherwise silent. Everything about his expression was distant and vacant, which left his mother slightly worried.

"Well, come on," his mother said, trying to warm him up with a smile. "Tell me...Is there a girl?" Steve's cheeks flushed and he looked down at his plate.

Moms must just know these things, he thought. *Or maybe there's a handbook.* His mother just chuckled quietly and smiled triumphantly. Steve certainly wasn't beaming about his bowl of soup.

I've still got it, Patty thought. Since Steve seemed to be opening up, she decided to wait patiently for him to continue. It was a subtle victory and she savored the fact that she hadn't completely lost touch with her son.

"Well, I got a really strange fortune at this Chinese restaurant I like to go to," Steve said.

"What did it say?" Patty asked.

"It said that *my charms hadn't gone unnoticed by all the angels,*" Steve said, imagining the tiny slip of paper that was tacked to the cork board that hung in his room.

"Yeah, that sounds like a good fortune," his mother offered. Steve nodded.

"The next day I left to go on a day trip for work and that afternoon my return flight got delayed," Steve said. He was trying to slowly build to the wonderful encounter with Clare.

That doesn't sound very fortunate, Patty thought.

"Does that happen a lot?" she asked.

Clare R.

"Yeah, all the time," Steve said.

"And it doesn't bother you?" Patty wondered out loud. Steve shook his head sideways. "Wow. It's why I don't like to fly much anymore."

"Well, it definitely didn't bother me that night," Steve exclaimed. He was grinning wildly now. "I met someone...sort of."

"That's great! But 'sort of'?" his mother asked. "Either you did or you didn't? Right?"

"I'll get to that, but her name is Clare and she was amazing," Steve said. For the first time since their fateful meeting, Steve was getting to express his excitement because he was finally able to tell someone about that wonderful afternoon. He didn't want to talk to Jimmy about her and Steve certainly wasn't going to talk to his other coworker Lucy about it because he was fairly certain she liked him.

"I had just made it through security and I was looking over the flight boards to see what was happening with my flight," Steve said. "When I saw it was delayed, I went to sit down. I guess Clare had noticed me smiling about the delay and she came over to ask me why I was so happy about it and we hit it off." Patty chuckled again.

"What else happened?" she asked, eager to hear more.

"Well, we talked for a long time...about books and movies. Then we got some tea and even ended up getting dinner," Steve said. The look of surprise on Patty's face continued to grow as she listened to her son's wonderful story.

"You got dinner? That sounds like a date," his mother said.

"Ma, if it was a date, it was the best one I've ever been on," Steve said. The elation he felt from thinking about Clare made him feel like an excited teenager again. Patty continued smiling, but this statement left her feeling a bit confused, but she neglected to say anything until the story was finished.

"Steve, it sounds wonderful! I can't say that I've had that great of an experience at the airport," his mother said. "I'm really happy for you, Steve. Are you going to see her again?" In no time at all Steve's expression changed from gleeful to glum.

"I'm not sure. That's why I said sort of," he said. "Clare was so great. She made me laugh and I made her laugh and when we got ready to get on our flights, she kissed me on the cheek."

"Well, that's great!" his mom said. Patty was relieved that her son was getting to experience something positive in his life. The harder he focused on that memory, the more Steve could almost feel Clare's lips on his cheek once again.

"It was amazing, but we both were in a rush to get to our flights and we didn't end up exchanging anything. No numbers or emails or anything," Steve confessed. Finally his mother understood why Steve was so vacant.

"Nothing?" she asked, looking for confirmation. "Not even her last name?" Steve shook his head sideways, but after a moment another half-smile crossed his face.

"Well, Clare did leave me her book," Steve said. "I think she shoved it in my bag when I got up to use the bathroom and I found it when I got home later that night. Her name is written on the inside cover and I know her last name starts with an R. But that's it." A playful titter escaped her lips.

"I don't think you have much to worry about then," his mother said. "I think she likes you, too." His mother's confidence in the situation made Steve smile but he shrugged his shoulders again.

Clare R.

"I hope so. I haven't quit thinking about her but who knows if we'll meet again," Steve said. Patty set her fork down and stared at her son.

"If you're this taken by her, then you shouldn't give up. You'll think of something," said his mother in a very reassuring manner. "That or you will run into her again, I'm sure."

"Yeah hopefully," Steve mumbled. Patty could see that their conversation was perched on the edge of a cliff and the last thing she wanted was for the strange awkwardness to befall the dinner table, so she tried to keep their conversation going in another direction.

"You know your brother thinks that Katy might be pregnant again?" she said.

"Really?" Steve said. "That's awesome. How come he hasn't said anything to me?" Patty refrained from saying the obvious answer, which was of course, Steve being gone and incredibly difficult to get ahold of.

"I think because they're not absolutely sure yet," his mother said.

"Did you know John had a kid?" Steve replied.

"Really?" his mother replied. "You mean John from across the street?"

"Yeah. I saw him and Suzy earlier today while you were gone," Steve said. "They have a really cute baby girl. Her name is Anna."

"That's great! How exciting," Patty exclaimed. "I'll have to go over tomorrow and say hello."

"You should," Steve said. "I'm sure they would like that." Before she could stop herself, Patty changed the subject again to something she'd been wondering about while she was out running errands.

"How come you seemed upset after looking at the pictures in the den this morning? Were you just thinking about Clare?" his mother asked. "Or something else?" Steve knew exactly what his mother was implying by the use of "something else" since her voice took on a completely different tone.

"I don't know. I'm just sad and frustrated. I feel like that all the time. Dad's never going to see me get married or see my family if I ever have one," Steve said bluntly.

"Don't say that, sweetie," his mother said. "You know he's up there somewhere. I'm sure he's keeping tabs on you and all the rest of us." Patty hoped her attempt at a joke would make her son smile but Steve only gaped at her with a rather glum expression.

"I know, but you know what I mean, ma," Steve said. He could feel his stomach getting sour and his mother knew it, too. Patty's husband had been the love of her life and she missed him dearly every day.

"What's she like?" asked his mother.

"She's smart, very clever, and very funny. She works for a logistics company that handles the travel arrangements for film companies and their personnel," he began. "Clare has long, auburn hair, bright blue eyes, and a gorgeous smile. Oh my goodness, does she have a beautiful smile. She's a bit shorter than I am but she had heels on, so I didn't notice at first, and she was wearing these pretty white earrings."

"Do you think she's in a relationship?" asked his mother. Steve shrugged again.

"I don't think so. I hope not. I mean, she did give me a kiss on the cheek before she left and we sort of held hands," Steve said.

Clare R.

This took Patty completely by surprise. In all honesty, she had expected Steve's return home to be accompanied by a great deal of unresolved baggage regarding his father's passing. But instead, he brought news that was much more cheerful.

"I'm really surprised you didn't start with this," his mother exclaimed. Steve finally laughed.

"There was so much that happened that night," he said. "I've spent so much time trying to remember every detail. There was something about her, though. Clare has this sense of confidence that's so intriguing but at the same time she was kind of reserved, almost shy. It was like we were both really nervous and excited at the same time." Patty chuckled again.

"Clare probably really enjoyed talking to you," she said.

"I hope so," Steve said. "It was so easy to talk to her and her sense of humor was amazing...the perfect amount of sarcasm." His mother smiled again. Hearing Steve talk about Clare sparked a wonderful memory of her own.

"You know that's sort of how your dad and I met?" she said.

"Really?" he asked.

"Yeah, well not at the airport," Patty clarified. "I had just finished a shift and I was starving. When I first started at the hospital the shifts I worked were insanely long and there used to be this great twenty-four hour diner downtown that I would go to after work. We were both picking up takeout and your dad was in such a rush."

"What was he doing?" Steve asked. Patty laughed as if someone had just told the most hilarious joke.

"He was picking up an order for him and his buddies. I think they were planning to hang out and watch a game or something.

You should have seen him...all dirty from being on the farm all day with your uncle," Patty explained. "I had just filled my drink cup up at the soda machine and your dad was moving a little too quickly and he knocked my drink over. It spilled all over my pant leg." Steve laughed because he had several memories of his own in which his father had done goofy things because he was moving with a little too much enthusiasm.

"Sounds familiar," he said.

"Yeah, I don't think I've ever seen your dad so embarrassed, and let me tell you, he slowed down after that," his mother explained. "He said *sorry* I don't know how many times and bought me a dessert. Then he ended up bailing on his friends and we ate dinner together on the bench outside the restaurant. It was so nice that night..."

"Seriously?" Steve asked. "That's how it happened?"

"That's how it happened," she repeated. "It was so wonderful and completely unexpected."

After dinner, Steve offered to do the dishes and Patty gratefully accepted. She had picked up a new book while running errands, so after making a cup of tea, she went to read in the living room. Once the tea was gone, it didn't take long for drowsiness to set in and soon she was heading to bed.

"Steve, I know things have been different the last couple years," his mother said. "But you have always been a strong and thoughtful person. Don't be too hard on yourself." Patty had come into the kitchen and put her hand on his back in a very motherly fashion.

'Different' is a bit of an understatement, ma, he thought.

"Clare sounds like a wonderful young lady and I think you

Clare R.

should definitely keep her in mind. Besides, you do have to give Clare back her book and I would love to meet a girl who can make you this happy. Just don't do anything rash, OK?" Steve nodded with a smile. Then he wiped off his soapy hands and gave his mother a hug.

Once the dishes were done, Steve returned to his room and scrounged in his bag for Clare's book. Ever since he was little, he loved reading by the light of the desk lamp. The soft glow pushed away the darkness just enough so that his world became the small area around his bed where the light reached, and in that tiny world, it was quiet and peaceful.

Over the years there had been countless nights that Steve had gone through this very routine, turning the pages on an innumerable amount of books and magazines until heavy eyelids signaled it was time for bed. But before he continued reading the newest installment of the *Lunar Chronicles*, Steve breathed in the distinct smell that lingered on the pages of Clare's book.

With each breath, Steve continued to ponder his parents' first meeting. It was fun to imagine his father making an absolute fool of himself in front of his mother. It eased Steve's worry about being goofy during the unique time he and Clare had shared. Nevertheless, Steve was still left with the conundrum of finding her again, so instead of reading that night, Steve fell asleep thinking of possible scenarios in which he and Clare could meet again.

The next day Steve had an early breakfast with his mother prior to heading home. Before leaving, she made sure to give him an extra hug and a bag of useful things that she thought would make for a belated house warming gift. The return trip was pleasant and Steve had fun singing along to several love songs that came on the radio. With each tune, thoughts of Clare came to mind and he replayed that moment of their hands touching over and over again.

By the time Steve made it into town it was nearly dinner time and he wasn't eager to do much cooking, so he picked up Chinese takeout on the way. When he finally returned home, Steve made his way through the dark house with his dinner atop the box of dusty books and movies he'd scavenged off the bookshelf at his mother's house. After turning on some lights and the kitchen radio, Steve sat down on the living room floor and opened up the takeout container. A fresh wave of flavorful steam wafted into his face and his stomach growled in anticipation.

Steve eagerly put down a few bites of his dinner before his gaze once again rested upon the box on the floor beside him. Finally, he began pawing through the box. It didn't take long for the floor surrounding Steve to become covered with an assortment of books and movies and the only free space was devoted to his dinner. A grin spread across Steve's face as the various titles caught his eye. *The Belgeriad, Lord of the Rings, Star Wars, Jurassic Park, Lost Years of Merlin, Andromeda Strain.* There were so many thrillers and fantasy movies that he hadn't thought about in years and even more books that he'd hoped to read a second or third time because they were so good the first time.

A multitude of cheerful memories unearthed themselves in his mind. Many were of trips to the movies with his friends. Steve snorted with laughter when he recalled a particular evening when they all had fallen asleep on the ride home while listening to soothing melodies of Al Green.

It occurred to Steve as he studied the assortment of books and movies that he hadn't opened *Coping with Death* in weeks.

Clare R.

Between cooking classes, work, and searching for Clare on the Internet, Steve had been too distracted to think about the negative thoughts that had plagued him for so long. Steve was proud of himself and yet, he was worried. He didn't want to be swallowed up by the sadness and negativity ever again.

Steve continued to gape at the collection spread out before him and tried to imagine Clare sitting there with him, digging through everything, and sharing her own funny stories. In the short time they had spent together, it was clear to Steve that Clare valued a good book or movie and he was certain that she'd been a bookworm most of her life.

He pushed aside the takeout container and that was when he noticed the tan fortune cookie resting in the bag his meal had come in. Steve leaned forward and pulled the cookie from the bag. Gently, he broke the cookie in half with his fingers and pulled out the tiny slip of paper. When Steve realized that it was another promising fortune, his heart started beating in earnest.

Even on the rainiest of days, love and happiness will find you.

Steve found himself smiling uncontrollably and with shaking hands he set the fortune down carefully on the coffee table like it was a fragile piece of china. While he cleaned up the rest of the mess from dinner, Steve peered out into the rainy night beyond the kitchen window, wondering if the fortune could ever come true. Every now and again the headlights of a car shined through the intersection, but for the most part, nothing exciting was going on outside. Then Steve chuckled to himself as he imagined Clare sitting at home, wherever that was, wearing her sweatpants and reading one of their books on the couch.

Steve went upstairs and got ready for bed. Among all the thoughts floating around in his head, the fortune stuck out most prominently. He found the new fortune so intriguing that he read the tiny slip of paper several times before climbing into bed that night, hoping that it would reveal some novel idea on how to reach Clare. But when no exceptional ideas came to mind, he tacked the newest fortune on the cork board beside the first one and collapsed into bed with his laptop in hand. Steve searched and searched for logistics companies that handled movie projects. Only when the lines began blurring together did Steve give in to sleep.

Chapter 7

Like any of the other jobs that Steve had held in his lifetime, he found that engineering had its fair share of slow periods. When Steve became bored or found that his eyes were strained from staring at the computer, he would lean back in the clunky, worn out office chair and let his eyes wander across the ceiling.

There was no drop ceiling installed in the office which meant all the steel truss work was exposed. Huge, white I-beams stretched across the ceiling like a giant's arms holding up the weight of the building. Smaller trusses filled the remainder of the ceiling and provided further support for the floor above as well as other utilities. Steve allowed his mind to go blank while his eyes followed the pipes, duct work, and wiring that snaked through the maze of metal triangles. It had been a few days since his return from visiting his mother, and the week was by no means a fast one. At the moment, Steve was biding his time until he could leave work, and in order to distract himself from his grumbling stomach, he chose to count all of the sprinkler heads that he could see in his vicinity. Simultaneously, he wondered what Clare did to amuse herself at work if she ever got bored.

Actually, Clare didn't often get bored at work because she didn't have time. Normally she was processing documents required for their projects, in meetings, making phone calls, or she was traveling. But this afternoon, it just so happened that Clare's office door was shut and she was spinning in her swivel chair. To any of her coworkers, this behavior would be seen as very unlike Clare because she usually worked very diligently. In truth, she was in such a good mood that she had finished the majority of that day's workload before lunch, and now she was spending some time pondering more important matters.

Clare had kicked off her dress shoes and placed a fresh notepad on the table. Her eyes were closed and she had a pleasant grin on her face as she leaned back against the headrest. Every so often she would giggle and lean forward to write something on the notepad.

What else could I ask him? Clare wondered. Then she laughed again.

What's your most embarrassing memory? She added the question below several that were already on the list. Clare leaned back again, satisfied with the progress she'd made.

But she wasn't done yet and the grin on her face continued to grow as she continued spinning around in her chair. She had to fight herself to keep from laughing at the especially humorous questions that were forming in her brain, and it wasn't long before Clare filled up the first sheet of paper with questions. Once again, she paused to admire her "work" and gave herself a mental pat on the back.

Then with a glance at the clock in the corner of the computer screen, Clare realized she was almost late for her afternoon meet-

Clare R.

ing. While trying to put her dress shoes back on, Clare bit her lip trying not to laugh. After taking several deep breaths to help regain her composure, Clare opened the door and hustled down the hallway to the conference room.

The meeting Clare had to attend wasn't ever that fun. "Information and Activity" sessions were always something of a chore for Clare. Because of her position within the company, these bi-weekly meetings were often of no use to her since the majority of her work was dealing with third parties and traveling to other meetings. However, Clare was still a company employee and therefore required to attend. This in turn meant Clare often sat in the back of the room, falling asleep in the palm of her own hand.

Clare opened the door as quietly as she could and mumbled a couple of "sorrys" and "pardon mes" as she took the last available seat in the back row. Earlier in the day Clare had skimmed an email, and as she understood it, the first half of this hour long session was going to be about implementing the new plotters their company had recently purchased for making large scale posters. The second half promised to be even more thrilling, following the topic of companywide budget changes.

As Clare looked around at the other people who were all ready with pens and notepads to take notes, she decided to play along until her impending boredom sent her into an hour long stupor. But when Clare flipped open her own notepad, she was pleasantly surprised to find that she had brought the one with her questions to Steve, and a gleeful grin spread across her face.

While she feverishly wrote down more questions, Clare noticed out of the corners of her eyes, several people looking between her and the presentation screen wondering what they were missing and many of them began taking even more notes. It was enough to make her giggle quietly and she found herself writing a note to tell Steve about this very afternoon.

In what seemed like no time at all, Clare had written another page worth of questions and in the process she received a boatload of disapproving glances from coworkers around her due to her random squeaks and titters.

"Are you all right?" a coworker finally asked. It took everything for Clare not to snort with laughter.

"Yeah, I'm great!" she whispered. "I'm just really into this presentation today! It's so interesting!" Then she dropped her pen in excitement and had to ask the person in front of her to retrieve it for her. When Clare finally left work that afternoon, she was nearly in tears from laughing so hard. To make a pretty stellar afternoon even more amazing, Clare was surprised to hear her favorite song come on the radio when she got in the car. If there was one song that she wanted to dance to with Steve, it was this song.

I wonder if Steve even likes to dance, Clare thought when the song finished.

~~~

Maggie pulled her hair free of the ponytail and flipped it back over the hood of her jacket. With a quick hand movement, she pulled down the visor to make sure she didn't look too tired to be in public. Maggie's shift had finally ended and after working ten hours, bar food sounded amazing and she had no desire to do the dishes associated with making dinner herself. When she was satisfied that she looked presentable, Maggie got out of the car and walked across the street.

A wild wind whipped cold air down the street and the fallen leaves could be heard skittering across the pavement. There wasn't much she could do to stop her hair from blowing about wildly.

So much for looking presentable, Maggie thought. *Should have kept the ponytail.* As she walked up the steps to the bar's front door, the outdoor area caught her attention and she stared longingly at the empty volleyball court and covered pool. Living in this particular suburb had several nice perks and the bar with these adjacent amenities was certainly one of them.

Eventually Maggie reached for the door handle and once inside, the appetizing smell of fried food alongside the conglomeration of music and TV was enough to quickly make her forget the chill outside. Maggie made her way to the counter and was just about to take a seat when she noticed someone very familiar sitting farther down the bar.

Normally, she was poking and prodding in their mouth for an hour while they sat uncomfortably in the chair waiting for the unpleasant experience to be done. Thankfully, residing in a large metro area meant that Maggie rarely saw her patients outside the dentist's office. But sometimes there was the occasion when she did have an awkward encounter and Maggie would do her best to escape a conversation that would undoubtedly be about teeth.

After casting a few sideways glances to confirm her suspicions, Maggie was sure it was one of her patients. Several months before, Maggie had met Steve through her job as a hygienist. It had been shortly after he moved to town and since Steve was a new patient, the appointment lasted a little longer than usual because she had to collect more information.

However, Maggie quickly found that Steve didn't say much. He was rather quiet and reserved, which she found oddly intriguing. If Steve was at all nervous he didn't show it, and he hardly reacted to the pokes and prods like the other patients did. It was almost as if Steve didn't feel the pain caused by the stainless steel pick nicking his gums and teeth.

During periods of conversational silence, Maggie was able to make numerous observations about Steve other than his teeth. He had a nice smile and very pretty green eyes, but they seemed distant and almost sad. His hair was cut fairly short and she wondered if he was, or had been, a service member.

But since Maggie hardly knew him, she wisely decided not to pry. The short bouts of conversation they did have, however, were pleasant. Steve was polite and when there weren't any metal tools or fingers in his mouth, he asked what she liked to do. By the time Steve said goodbye, Maggie was hopeful that they might get to hang out again. She even considered giving him her number before he left the office but then decided otherwise. As it turned out, she never ended up hearing from him and this was the first time Maggie had seen Steve since.

A bulky winter coat was slung on the back of his bar stool and he still had a hoodie on, which Maggie surmised was to combat the colder weather that was blowing through the area. Steve was also perusing a menu, so hopefully he'd be sticking around for a while.

Maybe we'll have a chance to chat again, Maggie thought, and she grabbed her bag and walked the short distance to take the empty seat next to him.

After counting a dozen sprinkler heads in his vicinity, Steve

Clare R.

had finally escaped the confines of the office, and after making the short trip down the street, he was now sitting comfortably at the bar trying to decide upon something to eat. Before he could make a decision however, the rustling of a person next to him broke his concentration. When he saw that it was a woman grinning at him, Steve's heart leapt.

But just as fast as his heart leapt, it fell back to earth with a resounding thud. It wasn't Clare and it took Steve a moment to remember who she was.

"Hey Steve!" she exclaimed. "How are you?"

"I'm good," he replied. "How are you?" Maggie nodded enthusiastically and brushed the hair out of her face once again.

"Great! Can't complain. Done with work for the day!" she replied. When Steve's eyes shifted back to the menu, Maggie stole another glance at him. His hair was longer now and it was all stirred up from wearing the hat that was sitting on the bar next to his drink.

"I thought you said you were an engineer?" Maggie said, motioning to his hat. Steve had so many hats that he didn't even remember what one he'd grabbed that morning and he glanced at the logo on the front. Above the brim of the hat, brilliant, yellow letters were embroidered into the cap that spelled out the name of a well-known farm equipment manufacturer. Steve chuckled.

"Oh, I am. I did a lot of farm work growing up though, so I have a few of these lying around," Steve said.

"Very cool," Maggie replied. "What kind of farms?"

"Cherries mostly, but I did some work with apples, cows, and goats, too," Steve answered. While Maggie mulled over his answer, Steve found himself smiling inside. It had been a long time since he'd thought about the farm.

The bartender came over and Maggie ordered a drink and when the barkeep set it down in front of her, she immediately took a sip in hopes that it would take a little bit of the edge off. Steve seemed happier than when she'd first seen him. But he still seemed distant, like he was perpetually distracted by something.

"You have any idea what you're going to get?" he asked suddenly. Maggie smiled and picked up a menu. "If you're going to get something…" She looked over at him and nodded.

"I think I'll probably have a salad and chicken wings. What about you?" Maggie said.

"A burger probably," Steve replied. He did his best to pay attention to the things Maggie was saying but her voice seemed to fade in and out like a badly tuned radio station. It wasn't because he found her boring, but rather because Steve had begun day dreaming about what it would be like to be on an actual date with Clare. Maggie was beginning to notice as well.

She didn't think he was being rude by any means but she was certain that Steve was distracted by something or someone. Their conversation flowed at times and then it would become choppy and inconsistent. After Maggie finished eating, she placed her napkin on the plate and pulled her wallet from her purse.

"She's a lucky girl," Maggie said, making a fairly confident stab in the dark. Steve felt his cheeks redden and a sheepish grin crossed his lips. He opened his mouth to speak but no words came out.

"It's OK, Steve," she said. "I'm glad you found somebody." After scribbling a signature on the receipt, Maggie donned her coat and gave him one last smile.

"So, I'll see you for your next appointment?" she said, back-

Clare R.

ing away. Steve moved his head up and down.

"Yep," he said.

"All right," said Maggie. "Have a good night." Steve gave her a little wave before she slipped out the door and disappeared into the growing darkness. After Maggie left, Steve tried to finish his dinner but the food left on the plate tasted bland and the fries were chalky in his mouth. It hadn't really occurred to Steve that Maggie had taken an interest in him. They had only met for a short time at his last dentist appointment.

Steve paid for his dinner and then he, too, headed for his car. Once inside, Steve leaned back against the head rest and closed his eyes. He had been fairly confident after leaving the airport the night he and Clare met that she wouldn't leave the top of the "list" and now Steve knew for sure.

Maggie was a kind woman and a wonderful hygienist, but even now as Steve sat in the car, he had a difficult time remembering what she looked like. In fact, all the girls that he'd liked at one time or another just seemed like a blur. All of them except for Clare. She was painted on his mind as clearly as if she was standing right in front of him.

Chapter 8

"...that's going to be a designated change order..."

"...does anyone know the status of the addendum for the project in Georgia..."

"...we're twelve thousand over budget on this project..."

Steve groaned and clamped his headphones over his ears. He closed his eyes and turned up the volume on his media player, letting the music drown out the sounds of the office. Every day, Steve noticed more things that irritated him about office life. The conversations, the work, the feeling of being stuck in the cube like an animal in a barn stall.

He tried his hardest to cling to those special memories of the airport. But as the days passed, Steve worried that the magical fire Clare had sparked inside of him was burning lower and lower. More often he felt anxious and ached to see her smile and hear her laugh again.

Other than thinking about Clare, the only thing that seemed to keep the emotional roller coaster from taking a permanent dive were the cooking classes. At the moment, they were the only thing that made him feel like he was actually moving forward in life. That week the lessons had been incredibly sweet. Literally. On

Clare R.

Monday Gus did a lesson on making jams and jellies. On Tuesday they made ice cream and Wednesday's lesson was all about pie.

Several of the other students were hanging around after the lesson ended, scooping their homemade ice cream onto slices of pie. Auggie, however, was hovering by the oven waiting for his pie to finish cooking. Gus stepped up next to him.

"So how's it going?" Gus asked.

"With the pie? Great. It's almost done," Steve replied.

"No, not the pie. The girl!" he replied.

"Seriously?" Steve said.

"Yeah," Gus said.

"Mr. Alero, are you one of those people with a super edgy exterior, but deep down you love a good love story?"

"Everyone loves a good love story," he replied.

"That's so sentimental," Steve said with a grin.

"Careful Steve," Gus said. "I'm the one with the red pen." He resisted the urge to make a comment about pens and just smiled. When the timer dinged, Steve slipped his hands into a pair of oven mitts and removed his pie from the oven.

"I'm not sure how it's going," he finally said. "I've joined literally every social media site there is and I've found...Nothing."

"Hmm," Gus replied.

"Was that for the girl or the smell of the pie?" Steve said. "Because it does smell pretty good." Gus scoffed and stared at Steve.

"The girl of course," he said. "Can I ask you something, Steve?"

"Sure. Would you like a piece?" Steve asked.

"Sure. My question is...Have you ever been this passionate

about something?" said Mr. Alero.

"No," he answered. The reply was quick and direct, which was sort of startling to Steve. "Why?"

"Just curious. You joined this class to impress a girl you spent hardly any time with," Gus said.

"What's your point?" Steve asked, handing him a plate.

"The heart wants what the heart wants, Steve," Mr. Alero said. Then he took a bite of the pie. "Muy bien, Steve. It's delicious."

Steve opened his eyes and resumed working and tried to get as much done as possible. When he pressed pause on his music player and slid off his headphones, a nearly overwhelming silence met his ears. Upon looking at the time, he realized why it was so quiet. The tiny digital clock on the bottom of the computer screen read *8:09.*

Wow, he thought. *I've been working for twelve hours and to think I asked Clare if she was a workaholic.* Many of his coworkers in the department and others throughout the office had left four hours earlier. Steve laughed quietly to himself and got up from his chair. His back and legs ached from sitting with such poor posture, so before saving his work and shutting down the computer, Steve did a few stretches.

Before leaving, Steve took the opportunity to use the bathroom and as he walked down the hall, he realized that the building was nearly empty. Every now and again, Steve would hear the clicks of a mouse at someone's computer and he noticed a janitor moving some furniture in order to vacuum. But that was it.

Steve paused and watched several banks of lights begin shutting off due to low activity in the building and he couldn't help

Clare R.

but think once again how much he disliked being at the office late into the night. Steve knew that the nomadic lifestyle he'd adopted over the last couple years was somewhat to blame. It had hindered his career advancement because he hadn't really taken the time to work up the ladder anywhere.

The office continued to go to sleep and when Steve heard the steady whirling noise of the janitor's vacuum dissipate after it was unplugged somewhere in the building, the phrase "cube farm" started floating around his brain again.

Steve didn't want to be stuck in an office forever. He wanted to do something more rewarding, something that he didn't mind doing late into the night, something that he could share with that special someone. Immediately, memories of Clare surfaced in his mind and all Steve wanted was to go home and spend time with her. But he couldn't...because she wasn't *there*.

~~~

Clare was actually relaxing at home. She was sitting on the floor, dressed in her warmest sweats, with her legs outstretched under the coffee table and a fresh mug of steaming tea on the table next to her computer. There was an optimistic expression on her face because that day at work, Clare was called into another meeting for their latest project and her next travel date had been set. She had kept her cool while she was still at the office, but as soon as she left that afternoon, a giddy excitement burst forth in the car and she hurried home to book a flight.

Clare was eagerly perusing travel sites looking for a connecting flight through the airport where she and Steve had met.

Several times during her search, she realized that her eyes had glazed over while daydreaming about another hopeful encounter with Steve.

With a shake of her head, she scrunched her face in concentration because now she was faced with another dilemma. In her excitement, Clare had somewhat foolishly hoped there would be a flight listed on the website that was earmarked especially for her. A flight that would take her to the airport at exactly the same time Steve was passing through.

Clare knew this was silly, but she still hoped. Her meticulous searching had generated a list of flights with several different times, and so began a battle of head versus heart. Part of her wanted early flights, but other parts of her wanted late flights since they had met later in the day.

In the end, Clare finally decided upon something in the middle that would bring her through the airport around midday, and she clicked through the necessary screens to complete her purchase. When the confirmation email popped into her inbox, Clare gave herself a mental high five. Then she sat back against the couch and took a sip of her tea. It had cooled off to the perfect temperature and she savored its delicious flavor.

Maybe, she thought. *Hopefully...*

Never had Clare been so excited to travel for work.

~~~~

After donning his sweater and jacket, Steve spent a minute or so trying to locate his keys, which had become mixed up in the papers that were strewn across his desk. Then he trudged down the

Clare R.

concrete steps of the echoing stairwell.

Finally, Steve thought. Another day was finished and he was overjoyed to be out of the office because if he heard the words *monies* or *tasks* one more time, Steve was sure he'd go berserk and that probably wouldn't be good for employment status.

The seasons had long since changed and the humid, summer breezes had been replaced by a refreshingly, cold wind that smelled like snow. Headlights burned through the growing darkness as other people like himself made their way home as well.

Steve stepped off the sidewalk and his footsteps echoed in his ears while walking across the nearly empty parking lot. But the closer Steve got to his car, the less he heard of his feet and the clearer Clare's laugh became in his head.

Please, he thought while gazing into the night sky. *It would be so wonderful to see Clare again.* A few stars peeked through the night sky but the only reply he got was a stronger gust of wind. Steve shook his head and climbed in the car.

Steve knew it was getting late but still he paused for a moment before turning the key, and stared dumbly at the steering wheel trying to think of some way they could meet again. But nothing was coming to mind. He had nothing substantial to work with and it was incredibly frustrating. Steve didn't have a number, address, or the name of the logistics company she worked for.

The only thing Steve had was her book and a strong hope of seeing her the next time he went through that airport again. It then occurred to Steve that he could check his calendar and see when it would be possible to schedule another site visit. He made a mental note and allowed himself a half-smile.

Without the prospect of his cooking class, it looked like it would be another uneventful evening. The thought of food made his stomach grumble since he hadn't eaten much of anything the entire day, but he didn't care because thinking about Clare satisfied him in a way that food could not. Steve's body took over driving, leaving his mind free to wander as he imagined other conversations that he and Clare could have if they ever saw each other again. Her smiles and goofy expressions glanced across his field of vision and he broke out laughing while thinking once again about the jokes they had shared together.

The drive across town took him to the gas station and the grocery store. Before meeting Clare this activity would have been a chore since traffic after work was always a bit thick, even late into the evening. Now, however, Steve hardly minded since it gave him more time to reminisce about Clare.

He wandered through the grocery store with a smile on his face while picking up the few items he needed. *Box mac and cheese, bread, Kleenex, peanut butter, lettuce*...Steve was searching the spice rack for a seasoning that Mr. Alero had suggested when out of the corner of his eye he spotted something that made him stop in his tracks.

That something was actually a woman leaving the end of an aisle and everything about her resembled Clare. The hair, her height, her fair complexion. But of course, Steve wasn't able to catch a glimpse of her face. Wishful feelings took hold faster than he could have imagined and Steve quickly crossed to the next aisle. However, the lady was still in motion and he missed her again. It was difficult to be casual as he walked briskly from aisle to aisle hoping to get a glimpse of the woman's face, but soon he ran out of aisles and Steve was left staring blankly at the case of

Clare R.

cold dairy products.

What am I doing? he thought. *Obviously that wasn't Clare.*

"Excuse me," said someone from behind him. Steve turned and found the woman he'd been following staring at him, and it certainly was not Clare. The full grocery cart she was clutching was between them like a shield. "Were you following me through the store?"

"Um, yeah. Kind of. Sorta. Sorry about that. You just looked really familiar," he replied.

"Oh, well all right then," she said. Her voice was snippy and irritating. "Next time, try being a little more casual." Steve tilted his head. He couldn't believe he was actually having this conversation.

"Yeah, sure," he mumbled. "Sorry again."

Chapter 9

By the time Steve got home and changed out of his work clothes, he had disregarded the strange incident at the supermarket and instead busied himself with preparing a quick, late night dinner. He turned, looking into the empty kitchen behind him.

"Clare, are you sure you don't want anything else?" Steve asked. Then he returned attention to the bowl in front of him and began drizzling a delicious, garlic vinaigrette over the salad. Her face filled his mind and he imagined a possible response.

"Nope, Stevie, I'm good. Thanks though," he said. This was followed by a nod and he smiled to himself.

"Alrighty," Steve said, turning from the bowl to the stove and flipping the grilled cheese sandwich that was cooking on a fry pan. A fresh sizzling sound temporarily drowned out the sound of the radio and the kitchen filled with the smell of hot butter and crispy bread.

"Mhmmm, that smells good," he said, excited to eat. His stomach growled in agreement. It was also at this very moment that the evening decided to get incredibly strange.

"Yeah, it does!" said a woman's voice from behind him. "Oh, Stevie. I'm so hungry."

Clare R.

It was one that Steve recognized instantly. One he would never forget. Even more startling was hearing this voice say his name the way he imagined Clare saying it, if they ever got a chance to spend more time together. Steve's eyes went wide with fright and he noticed his heart pounding and the hair on his neck stood on end. Goosebumps rose across his body. He looked up at the wall in front of him and wondered if he really was nuts. He had been talking to himself like this for weeks.

"Are you OK?" asked the voice. Steve didn't answer. Every neuron in his body felt like it was firing and he had no idea what to do. Not even his most unnerving memories like cliff jumping or falling out of trees seemed that scary, and Steve tried to steady himself by taking a few deep breaths. After shutting off the burner, Steve set the spatula on the counter and turned around very slowly. He felt terrified and energized at the same time.

There was beautiful Clare, leaning against the kitchen wall, with a steaming cup of tea in her hands.

There is absolutely no way she is here, he thought. *I was stupid and never gave her a phone number and least of all...my address.* But then she stepped forward, set her tea down on the counter beside his spatula, and put her hands on his waist which caused his heart to beat uncontrollably.

My goodness! What is happening? Steve wondered. *Please don't let me have a heart attack! I don't want to die yet!*

"Stevie, are you OK?" she repeated. Her voice was just the way Steve remembered and he still had absolutely no idea what to do, so he did the only thing that made sense. He decided to play along.

"Yeah, I'm fine. I'm just really happy to see you...That's

all," Steve said. He was thoroughly surprised that any words came out of his mouth at all. But despite being very alarmed at her sudden appearance, Steve was so happy to see her.

"Good," she said. Then Clare turned and looked up at the tiny black radio that sat atop the refrigerator. The smell of her perfume came to his senses and he felt his legs get rubbery, so Steve clutched the counter, afraid that he might fall over. Since their meeting, Steve had come across many wonderful love songs and one of them had just come on the radio.

*...the way I see it, the whole wide world has gone crazy, so baby why don't we just dance...*Even though Steve didn't consider himself much of a dancer, he found himself more and more inclined to dance, especially if it was with Clare.

"Come here, you. I know you love this song," she said with a beautiful smile that he'd been musing over continuously. Then she reached for his hand and somehow it felt so real.

After so many nights of pretending to converse and dance with the love of his life, somehow Clare was there. Her voice rang out in his kitchen as she began singing along to the song and he felt an overwhelming tingling reach every extremity of his body. Even his hair felt like it was charged with electricity. They laughed and danced around the kitchen and when the song neared its end, Steve picked her up in a hug like he hoped to if they ever got a chance to see each other again. Somehow she hugged him tightly in return.

"I love when you do that," she whispered in his ear. Then Steve felt a warm kiss on his cheek. When he set her down, his heart was still racing, but now it wasn't out of fear. Instead it was a mixture of immense happiness and exhilaration. Steve had wanted

Clare R.

to kiss her goodbye that day in the airport and berated himself so many times for not trying harder.

She laughed again and Steve turned away for just a moment to get her plate. But when he turned around, the kitchen was empty. Clare was gone. Steve walked in the living room, but it was empty as well. Then he went upstairs even though he knew she wasn't there. Steve returned to the kitchen, grabbed the grilled cheese, and sat down on the stairs where he proceeded to ponder what had just happened.

Terrified was certainly a good way to describe how Steve had felt initially. Then the excitement had taken over while dancing. But now he was befuddled. Steve took a bite of the sandwich. The girl of his dreams had literally been in his kitchen and they had danced and she had kissed him!

No matter how fast Steve's mind raced trying to come up with an explanation as to what had just happened, nothing seemed plausible. Using his free hand, Steve pinched his calf as hard as possible. Not only did it hurt, but he pinched hard enough to leave a small bruise.

That was dumb, he concluded. Satisfied he was indeed awake, Steve took another bite of the lukewarm sandwich but the more he chewed, the less flavor it seemed to have and the more empty he felt.

Try talking to her again, he thought.

"Clare?" Steve said, but nothing happened. Everything in the house had gone silent and Steve found himself speaking in hushed tones. He tried again, this time closing his eyes.

"Clare, am I going nuts?" Steve asked.

"Why would you be going nuts, Stevie?" She replied. The

sound of her voice caused him to jump slightly and when Steve opened his eyes, she was sitting right next to him on the stairs. Her beautiful, blue eyes had a sparkle that no gem could hope to replicate and the longer she stared at him the harder it was for Steve to look away. Her long, reddish-brown hair dangled around her face and her fair skin had the faintest glow around the edges. Then she reached over and took a bite of the sandwich.

Well that's a good place to start, he thought again. *You just took a bite of the sandwich I made. How's that possible?*

"Gosh, you make good grilled cheese. Is our salad still in the kitchen?" imaginary Clare asked.

"Yeah, it's on the counter," he replied.

"All right, let me go get it," Clare said. As she stepped down the stairs, he snapped back to reality.

"Clare, wait!" Steve called out. He was desperate to know what was really going on and she turned back to him as if she was really there.

"Yeah?" she replied. He reached out for her hand and she took it gracefully.

"I know I'm not crazy, so I know you're not really here," he blurted out. Clare smiled at him and nodded.

"No, I'm not. But I sort of am. We'll talk more about that later. I was hoping we could finish dinner and go to bed because I'm pooped." Steve was at a loss for words. Hearing she talk like she was really there, like they were already in a relationship, sent his mind reeling. Now he was completely unsure of what to say, but because he missed her so much, Steve decided to continue playing along...with whatever this was.

"OK. I hope you don't leave again though," he said. "It's really great to see you."

Clare R.

"It's great to see you, too," she said. "I won't leave for a while and you should know— I'm not really gone either. I'm right here." Gently, Clare pressed a finger against his chest, right where his heart was. Then she stood up on her toes and kissed him on the cheek again.

Steve was certainly perplexed by the strange set of events that had unfolded in his home that evening. But somehow, they shared their simple dinner of salad and grilled cheese while watching a show on the television. After they finished eating and the show they were watching ended, Steve and this phantom Clare went upstairs and got ready for bed.

Despite knowing that she wasn't really there, Steve couldn't help but appreciate how nice it would be to fall asleep next to Clare. He smiled while watching her climb into his bed.

"Come here you dork," she said. After shutting off the desk lamp, Steve lay down next to her and waited for her to get comfortable before asking her the question that had been bouncing around his skull the entire evening.

"What?" Clare asked. Steve continued to stare at her.

"What are you doing here?" Steve asked. "This is all I've wanted since we met, but I know it's not real." Clare leaned her head against his and put a hand on his cheek.

"I don't want you to give up on me," she said.

The ensuing explosion of energy in his system was insane, and all of a sudden Steve had an urge to jump out of bed and run down the street as fast as possible. But he chose to stay in bed and keep staring at the strange apparition that had appeared out of nowhere. She continued to smile at him and brushed her hand across his cheek again.

"Do you like the book I gave you?" imaginary Clare asked.

"Yeah. Last week I finished the one I was reading at the airport and then I started yours. It's great so far," he said. "It smells like you, too."

"Good, I'm glad," she said. "I didn't want you to forget about me." Steve lifted his head off the pillow slightly.

"How could I forget about you? You're the most wonderful woman I've ever met," Steve said. "I haven't quit thinking about you." Imaginary Clare laughed quietly and shrugged. Even though he knew she wasn't real, Steve felt it was still worth saying.

"I know. That makes me happy," she said. While Steve tried to wrap his head around what was happening, a really important question popped into his head.

"What's your last name?" Steve asked.

"I can't tell you, Stevie," she said. "I'm sorry." The happy expression on her face didn't falter much but her voice sounded sad.

"What? Why?" Steve asked.

"I can't tell you because you don't know," she said simply. Steve let out a frustrated sigh that just made her chuckle. Her answer, however, made complete sense and he felt dumb for even asking the original question.

"Well, is something like this happening to her?" Steve wondered. Imaginary Clare adjusted her pillow slightly.

"I'm not sure," she replied. "I'm here because you want me to be."

"OK. Is she thinking about me?" Steve asked, figuring that she would say something similar to the first question.

"She thinks about you all the time," Clare said. Even in the

Clare R.

darkness of the room, Steve could see her beaming smile, and before he could ask another question, she cut him off. "The reason I can tell you that, Stevie, is because you know it's true. You could see it in my eyes when we said goodbye at the airport." His eyes shifted to the ceiling and their final moments together began playing across the ceiling like he was watching a movie. Her smile and eyes seemed more wonderful than ever.

Anything is possible, the real Clare had said.

"Stevie, can I ask you something?" she asked. He focused back on the figment lying in his bed.

"Yeah, sure," he replied.

"Can you promise me that you won't give up?" imaginary Clare asked. It was strange to hear her ask such a question because Steve was unsure of who he was really making the promise to. He knew it was to himself because she was just part of his imagination, but he couldn't help thinking that he was really making a promise to her and Steve knew he would never meet anyone like Clare ever again.

"I promise, Clare," Steve whispered.

"Good," she said.

"I thought you were tired," Steve said, letting his own hand run across the skin of her cheek.

"I'm just as tired as you are, so when you go to sleep that's when I will, too," Clare replied.

"Well, come here," Steve said. The figment scooted closer to him and he watched her wrap her arm around his chest. There wasn't exactly warmth, but it wasn't cold either. It was just pleasant and Steve could almost feel her body rise and fall with every breath she took. "Goodnight, Clare."

"Night, Stevie," she said, lifting her head slightly to give him a kiss on the cheek. Then he drifted off to sleep. When Steve woke the next morning, he relished in the thought that Clare was lying next to him. Strands of her beautiful hair tickled his face and he chuckled sleepily. She made a cute noise and kissed him softly on the cheek which made Steve smile further.

For a brief few minutes, Steve had the opportunity to imagine what it would really be like to wake up next to the woman of his dreams. But then his alarm went off, interrupting the wonderful moment. Steve rolled over to turn off the annoying piece of technology.

"Sorry about that—" he began. But when he turned back over, imaginary Clare was gone and tucked in his arms was an extra pillow. Steve shook his head in frustration but a smile still crossed his face. He rolled onto his back and stared at the ceiling, lost in thought.

What the hell is going on? he thought. I really hope I'm not going nuts. But when nothing conceivable came to mind except for what she had said to him the night before, Steve shook his head and got ready for work. At least it was Friday.

Chapter 10

Ever since that magical moment when they suddenly became "interested" in boys, Amy and Clare had kept an unofficial agreement that they would never interfere with each other's love lives. This wasn't to say that they weren't there for each other during a bad break up. On the contrary, this pair of best friends always had each other's back, especially in the worst situations.

The beauty of their silent arrangement was that it prevented unwanted, awkward dates from occurring with people who neither one of them would ever be interested in. She and Clare had a spectacular relationship.

But as Amy stood outside the break room, letting the gum in her mouth smack loudly, she stared out at the members of her marketing team wondering if one of them would indeed be a good match for Clare. Amy became so engrossed with mentally surveying several of the guys, one of the interns had to nudge her arm to get her attention.

"Yeah, sorry. What's up?" Amy asked. The intern looked a bit startled and Amy quickly apologized. "Sorry."

"I was just wondering which color you liked better for that poster we need to make for the benefit dinner?" asked the intern. One rendering was decorated in hues that corresponded to the fall season and the other displayed a variety of vibrant party colors. Along with being distracted, Amy was feeling rather indecisive at the moment, so her answer was very neutral but honest.

"I really like them both, so print fifty of each to start," Amy said. "And make sure a couple people check for spelling and grammar." The girl beamed and nodded. Then she hurried off and Amy resumed the survey of her male coworkers. Amy was not about to break the arrangement that she and Clare shared, but if things didn't work out with this Steve fellow, she wanted to be prepared.

By the end of the day, Amy had narrowed her prospective list down to three guys and they also happened to be three of the guys she also thought were cute.

Oh, Clare. You better appreciate this, Amy thought. Deep down though, she knew it was worth it because Clare was her best friend.

~~~~

Click. Click. Click.

An open takeout container sat on the desk next to Steve's computer and he picked at the cold remnants of that evening's cooking class like a nervous chicken. Since getting home, Steve had been investigating everything the Internet had to offer regarding figments and apparitions. Initially he'd begun his search by tearing through the pages of *Coping with Death*, but having read the book cover to cover several times, Steve already knew that it contained nothing about spiritual phenomena.

Either way, Steve was becoming increasingly aware of the fact that he loved and disliked the apparition that was appearing from time to time. He didn't feel crazy because he was sure he

Clare R.

was imagining her. But Steve knew that if he tried to explain the situation to anyone, they would most certainly think he was delusional, send him to a psychiatrist, and begin pumping him full of medication.

Maybe it's PTSD, Steve thought. *But what's so stressful about meeting a beautiful woman in the airport?* He shook his head sideways and moved on.

The next few articles dealt with the consumption of contaminated food and the hallucinogens found in certain mushrooms. He didn't even make it to the end of an article before he went through his entire kitchen to make sure he hadn't consumed anything that was expired or covered with fuzz. Satisfied that he was safe from some food borne illness, he resumed his search on the computer.

When Steve looked at the clock again, it was well after midnight. He let a heavy sigh escape and closed the lid of the laptop, frustrated that he was no closer to an explanation for the figment than when he started the search several hours before. Steve put on a sweater and took a seat on the steps outside his shabby townhouse.

The days and nights were slipping by faster than Steve could count, and each day he felt farther away from her. Doubts flitted in and out of his mind, but unfortunately some stuck like bugs on fly tape. Steve could just imagine what people would say if he told them how much time he was spending on trying to find Clare.

"...just forget about her..."

"...so many other girls in the world..."

"...why bother? You're living a fantasy..."

But he couldn't give up. He wouldn't. He had spent the last two years of his life moving, giving up, and moving again. He knew he had to keep trying. A chilly breeze whipped at him and he tried to focus on the last appearances of imaginary Clare to see if he'd missed something.

Earlier that week, she'd appeared at work during a meeting in the conference room. After sharing a big lunch with Jimmy, Steve was steadily nodding off and that was when he noticed the gentle touch of her hand on his knee. She was sitting in the chair beside him, dressed once again in her work attire, and chewing on a pen. After getting his attention, she stood up and proceeded to walk around the room. She made goofy faces at the other attendees and wrote jokes and humorous words on the whiteboard. Steve ended up having to leave the meeting because he was on the verge of laughing in front of everyone.

Later that afternoon, she appeared while he was shopping at the hardware store. She accompanied him through the aisles, and after checking out, they parked in an empty parking lot to eat some fast food. Steve reminisced about funny memories from high school. One of the best memories was about a mishap involving a pair of heels and a classmate falling off her desk.

Steve bowed his head and ran his hands through his hair. It had been a funny and enjoyable day but he was uncomfortable. Before leaving the office that day, he shared an unpleasant conversation with Jimmy.

"Steve, you've been off lately," Jimmy said.

"Yeah, I know," he replied.

"Well, what was up with that meeting today? Did you get food poisoning from lunch?" Jimmy asked.

"No," Steve said.

"Are you taking recreational drugs?" Jimmy asked.

"Are you kidding me right now, Jimmy?" Steve asked, shaking his head in bewilderment. "I've never done drugs in my life."

Clare R.

"Well you tell me then," Jimmy said. Steve hated lying but there was no way he would be bringing up his phantom dream girl.

"I don't know what happened at lunch. Maybe I did get something. But there's nothing wrong with me. I've been taking late night cooking classes so maybe that's why I'm a bit off," Steve offered. Like the flip of a switch, Jimmy's character changed completely and it irritated Steve immensely.

"Oh really? No way! That's awesome!" Jimmy exclaimed.

"Yeah, it's cool," Steve said.

"All right, well, get some sleep, huh," Jimmy said. "You gotta keep your shit together. We're really busy."

~~~

Steve lifted his head and stared at the stars that were peeping through the partly cloudy sky.

Maybe I am going nuts, Steve concluded. He was certainly grateful that he'd run into Clare at the airport because she had given him something to tether to as he drifted through life, but at the same time, what was it going to cost him? His job? His sanity?

"You're not crazy, Stevie," said a familiar voice. Steve shifted his gaze from the star filled sky to imaginary Clare who was leaning on his car.

"Really? Are you sure? Because I'm finding it hard to explain this," Steve mumbled. "And I'm sure other people would jump to that same conclusion."

"Who cares what other people think and why do you need an explanation? I'm here because you want me to be. I told you that already," imaginary Clare said.

"I know but—" Steve began, but she cut in.

"But what, Stevie? Look at what's happened since you met me. You've come back to life. You've been laughing and smiling. You joined a cooking class and you finally went home to see your mom." Steve couldn't argue with that, and despite the anxiety he felt about wanting to see Clare again, he was definitely happier.

"I think I was close to getting fired," he said.

"I know," she replied.

"That's not good," he said.

"Nope probably not," his figment said. "But then again..." The shiny orbs that were eyes glinted in the starlight and Steve continued to peer at her wondering what she might say.

"Then again what?" he asked.

"Then again...Do you really want this job forever? Do you want to come home every day still sad and unhappy? Do you want to keep burying your nose in that book about death?" she asked.

"*Coping with Death*," he corrected.

"Whatever," she replied. "Same difference."

"I don't know," he said. "This life isn't what I thought it would be like."

"Well, don't you think it would be better if you spent your life doing something you enjoyed?" imaginary Clare asked.

Before he could answer, a siren screamed into existence somewhere down the street and Steve timidly looked in the direction of the apartment complex driveway. It wasn't long before an ambulance with its lights ablaze went zooming by. Chills ran across his entire body.

"What if I never get over it?" he wondered out loud. The apparition came to sit next to him on the steps and they both stared in silence at the stars.

"You will," she said, and wrapped an arm around his.

Clare R.

"Are you a ghost?" he said.

"No!" she said. "I'm not dead."

"Good, I hope not," he said. "Are you a hallucination?"

"Are you on drugs?" she asked. They both laughed.

"Nope," Steve replied.

"I guess that's not it then," imaginary Clare said.

"Why are you here?" he asked, but she only answered his question with another question.

"Why do you like me so much?" she replied. Steve started to speak but the words caught in his throat.

Why does anyone like anybody? he wondered. Imaginary Clare waited patiently for him to answer.

"There are so many reasons," he finally said. "You make me happy and I love thinking about you." She nodded.

"I know, and I'm not looking for some answer in particular. Not right now anyway," she said. "But you believe in me?" Steve nodded.

"Good. Keep up with the cooking thing, Stevie," she said. "It's good for you." Steve smiled but when he turned, she was gone.

Chapter 11

It was a blustery Saturday morning and the weather was having a hard time making up its mind if it wanted to rain, snow, or be clear and sunny. Clare and Amy, however, had decided to go out for breakfast and it came down to two restaurants, a pleasant cafe farther into town or a mom and pop shop not far from their homes. The cafe was great but it had a tendency to get stuffy from a healthy supply of coffee snobs later in the morning. The mom and pop shop was small, quiet, and the steady flow of regulars always smiled politely. Clare and Amy chose the latter.

The food was always delicious and the restaurant itself had that old fashioned quality that left patrons feeling welcome instead of feeling like just another piece of cattle herded down the line. Best of all, though, was the bakery, which left the establishment smelling heavenly. Clare always smiled when she saw youngsters walk off between their parents, enjoying the delectable goodness of a cupcake or some other sweet treat that filled the case.

"Hey, I'll be right back," Amy said. "I gotta use the bathroom." Clare nodded and retrieved a magazine from her bag and tried to read in between yawns. For how late it was already, their breakfast date might as well have been considered brunch. After

Clare R.

being woken up by Amy's persistent phone calls earlier that morning, Clare had insisted they move their breakfast date to later in the morning because she had stayed up late the night before, binging on her favorite television show.

Amy had let out a hearty laugh when Clare got in the car that morning because her appearance was somewhere between zombie and exhausted.

"How many episodes did you watch last night?" Amy asked. Clare glowered at her friend but when she tried to make a mischievous expression, there was no overcoming the sleepiness and a huge yawn escaped her instead.

"A lot," she had said. "They were so good though. Totally worth it."

Amy had been focused on getting to the bathroom when a voice interrupted her thoughts. She turned in the direction of the voice and from across the counter, Amy noticed one of the bus boys staring at her.

"Hey, can I ask you something?" he asked. Amy had seen him around the restaurant a few times, but other than the miscellaneous chit chat or pleasantry, she hadn't ever really talked to him. Amy guessed that he was probably a little shorter than she was and his face was covered with light brown freckles that matched his sandy brown hair. The name tag clipped to his shirt read: *Nick*.

"Sure," Amy replied.

"That girl you're with," Nick started. "Your friend...Is she seeing anyone?" Amy certainly hadn't seen that one coming and the surprise that came about inside of her left her limbs tingling. She glanced back at their table. Clare was busy reading a magazine and when Amy returned her gaze to the bus boy, his cheeks had reddened significantly.

What the hell am I supposed to say? Amy wondered.

"I see you guys in here once in awhile and you seem pretty cool," he continued, trying to keep his composure. Amy really didn't know what to say. She definitely wanted her best friend to meet a nice guy and the bus boy seemed reasonably nice.

"Yeah. We like it here," Amy replied, trying to think of a suitable response. She was torn. Clare had apparently met a nice guy and his name was Steve.

But who knows if that's ever going to work out? Amy thought, casting another glance at her friend. It definitely surprised Amy when the next words came out of her mouth.

"Um, yeah. Actually she is. I'm sorry, man." Amy loved seeing Clare so happy and she didn't want to give up on the possibility of her best friend finding this mysterious airport man again.

"Oh, all right. That's cool," Nick replied. "No big deal." The busboy waved goodbye and continued on with his duties. Amy felt bad for lying but the busboy almost looked relieved, like he hadn't let out a breath while waiting for her to respond. Amy continued to the bathroom feeling somewhat distracted and then returned to their table.

Breakfast had been delivered while she was gone and Clare was taking a bite from a bowl of fruit while simultaneously spreading syrup over her pancakes. Amy couldn't help herself and eagerly nabbed a blueberry from the bowl. Clare chuckled.

"What took you so long?" she asked.

"Nothing, just got a little distracted," Amy replied. She waited for Clare to make a clever remark. But all that came was another yawn and a sleepy nod.

Clare R.

I hope you find him again, Clare, Amy thought while staring at her friend, *you deserve a good man who really cares about you.*

"Yummm," Clare said as she chewed her pancakes. Amy couldn't help but laugh. Her best friend could be serious when she had to, but most of the time Clare was so cute and goofy. She continued to flip through her magazine while they ate breakfast and finally curiosity got the better of Amy.

"What are you reading, anyway?" she asked.

"It's a business magazine I picked up from somebody at work," Clare replied. Only moments before getting to the restaurant, Clare had been falling asleep in the car but now after a few bites of breakfast, she was awake and alert as she absorbed page after page of the magazine.

"And..." Amy said.

"Well, I guess...I've been toying around with the idea of starting my own business," Clare said. Dwindling thoughts of her conversation with the busboy were swept aside as she tried to comprehend her friend's outlandish idea.

"Wait, what? Seriously?" Amy asked. Clare nodded.

"Yep," she said. Amy shook her head in bewilderment.

"Well, what's your business idea?" Amy asked. "How long have you been thinking about this?"

"Awhile, I guess. But I've been thinking about it a lot more since we started hanging out with Jenny. It's so cool that she runs her own business. That's an awesome bar," Clare said.

Amy ran her hands through her hair much like Clare did when she was overwhelmed with something. Although they shared most everything with each other, Clare sometimes had a tendency to be a bit withdrawn about revealing certain things. Amy was used to this because that's how Clare had always been and it didn't really bother her that much. Amy would just pry a little more.

"So, are you telling me you want to open your own bar?" Amy asked.

"No, no," she replied. That was the last thing Clare wanted. She looked over at the chest of mouthwatering desserts. "No, I think I want to open a bakery…" Then she returned her attention to the magazine. Amy was floored.

"Where did this come from?" Amy asked. Clare just grinned.

"You remember growing up, when we used to bake all the time with your mom?" Clare asked. Amy nodded.

Of course I remember, Clare, Amy thought. *There's no way I could ever forget those frosting battles.*

"Are you kidding me? We were on the fast track to be the next stars of *Cupcake Wars* or *Cake Bosses* on the Food Network," Amy exclaimed. Clare laughed so hard that several patrons turned to look in their direction.

"Well, I loved that. Cooking is so much fun. I mean, I love the job I have now. But I don't want to spend my entire life flying around to meetings, and there is no way I'm going to keep attending those bi-weekly seminars. I'd rather not die of boredom," Clare said. This time Amy let out a loud cackle and several more people glanced at their table with startled expressions.

Steve would have laughed too, I bet, Clare thought. *I wish you were here, Steve.*

"What about Steve?" Amy said. Clare's cheeks flushed slightly and she looked down at the magazine again. It amazed her how Amy could seemingly read her mind sometimes.

"I'm not giving up on him, Amy," Clare said. "Not a

Clare R.

chance." She hadn't quit thinking about Steve at all, and in fact, the more Clare thought about starting a bakery, the more fun she had thinking about her and Steve working there together. But she also wanted Amy there as well.

"Would you want to work there with me?" Clare asked. In no time at all, Amy's expression went from concerned and intrigued to surprised and elated.

"Hell yeah I would!" Amy said. "If you're leaving office life behind, I am, too!"

"All right then," Clare said, and resumed reading through the magazine. Amy smiled and took a few more bites of her breakfast.

"Wait, when is this going down?" Amy asked. "Like, should I quit my job on Monday? Because I will."

"Don't worry. I'm not gonna be rash about anything. I just think I really want to do this..." She shoved a bite of pancake in her mouth, "...because I fuckin' love cupcakes."

~~~~

Clare held her eyes shut when she woke up from another delightful dream. In the weeks since their meeting, it wasn't uncommon for Steve to make an appearance in her dreams and each time had been wonderful. This one was no exception and Clare tried her hardest to cling to the feeling of Steve's hand in her own. They had been standing side by side, staring at brightly lit movie posters, and when she smiled at him, Steve smiled back and led her by the hand into the theater.

However, the harder she focused, the faster the dream faded, and then sleep eluded her altogether. Clare let out a groggy sigh, pulled the blankets tighter around herself, and rolled over to stare at the bookshelf where her missing book had once sat. It was still dark in her room; the sun hadn't come up yet. But Clare's eyes eventually adjusted and the empty spot on the bookshelf seemed to stare back at her.

Several times after meeting Steve at the airport, Clare wondered if she would ever see that book again. She had high hopes for the possibility that Steve would someday be there, in her home, to put the book back himself. Then her imagination started to stir and as she succumbed to drowsiness once again, Clare closed her eyes. She allowed herself to fantasize what it would feel like to have Steve put his arm around her. A smile crossed her sleepy face and she eventually fell back to sleep.

When she woke again later that morning, Clare had an intense desire to keep reading her book and there was only one way to remedy the situation. After getting dressed and making a spot of breakfast, Clare wandered downtown to do a little shopping. Thankfully the weather was a bit nicer than it had been in recent weeks and the walk was invigorating.

A set of bells gave off a cheerful jingle as Clare walked through the door of a small bookstore that she enjoyed visiting from time to time. Even though she could have ordered the book online, there was a certain excitement that came from being in the atmosphere of a bookstore. Shelves upon shelves of book titles caught her eye and she smiled, loving all the hard work and countless hours that authors had put in to fill these shelves. The delicate smells of freshly baked pastries and coffee wafted out of the small café, and an array of comfortable chairs invited people to stay and read awhile.

Clare R.

She undid her scarf after finding a display of the *Lunar Chronicles*. Her eyes moved side to side and in an instant, she recognized the title in question but her reaction wasn't what she anticipated. All of a sudden her stomach was swirling.

Clare had walked into the book store with a feeling of purpose and determination, but as she stood there debating whether or not to buy another copy, she found that her purpose and determination were fading. The sandy-haired clerk spotted what he thought to be a look of indecision on her face and came over from the counter to provide assistance.

"Do you need help finding anything, miss?" he asked. At the sound of his voice, Clare looked up and smiled politely in return. There was a kind expression on his face even though Clare could tell he was scraping the bottom of the bucket looking for something to do. It was still fairly early in the morning and the store wasn't that busy.

"No. Thank you. I'm just looking today," Clare replied.

"Well, let me know if you need anything," he said. Clare wondered if he was going to linger, but to her relief, he turned back to the counter. She returned her gaze to the display of her favorite novels.

Do I really want to get you? Clare asked herself as she reached out to pick up a copy of the book she'd given to Steve. Once again, the wonderful artwork on the cover teased her and she felt herself itching to continue the deceptively thrilling tale that was written on its pages.

But then Clare thought about the wonderful conversation she and Steve shared about the series, the jokes they had shared, and the feelings that gushed inside of her whenever she mused about him. Clare couldn't help but think that if she bought another copy it could be taken as a sign that she was giving up on him.

Clare wasn't even that superstitious but she didn't want to take any chances. She argued back and forth with herself but in the end, Clare carefully placed the book back on the shelf with its companions. Another smile crossed her face and she gave the display one last hopeful glance before walking down the aisle to look for something that could amuse her for.

A short time later, Clare stepped back outside into the cold breeze with her scarf wrapped freshly around her neck. A decorative bag from the bookstore hung from her gloved fingers, and inside were two smaller books that had caught her eye. She knew they wouldn't be nearly as good but they would have to do for the time being.

People walked past her as she lingered on the sidewalk, trying to decide what to do next. Clare checked her phone, but there were no new messages of any kind. When she looked up from the screen, she found herself imagining how wonderful it would be to have Steve walk past her.

Hell, I would be happy if you ran into me and spilled tea on me. The thought made her grin. But Steve didn't walk by and she glanced back at the screen of her telephone. Her daydream from that morning came to mind and she recalled that there were a few good movies out in theaters.

Sometimes on the weekends, if she didn't have an episode of her show to catch up on, Clare would take one of the city buses farther into town to watch a movie at one of the local theaters. This was something she had done and since moving to town, mostly because of her love for movies. Clare decided this would be a fine

Clare R.

idea and walked down the sidewalk to the nearest bus stop.

In between taking sips of tea, Clare scanned the faces of everyone she saw hoping for one face in particular. But there was nothing and a moment later, a bus screeched to a halt in front of the bus canopy. As people filed up steps at the front of the bus, Clare caught sight of a passenger leaving the back door. On his head was a pale green hat and the work boots on his feet were rough and worn. Everything stopped and Clare found herself rooted to the spot. She was the last person to board and yet she held her position, hoping to see the man's face.

"You getting on board, miss?" The bus driver called to her, but his voice was faint in her ear.

Come on! Turn around! Steve, if that's you—

"Miss, are you getting on the bus?" the driver asked. Clare still hardly heard him and was seriously considering shouting to the doppelganger. But just as Clare was about to let go of the railing, the man turned to talk to someone and Clare saw that it wasn't Steve at all. In one swift motion, she climbed the steps and mumbled sorry to the driver. Several blocks went by before she regained her composure. At least she thought she had.

A couple times Clare looked at the bus driver who had been trying to get her attention. She was grateful that he was somewhat patient with her and hadn't simply driven off. Clare found the weekend bus drivers to be much nicer than some of the weekday drivers. One driver that she remembered distinctly had been so ornery, and he barked out the stops with such ferocity, that Clare was positive he hadn't eaten something in days. She came to this conclusion because every time they drove by any type of establishment that served food, Clare heard a discernible grunt from the head of the bus. When Clare got off that day, she tried to give the driver the most cheerful smile she could muster, but inside there was only one thought going through her head. *Next time pack a lunch, buddy!*

Today, Clare had taken a seat about halfway down the bus and was staring out the window watching the street go by. At each stop, she would glance at the passengers getting on and off the bus. Sometimes Clare was privy to seeing something especially humorous and usually enjoyed retelling the story to Amy the next time they were together. But after seeing the look alike, Clare searched in earnest for Steve.

That morning though, the search would only disappoint her further. The frequency with which she ran into couples had increased dramatically since her encounter with Steve, and they always seemed to be displaying their affection for one another. While scanning the exchange of passengers at another stop, Clare spied a couple standing near the bus driver that were talking and laughing together.

Normally this didn't matter to her, especially since there were other people on the bus talking just as loudly. Yet the sound of their raucous flirtation continued to distract Clare, and when it got to be too much, Clare dug in her bag, searching for headphones. She plugged her ears to block out the mushy gushy talk that she admittedly wished she and Steve could share. Then Clare let her head thud against the window. It was almost as if she was being taunted for not taking more of a chance with Steve.

Why didn't I kiss him? she thought once again. *Or give him my number...Why?*

But even with the music playing in her ears, Clare couldn't

Clare R.

help but glance in the direction of the couple who was now sitting in a pair of seats. The guy's head was resting on her shoulder and she was running her hand through his hair. Clare knew there was a pained and frustrated expression on her face, so when the next stop came she hopped off the bus and walked the last two blocks, not sure if she even felt like watching a movie any more.

By the time Clare arrived home later that night, the weather had taken a turn for the worst. The air was bitter cold and filled with an icy rain that bit at her cheeks. Before doing anything else, Clare got her tea kettle going and changed into comfy clothes. While she waited for the high-pitched whistle, Clare paced around the house, trying to sort out her roller coaster of emotions.

For so long it seemed like the two most important things in her life had been Amy and her job. That was all she had needed. Guys were fun to hang out with once in a while. There had been some good times, but it hadn't been a priority for her because none of those guys had been good enough. That was it. Plain and simple.

But as Clare sat curled up on the couch with her nose buried in one of the new books, she was unable to read more than a paragraph without losing focus and having to start over. Clare let the book flop down on her blanket and stared at the steaming cup of tea that was resting on the coffee table. She found herself imagining how wonderful it would be to have Steve walk into the living room and sit down next to her. A half-smile crossed her face as she pictured herself laying her legs across his lap.

I bet that would make him laugh, Clare thought. She reached over to pick up the cup of tea and took a small sip to test the temperature. Between her sweatpants and the cup of tea in her hand it was hard to think of anything or anyone else but Steve. But as she watched the steam rising off the cup only to disappear into thin air, Clare noticed an inkling in her brain. Something was nagging at her.

When the business magazine sitting next to her tea cup caught her attention, the inkling became a loud murmur, and then all at once Clare found her direction. She exchanged the book on her lap for her computer and began a serious endeavor to make her dream of a bakery come to life. If there was going to be any way that she got a hold of Steve, it would be by doing something she loved.

Chapter 12

On the morning of her latest trip, Clare woke much earlier than she intended. But she didn't feel drowsy or exhausted. On the contrary, she felt alert and incredibly excited. It was her first trip since meeting Steve, and for the first time in her life she prayed for a delayed flight. Clare deftly reached into the darkness next to the bed and found her phone on the floor.

She squinted when the bright screen lit up the room, and once her eyes adjusted she navigated through the menus to her email inbox. While lying in the comfort of her bed, Clare read through her trip itinerary and smiled when she reached the return flight that would go through the same airport where she and Steve met. When she could no longer stare at the bright screen, Clare let the phone fall in the blankets and closed her eyes.

All right. Seriously. I wish that Steve and I could see each other again today. Please. It had been such a long time since Clare had truly wished for something, because after losing both her parents, there hadn't been much left to wish for. But this one felt good and Clare got out of bed with a wide hopeful smile on her face.

She followed all her normal routines before leaving for the airport and she carried them out with much more enthusiasm. The flight that morning was a direct one and she made it to her meeting without any interruptions. The meeting itself went without a hitch and as it neared its closing, Clare felt herself itching to get in a taxi and head back to the airport.

Despite the fact that Clare knew she had plenty of time to get there, a weird, anxious feeling was creeping up inside of her. It felt like every second was crucial to her and Steve having another chance meeting, so she was a bit annoyed when another one of the meeting's attendees stopped her to verify a few of the dates on the schedule.

It's all on the paper, she thought. *Weren't you listening? I have places to be.*

Of course, Clare was polite and helpful and even felt guilty for thinking such a thing. She nodded and listened to each question and showed off her savviness by getting the matter situated very quickly. Finally, Clare escaped the conference room and walked as fast as she dared through the lobby while trying to maintain a professional appearance, but she couldn't help grinning the entire way. To her surprise, people appeared to move out of the way as she crossed the sidewalk to hail a cab.

The taxi driver was incredibly friendly as well, and seemed to pick up on the sense of urgency that was radiating from her person. He was a man of few words while he focused on driving, and the route the driver took was very sneaky and shockingly quick. This left her smiling even more, although a few of his quick, hair pin turns had left her slightly white knuckled.

"Thank you, miss!" the driver called out the window. She waved after handing him some cash. "And good luck!" His last sentence caused her to pause, but before she could ask what he'd

Clare R.

meant, an impatient business man bumped past her and the taxi zoomed off with its new customer.

How strange, she thought. But then her excitement took over once again and she continued on her way. Roughly an hour later, the first part of Clare's return flight landed and she promptly went to check the arrival and departure boards. She was pleasantly surprised to see that her flight was indeed delayed. Grinning to herself, she went and sat patiently at the gate. But it was difficult to sit patiently, because for the first time in a long time, she was aching to hug someone.

Because of old habits, Clare took a chance to look away from the passing crowds and dug in her bag, searching for her book. Then Clare remembered that she'd given it to Steve and for the millionth time, she wondered if he'd read it yet. When a half hour or so went by, Clare stood up and decided to wander around the concourse and see if Steve was by chance in another gate.

The continual clattering from the luggage wheels rang in her ears as Clare scanned each gate while walking by. Even though she was very comfortable in airports, Clare admittedly felt nervous about leaving her designated gate. Normally, she would sit down and read or work on the computer once she made it through security because the thought of missing any important announcements or gate changes was always stressful. But as Clare walked farther down the concourse she felt oddly exhilarated. It was as if she was trying to be inconspicuous, like a spy in disguise, searching for her target.

This is kind of fun, she thought, letting a grin momentarily replace the neutral expression that she assumed all spies kept on their faces during a mission. At one point on her walk, Clare's heart leapt because she thought she saw Steve. However, when the gentleman turned she realized it definitely wasn't him. Eventually, Clare ran out of gates to look in and returned to her seat. By this time, nearly an hour and a half had passed and Clare never ended up seeing Steve. An announcement for her flight came over the speakers and she again dug in her bag, this time looking for the remaining boarding pass.

A lock of hair fell in front of her face and she blew it out of the way in frustration. Of course Clare knew that the chance of seeing him again was probably slim, but she loved hoping for it. With a half-smile and a head of swirling emotions, she grabbed the handle of her luggage and stepped into the boarding line. Clare turned back one more time to look at the departure board, hoping she'd see him, but he was nowhere to be found. Shortly thereafter, the plane took off and Clare flew on home with a single tear rolling down her cheek.

~~~~

Leaving the plane's cabin behind, Steve made long strides up the tunnel, absolutely unaware of the drastic change in temperature because of the adrenaline surging through his system. It took everything for Steve to stay focused as he toured the project site that morning. But now, his visit to the job site was only a blip in the day because he was eager for two things—a delayed flight and the smiling face of the auburn haired girl who wore little white pin earrings.

Clutched in his hand was the book that Clare had hid in his bag, which he had just finished. When Steve stepped up to the

Clare R.

flight boards, he found that his flight was delayed and he couldn't have cared less what the reason was. Steve went back to the waiting area, sat down, and started scanning the masses of people who were moving down the concourse, hoping to spot Clare. After a few minutes, Steve decided to get a cup of tea.

"Thank you, sir," Steve said when the clerk handed him a cup of hot water. Steve picked a packet of tea from the assortment of boxes on the counter and then he returned to his seat. He had made sure to leave Clare's book on top of his bag in the empty seat next to him, hoping that it could be seen as a display that said something like, *Hey, Clare! I'm right here!*

As the delay progressed his grand feelings of excitement began to fade, only to be replaced by a nearly overwhelming feeling of sadness. When the announcement for his flight came, Steve placed her book carefully in his bag and went to board the flight. After scanning his pass, he took a free window seat, and for the longest time, the seat beside him remained empty.

Not even the apparition appeared though, and Steve let out a heavy winded sigh after leaning his head against the window. He stared into the growing darkness knowing the girl of his dreams was out there somewhere.

~~~

Clare skipped returning to the office after her flight landed. Instead, she came straight home and Amy came over not long after.

"Seriously," Amy said. "What if this Steve guy is just a total tool?" Clare knew Amy was playing devil's advocate on purpose, so the comment didn't bother her in the slightest.

"Trust me," Clare countered. "He's not."

"What if he has a fake leg?" Amy said, trying again with a suggestive wink. "That could make things totally awkward." Amy's expression only made Clare laugh even harder.

"Amy!" Clare exclaimed. "A fake leg...Really?" Amy was very curious to learn more about Steve, so much so that she had practically been waiting for Clare to get home that night to see if they'd met again at the airport. But when Amy saw Clare's doleful expression, she knew that portion of the trip hadn't gone well.

In the time her and Clare had been friends, Amy knew about all the instances when Clare had been blown off by guys, so she wondered what Clare saw in this mysterious airport guy that was so remarkable. Her best friend had changed out of her work attire and back into sweatpants and a long sleeve tee. Currently she was occupied with unpacking her luggage.

Amy secretly admired Clare's orderliness as she put dirty clothes in the hamper and any clothes that had remained unused went back to their respective drawers in the dresser. Although she wouldn't have admitted it, Amy knew she probably would have just dumped everything on the floor and sorted it out later.

"Did you two have sex in an airport bathroom?" Amy asked, straight faced. When Clare looked at her with wide eyes Amy couldn't hold the face any more and a sassy smirk crossed her lips. She was pleased to see Clare finally laugh.

"My goodness, you are relentless tonight!" Clare said. "Where do you come up with these things?" After coming home and feeling so upset, Clare wasn't that surprised that she was now smiling. Ever since they were kids, they had been there for each

Clare R.

other and that was why Clare and Amy were best friends.

"Well, I don't have some wonderful guy to think about while I'm at work, so I can daydream about meeting some illustrious man in the airport, too," Amy offered.

"Illustrious? Really?" Clare replied.

"What can I say? After hanging out with you all these years, you're finally rubbing off on me," she replied with a casual shrug. Clare shook her head, still smiling, and carried the hamper off to the laundry room. Amy sat on the bed waiting for her friend to return.

Clare really likes this guy, Amy thought, and she decided that her next question wouldn't be humorous.

"What is it then?" Amy asked when Clare came back into the room. At first, Clare didn't say anything and simply shrugged, after sitting down next to Amy. But as she focused on Steve the highlights of their delay shined like neon lights in her mind.

"For one, it was so easy to talk to him," she said. "Steve's honest and funny and smart. He picked up on my sarcasm, too. A lot of guys just get that dumb look on their face, you know?" Clare got off the bed when she saw something else in her bag that she wanted to put away.

"There was no awkwardness either. He just made me feel awesome," Clare said. "I mean, I was all dressed up for work, you know. But he didn't treat me like a stuck up business person or anything." She turned from her closet to see Amy nodding and listening. Then she walked back to the bed and sat down again, letting another smile cross her face.

"And the way he looked at me..." Clare continued. "It wasn't like some drunk douche at the bar. It was like he was looking into me." Amy took the opportunity to interject by grabbing Clare's shoulders and pulling her close.

"You two should have made out...right there!" Amy said, unable to hold back her own laughter. Clare shook her head and shoved her friend. "Listen to how mushy you are getting. You're totally taken by this guy."

"I know it sounds corny. It's stupid, Amy!" Clare finally said. "Why does the coolest guy I meet have to be some random guy in an airport who I might never see again?" Normally, Amy may have agreed with her, but there was something about seeing her best friend in this situation. Perhaps it was because in all the time Clare and Amy had been friends she hadn't ever really seen Clare actually lovestruck.

Amy was well aware that Clare had always been focused on school and her career prospects, which left guys to fit in where they could. But in the last year or so, it became evident that Clare wanted someone in her life and thus far she hadn't had the greatest of luck.

"It's not stupid, Clare," Amy said. "I think it's kind of exciting and I'm kind of jealous of you. It would be really awesome to meet a cutie in the airport." Clare looked over at Amy with a look of bewilderment.

"Are you really, Amy, or are you just screwing with me?" Clare asked.

"No, I'm serious and I don't think you should give up on this," Amy said. "I like seeing you like this. I mean, I like seeing you happy about a guy and I'm sure Steve is great."

"Thanks, Amy," Clare said. This was followed by an exasperated laugh. "I should have kissed him."

Clare R.

"Whoa there, bestie," Amy joked. "Let's remember you don't even know his full name or phone number. There are some priorities before swapping spit." Clare gave Amy another push and laughed loudly at the mild mannered insult. Then Amy got up and headed to the door.

"Where're you going?" Clare asked.

"I'm going home," Amy replied. "It's late. You need to sleep and I'm going to think up some fantastic scenario where I meet some hunk in an airport." They both laughed and suddenly Clare was overcome with feelings of gratitude toward Amy.

"Just hold on, OK?" Amy said. "Don't give up just yet..."

"I won't," Clare said. Then she did a double take. "Wait, what? What did you say?" Amy turned and stared at her from the doorway, tilting her head in confusion. She knew Clare had heard her.

"I said, 'hold on'. Don't give up on him," Amy repeated. When Clare didn't say anything, Amy returned to her seat on the bed. "Why?" Clare shook her head.

"Tonight when I came home from the airport, I was pretty upset," Clare said, trying to rethink the whole trip home. As she recalled the two strange coincidences, Clare could feel herself getting more excited. "I just wanted to get back here. But when I put the radio on, this really nice love song came on and then I got stuck behind this car. Oh my goodness, were they driving slowly! But their license plate..."

"Yeah?" Amy said.

"It said 'hold on'," Clare finished. "You know, like one of those vanity plates."

"Huh," Amy said.

"I know," Clare said, shaking her head. "It probably sounds totally lame."

"No it's not. Maybe a bit strange," Amy said. "But really kind of awesome!"

"You think?" Clare asked. Amy moved her head up and down in quick movements. Clare wasn't one to typically read into these types of things. Her past wasn't one that was necessarily full of good fortune, so she usually approached things in life by being cautious and well informed. It was her way of avoiding disappointment and it worked...most of the time.

"Yeah, why not?" Amy said, getting up again. "I mean, yeah you didn't get to see Steve like you hoped. But why not be positive about it? That license plate thing is pretty cool and maybe it's not time yet." Then a ghostly sound escaped her lips and she waved her hands like a magician, causing Clare to break out laughing again.

"Yeah," she replied. "Yeah..."

"All right," Amy said. "I'm going to head out. Unless you have any more surprises I need to hear about?" Clare shook her head sideways.

"Nah, I'm good," Clare said.

"All right, g'night!" Amy exclaimed, and off she went. When Clare heard the front door shut, she went out to the entryway to lock up for the night. Since she wasn't feeling tired yet, Clare made a cup of tea and wandered around the house picking things up.

It was a habit that Clare had developed when she was a young girl. Whenever Clare couldn't sleep, she would wander around the house and put things away that had been scattered about. Blankets,

Clare R.

television remotes, chip bags, laundry, it didn't matter. Clare knew that most kids would have probably gone to their parents, but she had also known that her father had trouble sleeping, so she only woke him if it was really necessary.

Every so often she would take a sip of tea, and at one point, she stopped to admire the cup in her hand. It was her father's favorite coffee cup. But there was something more. Ever since she and Steve had met, each cup of tea that she made was so much more satisfying, and they all made her smile.

Eventually, Clare found herself back in her room, staring at a picture of her and her father. Amy's dad had taken the picture for them after her high school graduation. Her father was giving her a sideways hug and she was grinning while holding up her diploma. Emotions and memories from many years before began surfacing and everything except the tea cup in her hands began to feel very cold as she let a particularly sad memory consume her.

~~~~

"Clare, you are brilliant and I love you so much," her father said. "I'm so proud of you." He was tucked under the white linens of a hospital bed and she was sitting in the chair beside him. She hadn't left his side in three days.

"Thank you, Daddy," Clare said. "I love you, too." Tears were welling in her eyes but she wouldn't let them fall. She knew it was coming. The inevitable goodbye.

"Promise me you will keep working hard. I know I wasn't able to give you much and I want you to do everything you can to make your dreams come true," he said. His blue eyes were as kind

as she'd ever seen them.

"I promise," Clare replied. He was getting weaker, but that didn't stop her father from lifting a hand and brushing it across her cheek.

"You're so beautiful, baby girl," he said, and then his eyes closed for the last time. Clare took his hand and kissed it. The flat line sounded on the heart monitor and the tears started falling.

~~~~

Her father had become fatally ill shortly after her graduation, and after his passing Clare was notified that everything of his had been left to her. She spent numerous nights crying while sorting through his belongings. After collecting a few mementos that she wanted to keep, Clare eventually sold their tiny house and moved in with Amy's family for the remainder of the summer. That fall they went off to college together.

Clare sniffled and wiped the tears on her sleeve. Then she downed the rest of her tea, craving the warmth. When the cup was empty, Clare climbed into bed and stared at the bookshelf that was missing a book. She sniffled again but smiled, too, while imagining Steve lying in his own bed, reading her book.

Please don't give up, Steve, she thought.

Chapter 13

The point of curvature plus the tangent distance equals the point of intersection. Steve looked away from the dizzying table of numbers and tapped the corresponding numbers into his calculator. When the result appeared, he put a check mark next to the row in question.

The point of curvature plus the length of curve equals the point of tangency. Steve again clicked away on the keys of the calculator and after a new number appeared, he put another check next to the row. It had been an hour since he'd begun this mind numbing exercise of double checking the track geometry for their project and he was quickly getting tired of it. Thankfully there had only been one row that Steve needed to adjust.

He slid off his headphones and rubbed his dry, irritated eyes. The office was quiet for the middle of the afternoon, and when Steve glanced around at the other cubes he noticed that several people had already left for the day. Jimmy, however, was still in his office, talking loudly on the phone. A grin spread across Steve's face and all of a sudden he felt full of energy again. After minimizing the design software, Steve reopened the Internet browser and continued perusing for a certain book.

After finishing Clare's book, Steve had been in search of a new piece of literature and nothing sounded appealing. Not even anything he'd scrounged from his mother's sparked any interest at the moment. But that morning, Steve woke with such a strong desire to bake cupcakes that he spent much of the morning at work glancing between the Internet and his work, searching for good recipes. This small bit of distraction was rather enjoyable, but to Steve's dismay, Jimmy appeared after lunch and requested that he check through the geometry numbers one last time.

However, when he was roughly halfway through this assignment, it dawned on him to expand the search to a suitable cupcake cookbook. With the geometry check finished, Steve was back on the hunt and he was rarely disappointed by his favorite online bookseller. In an instant, Steve was sifting through an overabundance of cookbooks that the search yielded. After previewing several books and reading countless reviews, Steve found the book he wanted.

It was the cover that got him first. The simple, old fashioned font that made up the title gave Steve the impression he was stepping into a bakery from the twenties or thirties or even perhaps a magical bakery in some sort of fantasy novel that was radiating a heavenly smell from numerous, delectable treats. Then there were five mouthwatering cupcakes that adorned the cover. The delicious looking treats were smeared with frosting in pale hues, much like Easter colors, and topped with sprinkles.

I wonder if Clare likes cupcakes, Steve thought. *I bet she does. It would be awesome to make some for her...* As Steve continued to stare at the cover, it occurred to him that he couldn't recall the last time he'd had a cupcake. All of a sudden, a warm

Clare R.

feeling spread though his body and Steve found himself tittering quietly. Something about this book was so comforting and reassuring it left Steve eager to buy it. Normally, he preferred going to the bookstore because of the calm peacefulness that came with sitting in one of the big chairs while peering through books.

However, this cookbook was more of a specialty item and Steve was fairly certain that the local bookstore wouldn't have it in stock, so he clicked through the purchasing process right at his office desk. A moment later his phone beeped when a confirmation email appeared in his inbox. Steve grinned and sat back in his chair, taking the last sip of tea from his Christmas-themed mug.

Jimmy was still talking loudly on the phone but the frequent bursts of laughter coming from the office suggested they were no longer talking about work-related topics and the remainder of the office sounded even quieter. Steve took the hint and shut down the computer, put on his jacket, and walked out the door eager to get to cooking class.

~~~~

"Ughh!" exclaimed an aggravated voice. Steve looked up from his station to see the student next to him furiously scraping the contents of a pan into the trash. This evening's lesson was centered on making a roux for the base of soup or sauce and Steve guessed that his classmate had just burnt whatever was in the pan. Steve scanned the room for Mr. Alero, but he was busy helping another student.

Steve looked back at his frustrated classmate. Clearly he was upset and although Steve was no expert, he decided to offer a hand.

"You all right?" Steve asked.

"Yeah, I'm fine," snapped the guy.

"All right," he replied. "Well, would you like some help?"

"Nah man, I think I'm just gonna call it a night," said his classmate.

"What about your grade?" Steve asked. The trash guy shrugged. Steve didn't want to see another person leave the class, so he tried again.

"Come on. Let me help," Steve said.

"What's the point?" said the trash guy while he motioned to the board. "There are hardly any directions and I couldn't make it work."

"Eh, well I think there's a bit of a learning curve that Gus wanted us to figure out," Steve offered. "Seriously, you should give it another shot." His classmate looked at him and Steve was pleased to see that he actually went to clean his pan at the sink.

"All right," the trash guy said. "What am I missing? I added the flour and the butter on medium heat and each time it got pasty and then burned. The next time I tried it was lumpy and then it burned."

"First off, I'm Steve," he said.

"Mitch," he replied.

"OK, so what exactly did you do first each time?" Steve asked.

"I got the pan up to temperature and then I added the flour and butter," Mitch explained. "Is that not right?" Steve shook his head sideways.

"I think you're going too quickly," Steve replied. "Add the butter first and let it melt all the way."

"OK," Mitch said. He replaced the pan on the burner and

Clare R.

added the butter once the pan was up to temperature. "Now what?"

"Don't add the flour all at once. Sprinkle some and whisk it into the butter so it can cook," Steve explained. "I would probably lower the heat some just in case." Mitch nodded and did what Steve suggested. In short order, Mitch had the start of a roux that was neither burnt nor lumpy.

"There you go. Now you can add milk or beer or broth and make it even more awesome," Steve said. "I think we're adding milk today."

"Wow, thanks man," Mitch said and he finally grinned. "You are good at this cooking thing."

"Ha, thanks," Steve said. "Well good luck and uh, just take your time." Mitch nodded and Steve returned to his station. He didn't notice Mr. Alero staring at him, and after the class cleared out later that evening, Gus stopped at Steve's cooking area.

"You know, I think people find you less scary when you get rid of your Batman scowl," Mr. Alero said.

"What scowl?" Steve replied. "I have no idea what you're talking about." Gus laughed.

"The look of sour milk then," he offered.

"Seriously, Gus. That hurts a little," Steve said, and Gus laughed again.

"Thanks for helping Mitch out today," Gus said. "That was kind of you."

"It's not a big deal. It's cool getting to help people," Steve said. Mr. Alero stared at him while he put on his jacket.

"It's probably not my place to say this, but I think your dad would be proud of you," said Gus. "Don't be so hard on yourself. Everything will work out, Steve."

~~~

R. K. Blessing

In the fall before Thanksgiving, Clare's company held their annual fall charity event, and tonight Clare stood in front of the bookcase, wondering if she really wanted to attend. In years past, the evening had been enjoyable. People milled about before dinner, talking and schmoozing over drinks, and once everyone had eaten their meal, the results of the past year's fundraising were presented. When that was finished, the dancing would commence.

However, this year was different. Many of her friends from work had since paired off and several even had families now. This meant that when the festivities finally started she was sort of an odd one out. It wasn't because she didn't have anyone to talk to, but more so because of how many of the conversations were oriented. More and more, it seemed like everywhere she turned, someone was talking about wedding planning, getting married to their significant other, or babies. The last thing on Clare's mind was having babies.

So there she stood, apprehensive about attending. Nothing significant had happened in the past several weeks except for Amy nearly getting in a fight with a pet shop owner after a parrot called her "bimbo." Other than that, Clare spent most of her waking hours working or staring at the bookshelf in her room. But whether she was working or not, her thoughts were mainly centered on Steve.

What do you do in your free time? What are your friends and family like? Did you forget about me, Steve?

Clare had yet to come up with a good solution to the predicament of finding him and it was becoming increasingly frustrating. That was why, for the last several weeks, her new evening routine came to involve staring at the bookshelf for random periods of time. It didn't matter where she was in her room either, because her eyes always ended up fixated on the hole in her bookshelf.

Clare R.

Clare would stare from her bed, the desk, or sometimes even sit on the floor in front of the bookshelf while eating spoonfuls of peanut butter.

Tonight Clare stood in front of the bookcase in a pale white dress with a new pair of matching heels. A whimsical grin played across her face as she enjoyed a moment of fantasy while imagining Steve walking into her room dressed up as well and eager to dance the night away.

"Ugh," Clare sighed. She opened her eyes and stared once again at the bookshelf. There would be no dream appearance of Steve. Then her phone jingled. It was a text message from Amy, her plus one.

Where you at? There be some cuties here!

On my way. Keep your panties on! Clare replied. She was sure that she and Amy would probably do some dancing and that would have to be good enough. The charity portion of the night went without a hitch and Clare made small talk with several of the clients who were attending.

It's good PR, her boss had said. Clare rolled her eyes every time she heard him say this.

People are here to eat, drink and dance, dude, she thought. *Just relax.* When it came time to dance, the odds there weren't in her favor. For some reason, hardly anyone wanted to dance and many of the guys she would have considered dancing with were now paired off, meaning they were pretty much off limits.

If only Steve was here, Clare mused as she looked longingly around the room. When a good song came on, Amy tugged her onto the floor with a few of her other coworkers but even that didn't have the zah it used to. Prior to her finally calling it quits for the evening, a guy who she hadn't met before came up and asked her to dance.

He seemed nice and sort of cute. But for some reason he reeked of garlic. Clare loved garlic but she loved the aromatic ingredient in food. Certainly not as a deodorant, so she politely declined and made her way to the coat room.

As Clare made her way across the parking lot, the clicking of her heels echoed in the darkness and the sound was hauntingly familiar to the pendulum inside a grandfather clock. It was as if the very world around her was trying to tell her that time was still moving on, regardless of how much she wanted to see Steve.

But, just as she reached for the door handle of her car, Clare happened to glance up at the night sky. The benefit dinner was usually held at a nice restaurant well outside of Pittsburgh, and that evening in the cloudless sky, the celestial bodies were glittering like diamonds, uninhibited by the lights of the city. Clare looked away from the sky momentarily to see if anyone else was in the parking lot. As far as she could tell, she was all alone.

Why not, she thought. *It's worth a shot.*

"I wish that Steve and I could see each other again," she said quietly. It definitely felt strange talking to a sky full of stars and Clare immediately wondered if she was just being foolish. But to her immense surprise, Clare was witness to a dazzling shooting star that blew across the sky above her. Its long, white tail seemed to stretch across the entire sky as it burned through the atmosphere and Clare could feel a breath get caught in her chest.

"Wow, so that's what that feels like," Clare thought out loud. A sense of intense anticipation came about inside her and she couldn't help but smile.

Chapter 14

Although the roads were clear and dry, the farm fields on each side of the highway were quickly being buried under a white blanket as large, fluffy flakes fell from the sky. The light of the day was starting to fade away as dusk took hold, but Steve could still make out the dark shapes of deer tromping through the fields, scrounging for food before it was hidden away by the coming winter weather.

Thanksgiving was a couple days away and Steve was making the drive back to his mother's home where the festivities would be held. Other than the visit after meeting Clare, this would be his first time home for a holiday in close to two years. Steve had been unsure if he was going, but after his last cooking class, Mr. Alero had urged him to go in his own quirky fashion.

"I would offer for you to come home with me but you're not orphaned. Go home, Steve," he had said. That same day his brother sent Steve a short text message.

Hey man! Are you going to make it home this year? It would be great to see you!

A few hours later, Steve replied with a text letting his brother know that he would indeed be coming. Apparently, his brother's family was going to be there as well as his aunt and uncle. Steve was admittedly very nervous and several times before going home, Steve's eyes glazed over while working as he pictured very uncomfortable scenarios occurring when he walked in the door of his mother's house.

Despite the anxiety Steve was experiencing, this trip home did feel less daunting. Since meeting Clare, the notion of seeing everyone didn't seem so difficult anymore because she made him feel so much happier. After a couple hours of driving, Steve was ready for a break and he pulled into a gas station to refuel and get something to drink. He was feeling parched after all.

~~~~

Amy and Clare on the other hand, would be spending Thanksgiving with Amy's family. Ever since her father died, there had been a standing invitation for Clare to join them and she usually took them up on it. After all, it was better than being alone. For the first part of their trip, Amy gabbed away on the phone to her mother and Clare sat with her forehead pressed against the window, amusing herself with watching the gradual transition from city to country. The bustling streets of Pittsburgh became increasingly smaller and soon enough, they were on a simple two lane highway that snaked its way through the country. There were no more tri-colored lights and busy intersections, only stop signs and the occasional farm house tucked off-road.

Clare tried to focus on the few memories she had of her father taking her to visit her grandparents. Their long drives in his old truck bouncing down the highway, had been so much fun. But

Clare R.

they had long since passed and Clare's thoughts took a different tack, which ended being the first trip she made with Amy.

~~~

It was nearly Thanksgiving break and Clare had become very moody the closer the holiday came. She took to different parts of campus, not wanting to be around people. The library, empty classrooms, anywhere there were less people. But no matter where she tried to hide, it seemed like someone would appear and they were busy making plans for their trips home and it quickly became depressing and frustrating.

Thanks to the heavy course load she had graced herself with, Clare always had an abundance of homework, which she loved because it was sort of therapeutic. On the day that Amy would be leaving for break Clare intentionally left their dorm room early but not before leaving behind a note saying Happy Thanksgiving.

Campus was cold and vacant as she made the walk back to their dorm later that afternoon. The empty buildings looming around her only accentuated the loneliness that she felt. But when Clare opened the door to her dorm, she was surprised to see Amy standing in the middle of their room, holding her letter. Despite all the emotions Clare was experiencing, she almost started laughing because of the exasperated look on Amy's face. Amy, however, wasn't ready to laugh yet.

"A letter. Really?" Amy said. "This is bullshit." Clare didn't say anything and moped over to her desk.

"I thought you would like my letter," Clare said. She knew

she was being a smartass but it was the only thing that was currently stopping her from breaking down. Amy chose to disregard the comment.

"Where have you been?" Amy asked. "I've been waiting for you." Clare looked at her friend and shrugged. Then she pointed at her bag.

"I've been doing homework," Clare said. Finally, Amy laughed.

"You would, you nerd," Amy said.

"Amy, why are you still here?" Clare asked when the humor faded. "I figured you would have left hours ago."

"I was waiting for you," Amy repeated. "You're coming back home with me...aren't you?" Clare shrugged again. For as long as she could remember, she had spent every holiday with her father. Nothing about them had been super exciting or glamorous. But they were festive and most of all, Clare and her father were thankful to have each other. Now that was gone.

Not only that, but the last thing Clare wanted was to impose on Amy's family. Yet, she wasn't surprised when Amy seemingly read her mind.

"Clare, don't even try giving me some excuse about imposing on my family," Amy said. "You're like my sister and I'm not letting you stay here by yourself. Now come on, let's go." Amy then reached up on Clare's bunk, pulled down her duffel bag, and dropped it on the floor at Clare's feet. She felt like she could cry.

"It's already full," Clare stated.

"Yeah, I know," Amy said with a goofy grin. "I didn't have much else to do while I was waiting for you." Amy's sarcasm brought a grin to Clare's face and she gave her best friend a hug.

Clare R.

A few minutes later they walked out of the dorms and began the trip back to Amy's parents'.

~~~~

"Hey! You awake over there?" Amy said. Clare snapped back to reality and turned to her friend who immediately started laughing at her. "That's nice. Really cute." Amy was motioning with her finger to her own forehead. Clare got the hint and quickly pulled down the visor. There was a red mark on her forehead from leaning against the cold window for so long. She laughed as well and flipped the visor back up.

"What's up?" Clare asked.

"I was going to stop for gas in a bit if you want anything," Amy said. "My mom says hi, too, by the way. I would have told you earlier, but I thought you were sleeping." Clare just smiled.

"Hi to her, too," Clare replied. "I could use the bathroom." They pulled into the gas station and Amy offered to pump gas, so Clare could use the restroom. A few minutes later, Clare returned to the car with a fresh cup of tea.

"I'll be right back," Amy said. "Oh, I think I heard your phone ring, too by the way." She nodded and grabbed her phone out of the console. While Clare checked a message from her office, she didn't notice a very familiar brown-haired guy with worn boots walk by a short distance away from the car.

~~~~

After Steve finished pumping gas, he walked into the gas

station to get something to drink. He made a cup of tea instead of getting coffee and also got a soda from the cooler. There were several hours of driving yet to do and Steve knew he would be grateful for the caffeine after a while. Then he proceeded to the counter. A brunette in front of him completed her purchase after tossing a pack of gum on the counter and then headed for the door.

"Happy Thanksgiving," Steve said to the clerk after paying for his drinks, and then he also headed for the door. The brown-haired girl was fiddling with the pack of gum, so Steve held the door for her on his way out.

"Thanks," she said with barely a glance.

"You're welcome," Steve mumbled. The two drifted apart as they headed to their cars. Clare looked up when the door opened and Amy sat down, sticking a piece of gum in her mouth at the same time.

"Ready?" Amy asked.

"Yep," Clare replied while buckling her safety belt across her body. It just so happened that Clare turned away from the passenger window just as the same brown-haired guy walked by again carrying his green soda and a steaming cup of tea. Not long after, both cars left the gas station and continued on their way.

~~~~

Steve's arrival early that evening brought a great deal of commotion, but before going inside, he lingered outside the door of his mother's house letting the frosty air nip at his exposed skin. Hard kernels of snow were falling from the sky and bouncing off the sidewalk into the grass beyond.

Clare R.

Corn snow, Steve thought. *That's what dad always called it.* There was a sense of trepidation as Steve reached for the handle, and just before his hand grasped the brass knob, he hesitated. It had been two years and Steve knew that he could just as easily turn away and make it three or even more. Then imaginary Clare appeared and put a hand on his arm.

"Go on, Stevie," she said. "They want to see you." The smile on her ghostly face had a reassuring warmth that fought back the winter breeze.

"I wish you were here," he replied. Imaginary Clare gave his arm an affectionate squeeze.

"I will be...eventually," she said. "Just go." Steve let his gaze fall back to the door and then back to his figment but she had disappeared. Steve took a deep breath and grasped the handle.

Everyone, including his brother's baby, was in the living room relaxing or waiting anxiously. Steve wasn't really sure, but when he walked in the door, they all seemed to get up at once to greet him. Except for the baby of course, who was stuck in the high chair while his brother's wife fed him dinner. His mother was the first to wrap him up in a hug and was followed thereafter by his brother, uncle, and aunty.

In no time at all, his mother's home was abuzz with conversation. There was talk of work, the farm, and the coming Thanksgiving dinner, but Steve wasn't interested in much of it. Not at the moment, anyway. Instead, Steve skated past his family to find his brother's wife now sitting in the recliner with a squat baby in her lap.

His brother, Matt, had married his college sweetheart; a tall, blond-haired girl who apparently had been giving his brother the "eye" for years before they actually started dating. At least that's how Matt had told it to him.

"Hi, Katy," he said.

"Hey, Steve," Katy replied. "It's good to see you finally." Even though Steve knew she probably meant nothing by it, her remark stung slightly. Everyone had clearly taken notice of his absence over the past couple of years.

"You, too," Steve replied. He did his best to disregard her comment and smiled while watching Katy bounce her son up and down on her lap. With each bounce, he giggled a little more.

"How have you been?" Katy asked. She looked up from the baby and stared at him. Her expression was somewhat piercing like Clare's had been. Yet, Katy's stare didn't have the same loving qualities as Clare's did. Instead, it was more of a pensive stare as if she was trying to determine how Steve was really feeling.

"Pretty good. Can't complain," Steve said, trying to ease her worries. Katy moved her head up and down silently and looked back to the baby.

"Baby Jacob, do you know who this is?" Katy asked suddenly. The baby's face turned and his large, watery eyes locked onto Steve. The long, wavy locks of baby hair were a brownish blond as if they were still trying to decide which parent's traits would dominate. "This is your Uncle Steve." Baby Jacob looked back to his mother for a moment and then returned his gaze to Steve. He reached out with a tiny hand and Steve let it land in his palm.

"High five little man," Steve said with a grin, and the baby let out a gleeful giggle. Katy smiled as well and kept bouncing her baby. "So, you guys did name him that then?" Katy looked at

Clare R.

Steve and nodded, clearly unsure of how he would react.

"Matty and your mom really liked the idea," she said slowly. "I hope that's OK?" While Steve moved his head in acknowledgment, he realized that his brother and Katy had been worried he might put up a protest.

"Yeah," Steve said, trying to give his most reassuring expression. "It's great. He's a cute kid." Seeing the expression on his face left Katy feeling at ease and her smile broadened. Despite the grin on her face, Steve suddenly felt awkward and alone again.

Matt was only halfway engaged in the conversation he was having with his Uncle Charlie. They were talking about purchasing some new equipment for the farm, but Matt was busy casting glances at his younger brother. Although Matt was older than his brother by nearly a year, he often felt like Steve was the older one.

His brother had always been mature for his age and he had shared so much with their father, so it was no surprise that he had taken his passing as hard as he did. But Matt never expected Steve to drop off the face of the earth like he had.

*Then again...*Matt thought as he took a sip of coffee. *Steve hadn't really had anyone.* A lot of his friends had moved away. Matt and Katy were already married at that point. Uncle Charlie had his wife, and their mother had been a wreck as well.

It wasn't long before Uncle Charlie excused himself to go visit with Patty and his wife, so Matt took the opportunity to sit down at the table and continued to stare at his brother while clutching a warm cup of coffee in his hand. Steve seemed to like his baby and vice versa, which was good. He knew that Steve would be a wonderful uncle just like Charlie had been to them both.

Matt grinned to no one as he watched his baby giggle uncontrollably after receiving exuberant licks from his mother's puppy. That was a day he wouldn't forget either...

The car was stopped at a stop light and Matt took the opportunity to unroll the sleeves of the new flannel Katy had got him for his birthday. It was much cooler now as dusk faded towards the evening. A green glow filled the car, signaling that the light had changed and Matt turned his head away from the crate in the seat beside him.

He continued on and turned a short distance later onto another street, and soon enough he was parked in front of the house he'd grown up in. A pale glow from lights in the kitchen and living room could be seen through a variety of windows and Matt smiled. His mother was home and he hoped she would like his surprise.

After removing the crate from the passenger seat, Matt walked up to the front door and pressed the button for the doorbell. A short time later, footsteps could be heard and then the door opened, which caused the animal in the crate to start moving about excitedly.

His mother had looked tired as Matt knew she would. He knew she wasn't sleeping well. But that didn't stop her from being excited to see him.

"Hi, Matty," she said with a smile. The only times his mother had ever called him by his full name were when he had done something that upset her. So, for as long as Matt could remember, he'd been called Matty by everyone close to him. Especially Katy, who loved the nickname.

"Hi, ma," Matt said. "I'd give you a hug but my hands are full."

"Yeah. I can see that. Who's this?" she said. The puppy's

nose was pressed through an opening in the crate and its tail was wagging furiously.

"This is your new puppy," Matt said with a bit of apprehension in his voice. "Charlie's dogs had a litter and we both thought you would like one." Patty looked at Matt with a very surprised expression on her face.

"Charlie has a full-grown German shepherd and a basset hound," she said. Matt let out a very healthy laugh as he also considered what she said.

"Believe me, ma," he said. "Charlie and I were wondering the same thing and we had a good laugh about it, too." Patty's titter made Matt feel easier about the situation and she put a hand on her hip as she surveyed the puppy in the crate.

"Does it need shots and everything?" she asked. Matt shook his head sideways.

"Nope. Charlie took care of that already," Matt said.

"Oh bless his heart. OK, bring him inside," she said. "Can you stay for a while?" Again Matt nodded.

"Yeah, absolutely," he replied. "I brought some dog food and a couple bowls, too, so let me just grab those." His mother smiled and moved out of the doorway.

A short time later, Matt and his mother were sitting at the kitchen table making small talk while they watched the puppy investigate its new home. She had made him some coffee and tea for herself. Unlike Steve, Matt and his father had shared a love of coffee. Steve had always preferred tea like their mother.

"So," Patty said to break the silence that had fallen over the table. She was slowly spinning the cup of tea with her finger. "Have you heard from him?" Matt looked up from his cup of

coffee and the hopeful expression on her face made him sad. He knew his mother would bring this up. She always did when he came to visit and his response was always the same.

"No, not really," he said. "I'm sure he's OK, ma." Patty nodded but Matt knew she was incredibly worried about Steve. They all were. Matt and his mother each emptied their cups and then he headed home...

Matt let a sip of coffee soothe his dry throat. Many months had passed since that conversation and several times he had found himself wondering what it would be like to see his brother again. Now Steve was here. He looked strong, healthy, and a few inches taller. As Matt continued to study his brother, he thought Steve looked happier, too.

A thud on his shoulder jarred Steve from his thoughts. It was a firm grasp that felt very reminiscent of his father's hand, but when he turned, Steve found only his brother staring down at him.

"Looks like Jacob likes you," Matt said.

"Yeah, hopefully," Steve replied.

"He does," said Katy. "Jacob hasn't stopped grinning since you came over." Steve chuckled and shrugged. He leaned in and gave Jacob a gentle prod in the stomach, which unleashed another fit of gleeful giggles.

"Come on, buddy. Ma wants us to get something from the garage," Matt said. Steve said bye to Katy and the baby and then they skirted their way through the house to the garage. Ever since Steve could remember, their family had kept a second refrigerator in the garage for occasions such as these when the holiday season meant a need for more food storage. It also provided more room in the late summer when they brought produce home from the farm.

In spite of being gone for so long, Steve reached into the darkness with a seasoned familiarity and found the light switch on the wall. A single light lit up half the garage and the brothers made their way to the fridge.

They had barely talked since he arrived home and Steve surmised that this trip to the garage was about more than just getting something for their mother. His suspicions were confirmed when Matt slowed to a stop and leaned against the dust covered workbench. The expression on his face had changed from the cheery one in the living room to one that was strained and deeply concerned. With the garage door shut and only a single light turned on, numerous shadows still filled the garage and several were cast across his brother.

Initially, Steve had thought that Matt still looked the same but in the nearly two years that had passed since they last saw each other, Steve now thought his brother looked older, too. It was as if the sleepless nights of caring for Jacob had taken a toll on him. But the expression was deeper than simply losing sleep. It was pensive like Katy's but there was also a hint of frustration.

Matt found himself at a loss for words. He had spent countless nights, lying awake in bed, staring at the clock or the ceiling, while Katy slept next to him. Hours would go by as he worried about his brother, thinking about things he could say to Steve, good and bad. But now as they stood there, Matt realized that he didn't want to say something that would upset his brother and make him leave.

Steve, on the other hand, noticed the blatant look of hesitation on his brother's face, so he decided to jump in before things got awkward.

"Matt, I'm fine and I'm sorry I've been gone so long," Steve said flatly. Apparently, this brief comment was enough to take the edge off.

"Dude, you've been gone a hell of a long time," Matt said.

"Yeah, I know," Steve replied. "Time flies." Then he shrugged.

What else is there really to say, Matt? Steve thought. He knew it sounded somewhat selfish. *I wasn't ready to come home.* Matt also came to that conclusion as well. It was pointless to be frustrated or angry now. His brother had finally come home.

"I'm glad you're OK. It's really good to see you," Matt said. "What have you been up to?"

Steve replied with another shrug and peered at some of the dusty shelves. There had been so many times while growing up when they had been enlisted by their father to sort through nuts and bolts while he tinkered with a project on the work bench. "Working. Moving."

"Yeah, I got that," Matt said. "Where all have you been, anyway?"

"Well...Wisconsin, Minnesota, North Dakota, Utah, and now Ohio," Steve said. Matt tried to keep a cool expression on his face but it was difficult because he had no idea about the extent of his brother's relocating.

"Did you like it?" Matt asked.

"Sometimes. Fishing was fun," Steve said, looking up from the shelves. "The man-camps out in North Dakota were a little dicey sometimes and living out of boxes gets old. I still haven't

Clare R.

unpacked a lot of my stuff." Matt was shocked.

"Man-camps?" Matt stammered.

"Yeah. I did engineering work out in the oil fields for a while," Steve replied. But then his attention was diverted by a rusty, metal box he found on a shelf. Steve's name was still legible but faded and when he shook the container, a loud clanging came from inside. Their father had filled it with some of his spare tools to help Steve feel more important when they had projects to work on.

"I thought this was gone," Steve mumbled.

"No way. Ma's not getting rid of this stuff anytime soon," Matt replied.

"Hmm," Steve said and set the box back on the shelf.

"Are you planning on moving again?" he finally asked. Steve shrugged again.

"I don't know. I might hang tight for a while," he said. Matt saw right through the fact that Steve was being aloof on purpose.

"Because of the cooking class, or the girl," Matt offered. He let a smile cross his face and Steve did, too. "Ma mentioned you met someone..." A noise escaped Steve's lips much like the one that had when he and John had talked about ladies during his last visit. In the end, Steve just shook his head and went to the fridge. The smile never left his face.

That's exactly why I don't want to move, Matt, Steve thought. *I don't want to miss a chance at seeing her again.* But Steve didn't really want to talk to his brother about relationships at the moment. He was just happy they'd got past his extended absence.

"What did ma want anyway?" Steve asked. Thankfully, Matt took the hint and didn't pry anymore.

"Um, there are a couple different salads in there for dinner," he replied. Steve nodded and they each took a bowl and started back for the kitchen. Matt, however, stopped in the doorway.

"Come on, bro. You've gotta give me something," Matt said.

"She's amazing." Steve replied. "The most beautiful woman I've ever seen." It was a simple answer but it got the point across. Matt smiled and continued to the kitchen.

Chapter 15

Steve had grown accustomed to being alone and as much as he was excited to see everyone again, being in the company of so much family left him feeling a bit overwhelmed. After being at his mother's for only a couple hours, Steve had to slip away. But before leaving, he mumbled something to his mother about taking Toby for a walk. They all knew that Steve was still upset over the loss of his father. They all were. But unlike Steve, they had been able to move on somewhat.

Toby's floppy ears beat against his short legs as his head moved back and forth, sniffing everything in sight. Darkness had fallen fully now and Steve pulled his coat tighter while waiting for the dog to go to the bathroom. It wasn't long before imaginary Clare appeared at his side and she too was bundled up.

"He's funny," she said, smiling at Toby.

"Yeah, he is. I like him a lot though," Steve replied. Imaginary Clare leaned into his shoulder and wrapped her arm around his.

I sure wish you were here to do that, Steve thought as he peered at her. *I know my family would love you, too.* But before he could say anything, she spoke up.

"Your family seems nice," she said. "I think they're really

happy to see you and your brother's baby is so cute."

"I know," Steve said. Then he made a funny noise. "You know that's the first time I've seen Jacob. I've never even held him before." There was no hiding the glum expression on his face. He'd missed out on so much in his absence.

"Yep, I know," she replied. "You have been on the road a lot." Steve nodded and stared at the house. Through the living room window, he could see members of his family milling about, enjoying their time together. Then his eyes drifted up to the roof. The clouds had disappeared, leaving behind a star filled sky.

"How come you keep staring at the roof?" asked imaginary Clare. Steve was aware that she already knew the answer since she was just a figment of his imagination, but he answered her anyway.

"In the summer when my brother and I were little, my dad used to come wake us up after ma went to bed. We would sneak outside and climb up on the roof..." The more he told his figment, the clearer one of his favorite memories became.

A gentle nudging brought Steve out of his dreams. His older brother was pushing on his arm.

"Come on Steve," he whispered. "Dad wants us to get up." Steve remembered clearly the look of excitement in his brother's eyes and he quickly understood why. In an instant, Steve was awake and he slipped on his trousers and shoved his bare feet into his shoes. He was too excited for socks.

After grabbing a sweater, Steve and his brother tip toed out to the kitchen. Their father's excitement for the coming adventure mirrored Matt's and he led them quietly to the back of the house. Often times after these late night escapades, Steve and his brother would debate quietly whether or not their father had superpowers

Clare R.

because it seemed like he could see in the dark so easily.

Once they reached the TV antenna, the trio climbed up, one by one, and stood proudly on the roof. There was a light breeze but for the most part everything was still. The only sound that could be heard was the steady chirping of crickets. Steve's father spread out a ratty blanket that kept their pants from getting roughed up by the gritty shingles and then they all lay down and watched the stars.

It was like the sky was alive that night. Shooting stars flew across the sky, one after another before burning up in the atmosphere. Steve was silent on the blanket, completely mesmerized by the show that was going on above him. However, when his brother spoke up suddenly, Steve tore his eyes away from the sky.

"Dad, why do you like to come up here so much?" whispered Matt. Steve rolled over, so he could see his father, who was resting on his elbows.

"Because it's beautiful," he replied. His voice was barely audible. "When I was your age, I wanted to be an astronaut." Steve grinned while imagining him and his father floating together in space in those big white suits with the shiny helmets.

"I want you two to dream big," he said. "The sky's the limit." Never had Steve and his brother been so happy to spend time with their dad. They continued to watch the meteor shower until they fell asleep...

Never again, Steve thought as he shook his head in the cold night air. Imaginary Clare was still standing next to him.

"That's a beautiful memory," she said. Steve gave her a sheepish grin. "You know you'll be able to do that with your kids someday, if you want." It was a simple statement that Steve hadn't really considered before and surprisingly it made him feel better.

"Even when you're not really here you can still make me

feel better," he said. Imaginary Clare smiled and shrugged her shoulders.

"It's what I do," she said. "You still want to go for a walk?" Steve chuckled and gently tugged on Toby's leash.

"Yeah, sure," he said. "For a little bit." His figment grinned at him and they all turned and continued down the sidewalk.

~~~~

It seems safe to assume that there is something special about having someone of your own to share the holidays with that makes them that much more meaningful. Clare had learned this the hard way and although she had grown accustomed to spending the holidays with Amy's family, feelings of discomfort and loneliness always took root, no matter how hard she tried to keep them from germinating. This year, these pervasive feelings had grown exponentially after meeting Steve and many nights she dreamed about spending the holidays with him.

I wonder what Steve does for the holidays? Does your family decorate hardcore? Clare mused while meandering around Amy's house, admiring all the subtle changes that had occurred since her visit the year before. One room, for instance, had been painted a new color and another had new carpet. She was just about to peer into the little office her parents kept, when Amy walked up to her.

"I'm going to find my dad, OK? I'll be back in a bit," Amy said. Clare nodded. "My mom is in the kitchen. You should go say hi!"

"Mmk," Clare said. Amy smiled and disappeared into another part of the house. Clare and her warm cup of tea wandered back to the kitchen.

Clare R.

"You look cozy," said Amy's mother with a bright smile. Clare was still wearing her pullover but she had replaced her jeans with sweatpants and had also donned a pair of very warm socks.

"I am," Clare said. "Thanks for the tea, by the way." Amy's mother laughed. After learning that Clare had enjoyed tea as a little girl, Tracy had started keeping a stash just for her.

"Come here. Sit down," she said. "Do you still like to bake?" Clare obliged and took a seat at the counter opposite Amy's mother.

"Yeah, I do," Clare replied. "I don't get to as much now because I'm so busy with work." Amy's mother nodded as she pulled ingredients out of the cupboard.

"Well, you don't look too busy right now," Tracy said. "You want to help me make some cupcakes for tomorrow?" Clare smirked and took another sip of tea while Tracy stared at her. A large portion of her childhood was spent in the company of Amy and her mother and Clare especially loved when they had the chance to bake cupcakes. Quite often the best friends ended up covered with frosting and Clare's father would laugh at her when he found little clumps of frosting stuck in her hair.

"I would love to," Clare said. She set the cup of tea on the counter and rolled up the sleeves of her flannel pullover. "Are we making that same recipe?" Amy's mother nodded. Clare's memory was exceptional. That made her job so fun and easy for her. She could remember simple details that most people disregarded or forgot. But she also had a particularly good memory when it came to memorizing ingredients.

I wonder if Steve likes cupcakes, she thought. Picturing them baking together made Clare warm up significantly and she even let out a giggle as she pictured dusting him with flour or smearing his face with frosting.

"So, Amy happened to mention that you met someone," Tracy said. "And that you're pretty taken with him."

"Of course she did," Clare replied. She was slightly distracted while gently patting the side of a sieve, sending flour and baking soda into the bowl beneath. However, Clare was well aware that Tracy was applying friendly coercion to get gushy details out of her and it was one of the reasons Clare appreciated Amy's mother so much. Whenever they talked about stuff, Tracy never seemed to pry. It was always a patient, drawn out conversation based on comfort levels, so Clare wasn't even bothered when she asked about Steve.

"His name is Steve and we met at the airport when I got delayed on a work trip," Clare continued. Tracy made a sound of acknowledgment while pulling muffin tins from the cupboard. Then she pulled a pack of baking cups from a drawer under the counter and systematically began filling each spot in the tins. Clare assumed that Tracy's silence meant she wanted her to continue.

"We had a wonderful time," Clare said. "I mean, it was great. We talked about everything...books, favorite TV shows, work, food..." Amy's mother watched with a keen eye as Clare's movements started becoming more enthusiastic and erratic. The stick of butter needed for the recipe thudded loudly in the bowl as Clare unwrapped it.

"He made me laugh a lot," Clare said. "Oh my gosh, there were so many jokes." She could feel herself getting warmer. But it wasn't the same warmth Clare usually felt when she thought about Steve. It was an anxious warmth that Clare felt whenever she was nervous or super unsure of something. When she poured the milk in another bowl, it splashed up the edges and ran over the side, but she paid it no mind.

Clare R.

"Steve is the nicest guy I've met in a long time," she said. Then Clare finally cracked like the egg she hit too hard against the bowl. Pieces of egg shell scattered around the counter and the broken yolk ran down her hand. She looked up at Tracy who had quit placing baking cups in the muffin tins and was staring intently at her. Clare could feel her heart pounding and there were tears in her eyes.

"We didn't exchange any information. Nothing. I don't know if I'll ever see him again," Clare said. Amy's mother remained calm and handed Clare a damp wash cloth to wipe off her hands. The longer Tracy went without saying anything, the more foolish Clare felt for letting herself get worked up. Apparently, Tracy didn't mind though.

"Do you feel better?" she asked. There was no need to state the obvious. Tracy knew that Clare had lost the two most important people in her life and she didn't want Clare to lose anyone else.

"I don't know," Clare said with a shrug. "I guess...Sort of."

But it didn't make Steve appear out of thin air, she thought.

"Good," Tracy said. "Now what does your heart tell you?" The question sounded so cliché to Clare that she actually snorted with laughter.

"I know it sounds corny," Amy's mother admitted. "Don't laugh." This of course, only made her laugh even more.

"I think we'll meet again," Clare finally said. She was focused on her hand, trying to get all the gooey yolk off before it dried around her fingernails. "I really hope so anyway."

"Come on, Clare," Tracy said. She thought back through everything her and Steve had shared during their time together. Then in her mind's eyes she saw the bookshelf with its empty space for her missing book and she grinned.

"We will," Clare said more confidently. "We're going to because Steve has one of my books and I want it back." Amy's mother actually burst out laughing.

"I hope that's not the only thing you want," Tracy said, and she gave Clare a very suggestive wink. Clare picked up on the tone immediately. Not only did she start laughing, but Clare also threw the eggy washcloth back at Tracy.

~~~

Even after moving out, Amy's parents had kept her bedroom available, but she always chose to spend the night with Clare in the spare bedroom, which had two twin beds. There was one simple reason for this. Ever since Amy was a young girl, she could remember wanting a sister. The thought had always pleased her because Amy knew that a sister would be someone she could count on for everything— a best friend.

Amy could remember asking her parents several times if she could have a sister. The concept to Amy at that time in her life was fairly simple. If you ask enough times, then you shall receive... hopefully. Sadly, no sister ever came.

But, that didn't stop Amy from hoping and wishing and one day while waiting for the school bus, Amy met Clare. Before the bus even reached school, they were talking happily in the seat they had shared for the entire ride. That bus ride was all it took and since then they had done nearly everything together.

Amy often thought about the night when her mother explained Clare's situation at home. Clare had rarely mentioned anything about her family and Amy never wanted to pry because

Clare R.

keeping Clare as a friend meant a great deal to her. When her mother told her what happened, Amy was shocked and quickly understood why Clare never mentioned anything about her own family. That night when she went to bed, Amy vowed to always be there for her best friend and thus far, she had.

"Every time we do this, I feel like we're back in college," Amy said with a grin. Clare chortled.

"Good times," Clare said. "But why just college? You remember all the sleepovers we had." Amy nodded and then her cackle filled the room when a very funny memory came to mind.

"Do you remember that time I called you in the middle of the night to come get me—" Amy started, but Clare cut her off.

"And I walked into the wall of newspaper that you and the dorm mates taped over our door," Clare said trying to give Amy a stink eye. Amy enjoyed knowing that her prank still caused her best friend some frustration.

"*Clever* Clare didn't see that one coming," Amy teased.

"Wow, Amy," Clare said. "You haven't called me that in years." In truth, Amy hadn't called Clare by that nickname since her father passed away. The pair fell silent for a few minutes.

"Why was the kitchen a mess this afternoon?" Amy asked. "Mom wouldn't tell me what happened."

"I got a bit worked up," Clare mumbled. She didn't want to admit what happened, but Clare knew that Amy would know what she was talking about.

"Clare, it's going to work out." Amy said reassuringly. She nodded and gazed around the room. It hadn't changed much in all the years she had stayed there. There were even a few glow-in-the-dark stars still stuck to the ceiling they had put there as kids.

It wasn't long before Amy dozed off and the sound of her

gentle breathing filled the room. Clare, however, lay awake, staring at the stars on the ceiling. She had left the nightlight on as long as she dared, hoping that the stars would pick up a glow again. But after a while, Clare shut off the lamp because she didn't want to wake Amy. To her delight, a pale, luminescent glow was coming from the plastic celestial bodies they had super glued to the ceiling.

I hope you have a great Thanksgiving, Steve, she thought. *I wish that we could meet again.*

Clare pulled the covers tighter and let her head sink into the soft, down pillow. She continued staring at the stars until sleep took her away.

~~~~

Steve had always enjoyed the holiday dinners his family made, especially Thanksgiving dinner. The delectable smelling dishes would begin filling up the counter in his mother's kitchen late in the morning and by the time dinner was served, not even the mixture of emotions Steve was feeling could quell his grumbling stomach.

However, after filling up his plate, Steve looked longingly at the venison roast his uncle Charlie had brought. Every year, there was the standard assortment of dishes that made up their dinner but in addition there was always some sort of wild game available because Steve's uncle was a very proficient outdoorsman. This year, the wild game of choice was venison.

Everyone else had grabbed a slice or two but Steve almost felt guilty about taking some. Usually he, his father, and Charlie would go out hunting together at the farm a few days before the holiday. However, Steve hadn't hunted or been back to the farm

Clare R.

since his father's passing. Charlie noticed Steve's indecision and gave him a gentle nudge with his elbow.

"Go on, Steve," Charlie said. "Have some. It's really good!" Steve didn't want the others to notice his hesitation, so he reached for the fork and put a couple slices on his plate as well. It was delicious, and by the time dinner was finished, Steve couldn't have been more thankful to see everyone again. A variety of random stories were passed around the table and Steve even contributed a few tales from his time in other states. When dessert time came around, everyone enjoyed the humorous show that baby Jacob put on as he covered his face with whipped cream.

~~~

A few more members of Amy's family arrived for Thanksgiving dinner and Clare kept to the kitchen most of the morning and afternoon because she didn't want to interfere much. After all, they weren't really her family. But that didn't stop the flurry of feet from running into the kitchen to say hello to her.

Amy's two younger cousins, Billy and Sophie, had raced into the kitchen to find Clare, and following close at their heels was a very rambunctious puppy. No matter how distant Clare felt around this time of year, it was always enjoyable to see Amy's younger relatives. They didn't know about her past, so to them, Clare was just another member of the family.

"Clare! Clare!" a chorus of shouts came from the two children as each one eagerly moved to give her a hug and show off their new puppy.

"Who's this?" Clare asked once the kids had been hugged multiple times.

"Her name is Abby," Sophie replied. Clare knelt down to observe the puppy more closely, which was easy since it piled into her lap eager for a belly rub. It had a distinct mask around its dark colored eyes much like the mask on a raccoon. The mixture of black and white fur was long, soft, and poofy, which would be nice during the winter months. It also had large padded paws that Clare thought would be great in the snow and water. In the end Clare couldn't really figure out the breed but whatever it was, its tail was wagging furiously and as soon as she gave it a few pets, the puppy lunged forward to lick her face. Between the slobbering tongue and being tickled by the long, wispy whiskers, Clare couldn't help but laugh. Amy's younger cousins' squealed and giggled at the sight.

"She's beautiful," Clare said.

"Yeah," Billy said. "We got her a little before Halloween. Dad said somebody he knows at work had puppies and he let us pick one out!"

"Wow, that's awesome!" Clare said. "So, how have you guys been?"

"Good," the duo replied in tandem. Amy's cousins were very close and for a moment, Clare felt a pang of jealously. Then Billy tugged at his sister's arm.

"Come on Sophie," he said. "Mom wanted us to help bring stuff in." Billy got off the floor and ran out of the kitchen. Abby bounded after him.

"Will you play with us later, Clare?" Sophie asked. She had been watching the puppy run off and it took a moment for Sophie's question to sink in.

"Um, yeah. I will," she replied. "For sure!" Sophie grinned wildly and chased after her brother. Clare had just resumed frost-

Clare R.

ing cupcakes when she heard Amy's loud voice coming from the entry way.

"Where's that rice dish you always bring, Uncle Ben?" Amy asked.

"Eh, I decided to try something else this year," Uncle Ben replied. Clare chuckled to herself in the kitchen because for as long as she could remember, Amy's family had held a standing joke about Ben's name. When more of the family came into the kitchen, Amy locked eyes with her and made a humorous expression.

"Clare, Uncle Ben didn't bring the rice dish," Amy said. "Thanksgiving just won't be the same this year." Clare smiled.

"I heard," she replied. "Hi, Uncle Ben."

"Hi, Clare," he replied, after leaning in to give her a sideways hug. It was a formality more than anything to say *uncle*. Since she'd spent so much of her life in Amy's home, Clare knew most of her family. Uncle Ben and Amy were followed by Amy's aunt and her parents. Not long after, dinner was served.

An assortment of dishes were crammed on the counters in the kitchen and the family piled around the dining table that had been extended with two leaves to help accommodate the additional people. The smells of warm rolls and savory mashed potatoes mixed with the aroma of sweet potatoes and greasy, roast turkey. If it hadn't been for the clinking of dishes and cutlery, it would have been easy to hear a chorus of growling stomachs.

Conversation flowed smoothly around the table and many times Clare was included in the conversations. They treated her like one of the family and Clare was grateful for this. Several times one of the youngsters would tug on her arm to tell her something interesting that had happened in the year since she'd seen them last.

However, as Clare sat there taking bites of her dinner, she found herself losing track of the current conversation while she wondered about other things.

What would it be like to sit at the table with Steve's family? Would they like me? Would they like her cupcakes if she made them? Could she and Steve cook something together possibly? If Steve and I did get together, would he get a puppy with me? Would he want me there in the first place?

Belts were loosened a notch or two and the conversations around the table started to slow down as people began to reach their intake limits. That was when Clare felt a hand on her arm.

"Clare," Sophie said with a shy smile. "I think we should get a cupcake and go play with the dog." Every year it seemed like there were as many treats and desserts as there were entrees. Sophie, however, had always been fond of the cupcakes just like Clare.

"Sure," Clare said. "That sounds good." She put on a big smile and the duo went up to sneak a pair of cupcakes. Clare smiled again when Sophie motioned with her head to follow.

Apparently, she has a plan, Clare thought. She followed Sophie out to the entry way and watched her call for Abby. The fluffy canine came hurtling out of the dining room, expecting a treat, and sat politely at Sophie's feet. After hooking up the leash, the little girl leaned back in the kitchen.

"Momma, I'm taking Abby out to go pee," Sophie said. Aunt Sandy barely looked up when she replied.

"All right sweetie," she said. Then Sandy did a double take. "Are you going with her, Clare?" Clare's hair dangled in front of her face as she tried to slide a foot into one of her boots. Once it was on, Clare ran her hand back through her long hair and looked up at Abby's mother.

Clare R.

"Yeah," she replied and started sliding her other foot in the remaining boot.

"Will you make sure Sophie puts her coat on?" Aunt Sandy asked. Clare nodded quickly and turned to Sophie. The goofy, little brunette already had her jacket on and she had just taken a huge bite of cupcake, so her mouth was too full to answer. Sophie instead rolled her eyes as if she was smarter than her mother and grinned while trying to lick frosting off the tip of her nose.

Clare laughed and looked back to Aunty Sandy.

"She's good," Clare said.

"All right, have fun!" said Sophie's mother and returned to the conversation at the dining table. Clare slipped on her coat and pulled a hat over her ears.

"Is your brother coming?" Clare asked. Sophie shook her head sideways because she was still chewing. "OK, let's go then." Abby took the lead and pulled on the leash, excited to get outside. Before they walked out the door, Clare bit into her own cupcake.

Delicious, she thought. *Steve would definitely like these.*

~~~~

As far as Thanksgiving was concerned, Patty had designated it a major success. Everyone had shown up; even Steve, and for that Patty could not be more thankful. She once again picked up her knitting needles and continued working on her project. The socks she was making for baby Jacob were coming along very nicely. But more and more often, Patty would pause to comment on a conversation that was occurring between other family members. However, the conversations eventually came to an end as people fell asleep on the living room furniture. It wasn't long before she fell asleep as well.

Having eaten as well as she did, Patty expected to have a restful nap, but it was nothing of the sort. She was tormented by terrible dreams that were more or less, terribly vivid recollections of her past.

Patty was at the hospital again. She was rushing to the ambulance gate with a coworker after getting a call that an ambulance was coming in to the E.R. Patty could see it all happening from a distance. She and the coworker had made it to the receiving area when her superior arrived with another nurse in tow. He took Patty by the arm and led her away. She protested, insisting that she needed to do her job. Patty couldn't understand what was wrong.

Not even her superior could look her in the eye when he told her a second ambulance was coming in behind the first and her late husband was on board. Even in the dream that she tried her hardest to escape, Patty's stomach plummeted to infinity. She tried to turn away once again and everything went black...

When a world materialized again, Patty was home alone in her dimly lit kitchen. A box of stale crackers was open on the counter alongside half a bottle of wine. She had hardly eaten anything in days and her stomach was groaning painfully. She drowned it into silence with another gulp of wine. Then the tears started to fall. Hot tears that stung at her cheeks. Not only had her husband been taken away from her, but now her son had left, too, and she hadn't seen him in months.

Patty slumped to the floor and buried her face in her hands. After what felt like several minutes, she reached up with a shaky hand and retrieved her phone off the counter. Squinting at the bright screen, she tried desperately to dial Steve's number. But between her shaking and inability to focus on the numbers, she couldn't get the phone to work.

In a fit of frustration, Patty flung the phone across the kitchen and it shattered after colliding with the kitchen cabinets. She

Clare R.

cried even harder. Patty couldn't have cared less about the phone. She just wanted to see her son. She wanted to know he was OK...

Patty woke with a start. Beads of sweat had formed on her forehead and she felt like she'd been drenched with ice water. After pulling the blanket tighter around herself, she glanced around the living room, worried that she had woken up the others. However, no one moved and the only sound Patty could hear was the soft clinking of dishes being washed in the kitchen.

*Steve...*she thought. After taking a few deep breaths to calm her nerves, Patty went to see her son.

~~~~

Clare found it quite humorous watching Sophie try to finish her cupcake while the dog pulled on her arm every couple seconds. But she managed, and after the dog went to the bathroom, Clare and Sophie wandered around the yard watching the stars pop into the night sky.

"Are you still reading a lot?" Clare asked.

"Oh, all the time," Sophie said. "Do you have any good books, Clare?" She had plenty of *good* books but many of them were at a much higher reading level and the contents probably weren't appropriate for kids Sophie's age. Clare took another bite of her cupcake.

"Yep, I do," she answered. "But you'll have to wait a few more years."

"Oh, they're big kid books, huh?" Sophie asked. Again, Clare chuckled.

"Yeah, something like that," she said. It wasn't a warm evening and it wasn't terribly cold either but there was a chill in the air that signaled winter was coming. The trees around Amy's home stood still in the growing darkness and the only sound that could be heard besides them talking were their feet crunching against the fallen leaves. Before sitting down, Clare picked up a stick, which she handed to the puppy. To their delight, Abby immediately began chewing off all the bark. Sophie giggled and scratched the dog behind the ears.

"Clare, how do you know if a boy likes you?" Sophie asked.

There's an awkward question, Clare thought. *I'm not exactly sure I'm the best person to ask.*

"Ha!" Clare said. "How come you're asking me?" Sophie shrugged.

"I don't know...because you're really cool and I think you're fun to talk to," she replied. Sophie continued to pet her puppy and Clare tried to think about her question. For a moment though, Clare was distracted by the cakey goodness in her hand. All she wanted to do was smear frosting on Steve's cheek.

But Clare pushed that thought aside to continue pondering Sophie's question. She had known Sophie since she was a baby and Clare had even babysat for her family on occasions when Amy was unavailable, so they had become friends over the years. Yet, Clare didn't see Sophie frequently enough to know if she could provide a solid answer. Instead, Clare stalled for more time and responded with a question of her own.

"Why?" Clare asked with a smile. "Does some boy have a crush on you?" She pushed Sophie's shoulder gently, which caused her cheeks to redden.

"I think so," she replied. "How do you know?" This time, Clare turned her attention away from Sophie and looked up at the star filled sky. The image of the shooting star blazing across the

Clare R.

night sky filled her mind and she grinned wildly.

"Hmm...Does this boy smile at you a lot?" Clare asked. Thoughts of Steve started drifting through her mind. "Sometimes boys will try to tell you funny jokes, too."

"I guess...yeah," Sophie said. "I mean, he does smile at me a lot and when the other boys are rude, he is usually really nice." Clare smiled and gave Sophie a reassuring wink.

"I think he likes you then," she said and kept looking at the stars. Sophie continued to pet her puppy and it was a while before either of them spoke again.

"Do any boys like you, Clare?" Sophie asked. "It seems like they would. You're really cool!"

"Um, there's a guy, I guess," she said after a moment.

"How come he's not here?" Sophie asked. "I want to meet him!"

My gosh! She's tough, Clare thought. *Humor me...*

"Well, we met last month when I was on a trip for work..." Clare began.

"Did he smile at you and tell you jokes?" Sophie asked. It didn't really occur to her that she was interrupting. Sophie, after all, thought this was a very adult conversation.

"Yep, he smiled a lot and he got me a cup of tea," Clare said.

"All right, that's good. Keep going," Sophie said.

"He told a lot of funny jokes and we talked about books that we both like," Clare said.

"Oh really? My friend and I talk about the books we like all the time!" Sophie said. Clare scrunched her lips and nodded to Sophie indicating that she was in good shape.

"Then we shared some pizza and more tea," Clare said.

"I'm starting to think food is really important," Sophie said.

"Maybe, we should sit together at lunch." Clare let out a hearty laugh.

"Yeah, maybe!" Clare said. Sophie seemed excited but then she returned to the original question.

"But why isn't he here?" Sophie asked.

"Well, we got sort of rushed at the end because we had to get on our planes. I didn't get his phone number or anything," Clare admitted. "So...we haven't talked since."

"Hmm. That's super stinky," Sophie said.

"Mhmm," Clare replied. The puppy sat up and came over to lick Clare's hand as if to console her. "Gosh, I love dogs."

"Me, too," Sophie said. Once again, a silence fell and the only sound came from Abby as they continued to pet her. Clare found herself staring at Abby and all of a sudden she felt melancholy. Clare and her father never owned a dog. It was an expenditure that they hadn't been able to afford. But she also never had the opportunity to share a conversation like this with her own mother. Sophie had so much to look forward to and she was fortunate to have her own family to share her life with.

Clare turned her attention to the night sky again hoping to see another shooting star, and as she basked in the starlight her uncomfortable feelings faded somewhat. Sophie had wanted to talk to Clare for some reason and she was grateful for that. It was fun to see Sophie and Billy and spend some time with them. Her own mother had never spent any quality time with her after she disappeared, so if someone wanted to talk to her, Clare wasn't going to abandon them.

"Well, if you really want something, mom always tells me to wish really hard for it," Sophie offered.

"I did that already," Clare said.

Clare R.

"Did anything happen?" Sophie asked. Clare noticed the hopeful expression on her face, suggesting that Sophie wanted assurance that her mother wasn't just pulling her leg.

"Sophie, I saw the biggest shooting start of my life," Clare said, tracing her hand across the night sky.

"Wow," Sophie said. "Well you should probably hold on then. Don't give up. I bet he really likes you, Clare, if the shooting star was that big." They were profound words for a nine-year-old. Clare gawked at Sophie and then broke out laughing.

"I hope so," she said quietly. The dog came up and licked her face excitedly again. It wasn't long before Sophie spoke up again and it made Clare smile.

"Can we go have another cupcake, Clare?" Sophie asked.

"Absolutely," she replied.

~~~

"Just think, Stevie...A little bit of your dad lives on in him," imaginary Clare said. Everyone had retired to the living room after dinner and Steve decided to do the dishes because he didn't want to succumb to a food coma just yet. But with how busy and overwhelming the last two days had been, he was sure that sleep would have eluded him anyway. So, as everyone fell asleep in the living room, Steve and imaginary Clare talked quietly in the kitchen.

She was sitting on the counter next to him, holding a warm cup of tea and swinging her legs back and forth. She smiled at him and flicked a finger against his ear, which caused him to chuckle quietly.

"I'm glad you decided to come home, Stevie," she said. "Everyone was really happy to see you." He nodded and turned the water on to rinse off a plate.

"I know and it's been great to see everyone," he replied.

"Then why do you seem sad still?" she asked. Steve shut the water off and turned to look at his figment. Her blue eyes sparkled and locks of her wavy hair were curling around her chin. Steve could never remember a time where he could recall this many details about someone. Not only that, but Steve desperately wished that he could reach out and pinch her chin affectionately.

"Because I wish you were here, too," Steve said. "I know everyone would love to meet you and I just want to see you again." Imaginary Clare smiled at him and Steve felt his heart leap. He loved her smile.

"Don't worry," Clare said leaning over. "You will." Then with a light kiss on the cheek, she disappeared. Although it made him smile, Steve was a bit confused at how his figment could be so confident when he felt so unsure sometimes. Then he reached over to take a drink from the steaming cup of tea.

~~~

"Steve?" Patty asked. Her voice was hushed because she didn't want to startle him. But Steve wasn't surprised. The discernible creak of his father's old chair was all he needed to hear to know that his mother had gotten up.

"Hmm?" he replied. Her slippers flopped against the kitchen floor as she stepped closer and put a hand on his back.

"I'm really glad you came this year," she said slowly. "I don't want you to feel like you can't come home." Steve stopped washing the dishes and stared at the suds that were popping in the sink.

"This has been really hard and I've been worried about you

Clare R.

so much," she continued. "It was really great to see you earlier this fall. I wanted to say more then but I didn't want to make you uncomfortable." Hearing his mother talk about everything left Steve feeling selfish for being gone for so long. He knew that it had been rough for everybody. It was just easier being gone.

"I'm sorry," he mumbled. His mother just rubbed his back again.

"It's OK. I know that you were upset. We all were," his mother said. They stood in silence for a couple minutes and then Steve resumed doing the dishes. He much preferred the sound of clinking dishes to an awkward silence.

"I had no idea what to expect when you came to visit this fall," Patty said. "But this Clare must really make you happy."

"She does. I don't feel nearly as empty anymore," he said. "Ma, I really wanna see her again."

"Just don't give up on her and you will," Patty said reassuringly. Then a huge yawn escaped her. "I like seeing you happy again, Steve." She put her hand on his shoulder and gave it a squeeze that was followed with a sleepy "goodnight" before heading off to bed. Steve smiled and listened to the sound of her slippers flopping until the gentle sound of a closing door signaled that his mother made it to her room. It was a relief to feel some sort of weight lifted from his shoulders and Steve hoped that it would stay that way.

He reached over to turn on the radio, adjusting the volume so that he wouldn't disturb the others sleeping in the living room and continued to do the dishes. There were a lot of them because it was the remnants of Thanksgiving dinner, after all.

~~~

R. K. Blessing

After coming back inside, Clare and Sophie curled up on the couch and started watching a cartoon movie. The food coma was just starting to take over when Clare heard the ding of the doorbell. This was followed by disgruntled voices out in the entryway. Since she was so drowsy, it was difficult to discern what people were saying but then the conversation quickly escalated.

"Billy, no! Leave Clare alone," said Uncle Ben. But it was too late. Billy was already at her side trying to wake her up.

"Clare, there's some strange woman here. She wants to talk to you," said Billy. Clare untangled herself from the blanket and headed for the entryway where she could still hear voices.

"I think you should go," said Uncle Ben. Clare took her spot in the entryway and Abby came to stand next to her. They both stared intently, but neither could see anything because Ben's frame filled the doorway.

"No. Please! Can I see her?" said the voice.

"Who is it, Uncle Ben?" Clare asked. A heavy sigh could be heard as Uncle Ben turned to face Clare. His expression was anxious but he moved out of the way. In the dim glow of the porch light, Clare could make out a woman who had a haunting look about her. Abby let out a low growl that made goose bumps rise on her arms. Everything about this woman was discomforting and foreign, yet there was a hint of familiarity. Tendrils from a faint memory began creeping through her mind and the longer Clare stared the stronger the memory became. Her hands started to shake as she saw the handful of her father's worn pictures in her mind. Then all at once Clare knew and the air felt as if it was sucked from her chest.

"Mom?"

Chapter 16

All at once time slowed down. Billy joined Sophie on the couch and they hunkered under a blanket. Amy, her parents, and her aunt were crowded in the kitchen doorway wondering what was going on and everyone had a look of surprise on their face. Everyone except for Clare, who simply kept staring. She waited for the positive feelings to appear. But they never came. Tracy tried to hide her surprise behind her motherly generosity and hurried into the entryway with a plate of food.

"You look hungry," Tracy said. Clare's mother nodded and took the plate with shaking hands. "Do you want to come–"

"No," Clare said, cutting in with a tone that was cold as ice. "I don't want her in here. You can eat out on the porch." Clare pulled her jacket off the coat hook and climbed into her boots before finally crossing the entryway. Everyone parted for Clare and the hopeful look on her mother's face diminished slightly but she heeded her daughter's words.

Clare was almost shaking. Over the years, she'd come to grips with the fact that she'd never see her mother again, and yet here was this woman, shoving food down her gullet like a starved wolf. As she watched her eat, Clare knew she should have felt something akin to compassion, worry, excitement, but there was nothing. She was nothing like the beautiful woman who had given birth to her; the pretty woman who her father had fallen in love with and kept photos of until the day he died.

Her mother sat on the porch while Clare took up a position at the bottom of the steps where she continued to stare. Her mother's appearance was worse than Clare could have imagined. She was a disheveled mess. Her skin was stretched and wrinkles had formed just about everywhere. The clothes she was wearing were faded and worn and her hair was a gnarled mess, which she tried to hide by putting it in a ponytail. She looked nothing like what Clare imagined.

What the hell happened to you? Clare wondered.

"It's so good to see you, Clare bear," she said. "How are you?" Clare didn't say anything, so her mother tried again.

"Thank you for the dinner," she said.

"Don't thank me. Thank Tracy," Clare said. "What are you doing here?" Her mother moved her head up and down as if she was still a sentence behind. Then Clare's question seemed to register.

"I came to see my Clare bear. But apparently she's all grown up now," said her mother.

"Yeah. Grown up. That's what happens in twenty-five years," Clare said. "Or did you think I would still be that toddler you left in the crib?"

"No, no, of course not," she began, but Clare cut her off.

"What are you doing here?" she repeated.

"I wanted to see you," her mother said.

"How did you know where I was?" Clare asked.

Clare R.

"Your dad—" she began.

"My dad's dead," Clare said. Her mother stopped chewing and actually looked sort of upset.

"Oh," she finally said.

"Oh, give me a break. It's not like you care," Clare said. "Otherwise you would have stuck around."

"Clare, there's a lot to explain," she said. "Your dad wrote to me for a long time and he told me that you made friends with a girl down the street from our old house." This didn't surprise Clare in the slightest because she knew that her father had been so in love with her mother.

"But then he stopped writing and I figured he moved on," she said before shoveling more food into her mouth.

"You never wrote back? Not once," Clare asked.

"No, I was too scared," she replied. Clare snorted with derision and her mother looked up from the plate again.

"What was that for?" asked her mother.

"Are you kidding me?" Clare said. Her lips quavered but the adrenaline kept her going. "You ruined everything by leaving. Dad was a wreck for the rest of his life and I grew up without a MOTHER!"

"Looks like you did fine without me," said her mother. There was no remorse in her voice as she raised the plate of food Tracy had given her. "They like you and you've grown up into a beautiful woman, so..." All Clare could do was shake her head. The passive comment was lost on her.

"This is unreal. What happened to you?" Clare asked.

"I left town for a while. Stayed with friends here and there. Sort of started over," she said. "I got a new job and eventually got married again." Clare actually wondered if a horse had kicked her in the stomach.

"So you were just done with us," Clare said. "Did you have more kids? Do I have a string of half siblings spread around the country?"

"Oh, Clare, don't be ridiculous," said her mother.

"Me? Ridiculous? Seriously?" Clare said. "Do I have other siblings or not?"

"You have a half-brother, Chris, who is probably twelve," said her mother. "No, thirteen actually, this past September." Clare ran her hands through her hair and spun in a circle.

"And you're not with this new family because?" Clare asked.

"The marriage fell apart. I tried to make it work but…" she said.

"But you gave up!" Clare exclaimed. "Just like you gave up on us. On ME!" Her mother opened her mouth to speak but no words came out.

"I'm really sorry, Clare bear," she said finally. Then after setting down her plate, Clare's mother started rifling through her pockets.

"You smoke now?" Clare said. She watched her mother try to light a cigarette with shaking hands. Finally, the flame caught and a poof of smoke exited her mouth.

"Bad habit," she said.

"A pathetic one," Clare fired back. "Do you even care about anything that you left behind?"

"I think about it all the time," she said after taking another drag. The night she left Clare was burned in her memory like a cigarette burn on the couch.

Clare R.

It had been an incredibly warm day. Kids around the neighborhood could be heard laughing and screaming as they jumped through sprinklers trying to evade the heat and humidity. But now a cool, refreshing breeze was blowing in the open window and the sound of rain could be heard outside as a summer storm passed overhead. Everyone in the house was sleeping peacefully except for one and after a final, deep breath, she climbed quietly from bed leaving her husband to his dreams.

The house was dark, but she glided amongst the shadows making her way to her personal sanctuary. The glow from a lamp in the hallway lit up a small room as the young woman quietly came inside.

She sidestepped around toys and stuffed animals that were spread out across the floor and made her way to the crib that held her sleeping daughter. She clutched the railing as she stared down at the child with a half-smile on her face. But if anyone were to look in her eyes at that moment, they would have immediately noticed that they were weeping sadness.

Before going to bed earlier that evening, she had cracked the window to help keep her daughter from being uncomfortable while she slept, and now another cool gust of wind blew into the room. The air smelled sweet and the little girl's hair fluttered playfully in the breeze. She rolled over in the crib but didn't wake.

"You're so beautiful," she said quietly while reaching down to brush strands of reddish-brown hair from the toddler's face. Several minutes went by as she stood silently watching her baby sleep. For several nights she had done this and for several nights it had been enough to sustain her. Watching her baby sleep was incredibly peaceful and soothing to her. But tonight was different.

R. K. Blessing

Tonight her mind was made up.

"I'm going to miss you, baby girl," she whispered. With one last glance, the woman turned and crept from the room just as silently as she'd entered. She paused momentarily to take one last mental picture of the room and then continued on. The room grew dark as she shut the door and the toddler never woke.

A moment later she shut the door to the house and stood under the awning watching the rain fall. There was no thunder or lighting, just a steady downpour that seemed to feel as sad as she did. But her mind was made up. With her head bowed, she stepped off the porch and walked away into the night. She never looked back...

"Do you want me to tell you about it?" asked her mother. The cloud of smoke hung around her head in the cold air and the smell made Clare gag.

"No I don't want you to tell me about the day you left me and dad! Are you kidding me?" Clare said. "I think you should go." The flame of frustration was beginning to dwindle as Clare realized that she'd had enough. She may have not had a true family any more, but she knew there were people inside who cared about her.

"Fine. Whatever. I tried. But do you think you could help me out?" she said.

"Did you seriously come here for money?" Clare asked.

"Well no. I mean, I wanted to see you," she said. "But if you have a couple bucks."

"You're unbelievable. This is unfucking believable," Clare walked up the steps and stormed into the house. She grabbed her purse off the coat hook and pulled out all the cash she had. When

Clare R.

she walked back outside, her mother had lit a fresh cigarette and was puffing like a chimney. Clare shook her head in disgust.

"Just go, OK. OK! I don't know how much is there. But just go," Clare said. She could feel herself starting to quaver.

"Clare bear," her mother said, this time sounding sentimental.

"No. NO! JUST GO! You've been gone my entire life! Just go!" Clare shouted. She pushed past her mother and walked off into the night letting the darkness swallow her up. She heard Sophie run onto the porch.

"Wait, Clare!" she yelled. "Don't leave, Clare!" But Clare kept walking. She walked for a long time and the only thing she could hear was herself crying and her mother's words that were spinning around her head like they were on a perpetual marquee. *It's a bad habit... You did fine without me... Can I have a few bucks.* Clare walked until she found a corner grocery store that was still open. Clare set a fifth of something on the counter alongside a bottle of water.

"Can I see some ID?" asked the clerk.

"Seriously, dude?" she said. Her eyes were puffy and red as she held out a credit card. "I'm fucking twenty-seven years old." Apparently that was enough for the clerk and he took the card.

"Rough night, huh?" he said.

"Unbelievable," she said. "I hope you have a happy Thanksgiving, though, sir!" With that Clare turned and left the corner store. She walked back in the direction of Amy's house until she found a bench and then Clare started crying again. In one hand was the liquor and in the other was water.

How many nights did you spend drinking...mom! Clare

thought. *You left me!* Everything she had wished for about her mother was useless. In the event that her mother did return, Clare had foolishly hoped that she would have been some beautiful, successful person who had a top notch reason for leaving. But that wasn't the case at all. Her mother was nothing to her anymore.

The label on the liquor bottle was so much more appealing than the label on the water bottle. It was almost as if it was taunting her and Clare was so close to giving in. All she wanted was to forget this night ever happened. Fresh tears rolled down her face as she gripped the cap on the bottle with shaking hands.

"Clare! Wait! Is that you, Clare?" The voice was accompanied by the sound of running feet. When Clare looked up, she saw Sophie running toward her with Abby at her side. Clare ran the sleeve of her hoodie across her face to wipe away the tears. Then Sophie was at her side, pushing on her arm.

"What are you doing, Clare? Why did you leave?" Sophie asked.

"Because I'm upset," Clare replied.

"Yeah. OK. But you're not leaving for good, right?" Sophie said.

"My mom did," said Clare.

"You're not your mom, Clare," Sophie said. "What's that?" She pointed at the bottle Clare was trying to hide with her jacket.

"Nothing," Clare said. But Sophie was too quick and pulled the bottle out.

"This is bad stuff," Sophie said. "I don't want you to be like her." Without another word, Sophie chucked the bottle over the fence behind the bench. A moment later the sound of breaking glass met their ears and Clare tried to give her a stern glance.

Clare R.

"Why did you do that?" Clare asked.

"Because you're my friend," Sophie said. "You're not leaving are you?"

"I don't know what I'm going to do," Clare answered.

"Come home and have a cupcake with me," Sophie said, trying to put on a goofy grin.

"I'm not hungry, Sophie. I feel like I'm going to puke," Clare said.

"Yeah, OK. That makes sense. Maybe you should have some of that water then and think about that boy you like. I bet he'll make you feel better," Sophie suggested and Clare managed a weak chuckle.

"Yeah," she said. "Maybe he will."

"Here," Sophie said. She broke the seal on the water bottle and handed it to Clare who took a few gulps. Then she leaned back and looked up at the night sky. A plethora of twinkling lights stared back at her.

I wish you were here, Steve. That's what I wish for... But before she could think any more, her phone jingled and reluctantly Clare answered.

"Hello," she said.

"Where are you, Clare?" Amy exclaimed. "Is Sophie with you? My parents are about ready to call the cops. They're freaking out!"

"Amy, it's OK! Yeah, she's with me. We're coming back," Clare said. "Right now." The only sound for a few seconds was Amy's nervous breathing.

"Are you OK, Clare?" Amy asked.

"I don't know, Amy," she said, and without another word

Clare clicked off the phone. "Come on, Sophie. Let's get you home." Sophie, however, did not budge from her seat on the bench.

"Promise me you're not going to leave," she said.

"Sophie, come on," Clare said turning to leave.

"Clare! You can't leave. You're my friend," Sophie said. When she turned back to the bench, Sophie was still sitting, clutching the leash, and tears were starting to run down her cheeks as well.

If I leave, how does that make me any better than my mother, Clare thought. *I'm not my mother...*

"I've known you since you were a baby," Clare said. "I'm not going anywhere. I promise. Now come on. Your parents are worried." Sophie nodded and got up. Clare tried to smile when she felt Sophie's hand slide into her own but deep down she was crumbling like a landslide.

Upon their return, Sophie was swallowed up by her parents, and Clare did her best to sidestep the commotion. When Amy's parents tried to comfort her, she pulled away like a scared animal.

"I'm gonna shower," she said. Then Clare motioned at the entryway where her mother had first appeared. "I'm sorry about all that." Tracy shook her head sideways indicating that it didn't matter and tried once again to give her a hug but Clare pulled away again. Amy tried to catch Clare's eyes but there was nothing. Just an overwhelming sadness.

"I'm sorry," she repeated and walked upstairs. Clare grabbed clean clothes from her bag and went into the bathroom. After getting the water as hot as she could handle, Clare climbed in the shower and started washing her hair.

Soap, rinse, repeat. Soap, rinse, repeat. Soap, rinse, repeat.

Clare R.

Even in the steam of the shower, Clare could still smell the smoke from her mother's cigarettes and it made her wretch. By the time she was done showering, Clare had used half the bottle of shampoo.

Amy was waiting in the bedroom when Clare came in, lying in the twin bed opposite Clare's. The humor and excitement and happy exuberance that usually accompanied Amy was nonexistent. There was only worry. But still, Clare said nothing. She climbed into her own bed and curled up in the fetal position, clutching a pillow.

"Are you seriously not going to say anything?" Amy asked. Clare let out a heavy sigh and continued staring at the wall.

"What am I supposed to say, Amy?" Clare asked. "Happy Thanksgiving and oh, by the way, I'm glad you finally got to see my drug addled mother."

"Well that's a start," Amy said. "I've never seen you this upset before."

"Well, nothing really ticks me off more than being abandoned by a parent," Clare replied.

"You're not going to do something stupid, are you?" Amy asked and finally Clare rolled over.

"Why does everyone keep asking me that?" Clare asked.

"Um, because that was some crazy shit that just went down in my house... I mean that was like watching the best reality TV," Amy said. She chanced the remark hoping to make Clare smile and from the other side of the room came a noise somewhere between a laugh and a sob. Amy laughed when Clare held up her middle finger. After a while, Clare raised her head.

"I guess I thought she was dead like my dad," Clare said.

"But of all the things I thought she would be if I ever saw her again... That was not what I expected."

"Well at least now you know," Amy said. "You don't have to wonder any more. You can think about better things now."

"Ha! Like what?" Clare said. "That fucking crap my mom said is going to be stuck in my head for the rest of my life and the way she looked…"

"So, don't focus on that stuff," Amy said. "Think about that cupcake business you want to start. Or Steve. Think about him." Clare moved her head sideways.

"Amy, I don't know if I can. I don't want to get let down again," Clare said. "I have a good job that I enjoy most of the time and maybe Steve and I just weren't meant to be." The words tasted awful in her mouth but Clare couldn't handle going through something terrible with Steve as well.

"If Steve is half the man you made him out to be, he won't let you down," Amy said. "I don't want you to give up." But her attempt at reassurance seemed to fall short.

"I'm not giving up," Clare said. "I just don't want to get let down again." They both rolled over and faced their respective walls.

"I think that's bullshit," Amy said. "I liked madly-in-love Clare."

"I did too," she mumbled. Then the tears returned and Clare cried until she fell asleep.

~~~~

Before climbing into bed, Steve stared out the window and

Clare R.

beyond the panes of glass; a nostalgic snowfall was covering the ground with fluffy, sparkling flakes. *What if I never got to see a beautiful snowfall like this again? It's so important to appreciate everything in life.* Pages from *Coping with Death* flashed in his mind and then he was overcome by a shiver. Steve gave the big flakes one last glance and then buried himself under his patchwork quilt and flannel sheets, craving the warmth.

As he squirmed about, trying to get comfortable, Steve tried to pray his thanks for everything in his life. No matter how rotten the last two years had been, it was wonderful to see everyone in his family and he was especially glad to see baby Jacob.

Steve leaned over the side of his bed and lifted Clare's book from his bag. Every time he picked up her book, distant memories and thoughts would stir in the furthest crevices of his brain. Tonight it was the mythological monsters, heroes, and heroines that he wrote for his childhood plots.

Eventually, Steve cracked the cover and stared at her signature wishing he could know what her last name was. Then he ran his thumb across the pages, sending a cool breeze across his face that smelled like Clare. Despite not getting to exchange any information, Steve was also incredibly thankful that he and Clare had met because she had changed his life.

"Happy Thanksgiving, Clare," Steve said quietly. "I hope you had a wonderful day with your family." Toby nudged his hand and that night he fell asleep scratching the dog between his long, floppy ears. Clare's book sat safely on the nightstand and its shiny cover glinted in the lamp light.

Chapter 17

As the pair cruised down the highway back toward Pittsburgh, Clare was slowly being consumed by her doubts, which had been stewing for the remainder of their stay with Amy's family. Clare felt like a pot that was about to boil over. But somehow she remained quiet and after several hours of driving, the extent of their conversation went something like this.

"I'm stopping for gas," Amy said.

"OK," Clare mumbled.

"You want something to eat or drink?" Amy asked.

"Not hungry," Clare replied.

"OK," Amy said.

Clare knew that Amy was somewhere between upset with her and worried about her. Ergo, the uncomfortable silence. Her parents had tried to reassure Clare that everything was OK but she had only nodded to further the conversation along to its end. As she sat there in the car, staring at nothing in particular, Clare unintentionally kept replaying the encounter with her mother in her head.

My mother is a wreck. What if I'm destined to be a wreck as well? I don't want to ruin someone's life. Steve's life. I can't do that. Maybe I'm destined to be alone...

Clare R.

Amy, on the other hand, was trying her hardest to think of something to say. But each time she came up with something, the words got caught in her throat or another part of her brain would shoot down what she was thinking. By the time they got to Clare's house, Amy was feeling like the worst friend ever. Clare was hugging her backpack, clearly eager to get out of the car, and Amy still didn't have anything inspirational or helpful to say.

Clare, you're not your mom. You're a good person.

"So..." was what Amy said instead.

"Thanks for the ride, Amy," Clare mumbled.

"I'll call you tomorrow," Amy replied, but in a flash Clare was out of the car and the passenger door slammed in her face. Amy watched Clare hurry up the steps to her house. She opened and closed the front door and never looked back. It was an awful feeling to see someone hurt so badly, especially when that person was your best friend.

The tears were already rolling down her cheeks before Clare even closed the door behind her. Finally being home meant that she could break down in peace without people hovering over her or staring awkwardly wondering if she was going to snap. She made for her bedroom as fast as possible, but when Clare got to her room, she was confronted by a stack of papers on the bed.

There were weeks' worth of research on successful bakeries, sketches she made up for possible logos, real estate listings, and financing information from the bank. Clare's sobs increased as she picked up the pile of papers and shoved them into the trash can next to her desk before climbing into bed.

She woke several hours later to a damp pillow case. Her eyes felt gummy and her stomach was groaning painfully. But she didn't care. She simply rolled the pillow over and burrowed farther into the blankets. After staring into the darkness for what seemed like hours, Clare reached up and pulled the drawstring on her lamp.

The light cast deep shadows around her room and the first thing to catch Clare's eye was the vacant space on her overflowing bookshelf. The books were stacked side by side, series by series and every book was there in its respective place, save for one. Steve was the only person Clare had ever given a book to and although she didn't realize it at the time, Clare now knew that it was more than just a memento of their time together.

It had been her way of telling Steve that she was actually interested; that she was willing to open up. But Clare knew she had blown the opportunity. She hadn't put down a number, an email, or anything. And yet, she continued to study the void at the heart of her bookcase as if it held some elusive secret.

However, after pondering matters into the wee hours of the morning, Clare came to the conclusion that there was no elusive secret. She hated being alone. She absolutely hated the fact that she had no parents; that her father had passed way too early and that her mother's life was nothing short of a fucked up mess. She hated being alone and she wanted to be with Steve. Clare felt guilty about the conversation between her and Amy and wished she could take back what she said regarding Steve.

Eventually, Clare fell back to sleep and when she woke again the sun was just coming up. Gentle rays of light were cutting through the blinds on her window and bouncing off the shiny objects in her room. As a result, flecks of light dappled nearly every surface in her room and Clare lay in bed, baffled by the beauty that looked almost magical. It was something she assumed could only happen in one of her fantasy novels.

Clare R.

Clare had fallen asleep groggy, tired, and fully expecting the next day to suck horribly. But so far the day wasn't sucky at all. In fact, she felt hopeful. Her stomach ached from hunger, but she felt hopeful. She rolled over and retrieved her laptop from the night stand. In a flurry of precise finger movements, Clare clicked through as many websites as possible searching for one thing in particular.

When the search was over, Clare untangled herself from the sheets and headed for the shower. The laptop remained open on her bed and on the screen were the bold letters of an email confirmation.

Your Flight Confirmation number is...

~~~

It was Wednesday and the cooking class that Steve had come to love was at its end. Mr. Alero had decided they would make different kinds of pizza and have a party of sorts. The lesson itself consisted of how to make proper pizza dough, but after that it was a free for all, and just like the first day of class, Gus saved Steve's review for last. But instead of comments, he received something rather unexpected.

"So, Steve, I have a proposal for you," Gus said.

"What's that?" Steve asked.

"There's this cooking conference that I was going to attend up near Pittsburgh next weekend," he said. "Why are you raising your eyebrows? There are conferences for everything." Steve laughed and nodded.

"Anyway. I can't make it because I've got some other stuff going on and I was wondering if you would like to take my place," Gus finished.

"Really?" he said. "Why me?"

"Because Steve, half the people in this class were only here because they wanted a fun elective for their degree. Several others only wanted to be here because they thought they would walk out of here famous chefs. You're here because you love to cook," Gus explained.

"You're very blunt, you know," Steve said.

"Eh. Oh well," Gus replied. Steve was silent as he chewed a bite of pizza.

"Isn't everything registered under your name?" Steve asked.

"Yeah, but I can call and get everything sorted out. No big deal," Gus said.

"It would probably be kind of fun," Steve said.

"It is. There are cooking classes, new cookware, blah, blah, blah. It's a good time," Gus said. "You do like to have fun, don't you?" Steve shoved Gus playfully in the shoulder. He had certainly grown to appreciate his new friend over the past several weeks and didn't want the class to end.

"All right. I'll take you up on that," Steve finally said.

"Yeah?" Gus said. Steve nodded and they shook hands.

"It's been a pleasure cooking with you, Steve."

"You as well, Mr. Alero," Steve said.

"Seriously, call me Gus," he replied.

~~~~

Clare brushed aside the hair that was dangling in front of her face and took a sip from the warm cup in her hand while scanning the crowds hoping to see a familiar face. Ever since her mother's surprise visit, Clare had been plagued by doubtful thoughts and

Clare R.

even the simplest tasks at work had become incredibly stressful since she found herself second guessing nearly everything she did.

The only thing she wasn't second guessing were the spur of the moment trips she made to the airport. Clare had picked a couple days to take off work over the next couple weeks and she spent them curled up in a seat at the back of the gate where she and Steve had met. It was the perfect place really, because Clare wanted to be alone and being amongst so many people who had places to be, no one gave her a second glance.

She was well aware that coming to the airport was some sort of overly expensive and desperate attempt to salvage remaining hopes that she would see Steve again. But it seemed like a logical decision and her imagination also felt more alive than it had in days. Hypothetical stories for the other travelers began brewing feverishly as she searched through the herds of other travelers.

The first casualty of her overzealous mind was a middle-aged man with a scruffy beard and short hair. He was pacing around the gate opposite hers and he had on a leather jacket that Clare thought didn't necessarily fit his style.

My name is Earl Jenkins, I sell advertising, and I'm trying to grow a badass beard. I tell my wife I'm traveling for work, but really I just need to take a short vacation so that I can don a boat load of leather and tour with my gang of fellow bikers in some remote part of the country. I love to feel the wind on my face...

Clare chuckled quietly behind her cup of tea. The next traveler to fall prey to her mind was absolutely asking for it. You could see the woman coming from a mile off because of her bright red jacket and gaudy makeup. This prissy woman was radiating a strong vibe of arrogance and affluence as she strolled down the concourse. Following in her wake was the sound of clicking heels and countless stares from men in all directions.

"Holy diva," Clare said with raised eyebrows. "Talk about high maintenance..."

HEY EVERYBODY! My name is Tiffany Roland. I'm totally leaving Detroit and these sucky winters and moving to Georgia so I can audition for Real Housewives of Atlanta. I just love my heels and I'm a professional consumer of stiff drinks. I also know all about making rude comments about things I know absolutely nothing about...

Clare was shaking with laughter and desperately wished he would tromp into the gate area wearing his worn out work boots. Then she noticed a mother and father with their kids and the fun thoughts hit a brick wall.

"Ugh," Clare sighed and shifted her eyes elsewhere.

~~~~

Sleep. It's a beautiful thing; that satisfying feeling of going to sleep so exhausted and waking up completely refreshed. But it had been years since Steve had experienced this because since the passing of his father, sleep often eluded him most nights. He was plagued with restlessness or strangely, twisted dreams that would cause him to wake in a cold sweat, leaving him staring miserably at the clock or ceiling. Sometimes he would read but typically it was an hour, if not more, before he was drowsy again. As a result, Steve often went to work feeling exhausted. This was something he had done his best trying to come to grips with.

However, since meeting Clare, Steve became increasingly aware that his sleeping had actually improved and subsequently returned to normal. Steve was enjoying one of these rejuvenating

Clare R.

nights of sleep when he woke early in the morning before his trip to Pittsburgh. An incessant beeping was coming from the phone on the nightstand, and for a moment he thought it was Clare calling him. Desperately, Steve reached for the phone, not wanting to miss her call. But when nobody replied after giving a very groggy hello, he realized the beeping hadn't been the ring tone. It was actually a very persistent weather alert.

Steve grumpily got out of bed knowing that if it had snowed, he would have to get the car warming up so it was ready to go when he left for work. After throwing on some pants and a sweater, Steve went downstairs to find his boots. But when Steve opened the front door he couldn't help but chuckle because there was absolutely no snow. It was oddly warm and there looked to be a thin layer of ice covering almost everything. Apparently he wasn't the only one who had received the weather alert for severe freezing rain.

I should have known better, Steve thought. He had moved far enough south that the real snow came only in the dead of winter. During the other winter months, the temperature fluctuated enough that it could rain and snow all in the same day. Many folks in the complex had come out to turn their vehicles on and as Steve stood there, letting his eyes adjust to the blinding headlights, he couldn't help but think how reminiscent this scene was to a *Fast and the Furious* film.

The ironic part was that instead of there being souped-up street cars, gear heads, and a plethora of scantily clad women, there was a row of ice covered sedans, minivans, and the assortment of grumpy, bundled up, car owners scraping furiously at the ice, hoping to make it to work on time.

Steve let the heater do most of the work and only chipped off an area around the driver's side of the windshield. After helping the neighbor remove ice from her car, Steve went back inside to finish getting ready for work.

~~~~

Amy was nearly at her breaking point. It had been a couple weeks since the fiasco at Thanksgiving and Clare had been like a ghost ever since. Amy was well aware that Clare became a roller coaster of emotions as the holidays approached, especially at Christmas. But even this was unlike Clare. She was being much more aloof than usual.

Amy was determined to remedy the situation, so before leaving work that afternoon, she'd taken measures. Now she was walking briskly up the steps to Clare's house and before going inside, she paused to compose her thoughts one last time.

"All right, Clare, I've got some news for you," Amy said as she stomped into the house. Clare was trying to bury the disappointment of another fruitless trip to the airport by catching up on episodes of the *Lunar Chronicles* and enjoying a cup of mac and cheese on the couch. Having grown used to her friend's random interruptions, Clare kept the remote close at hand, so she could pause the show at a moment's notice. After pressing pause, Clare stared at Amy with a look of consternation.

"What's up?" she asked.

"Gosh, you look at me like that and it totally throws me off," Amy replied.

"Well, somehow you always manage to interrupt my show," Clare said. Amy shook her head and continued as if she hadn't heard Clare's comment.

Clare R.

"Where have you been? I came over earlier but you weren't home," Amy asked.

"I thought you had to go into work today," Clare said.

"I did but it only took a few hours," Amy said.

"Oh well, I was out," Clare said.

"Obviously," Amy said. "Where were you?"

"I was out, OK? Don't worry about it," Clare said. She turned her attention back to the television and unpaused her show.

"Clare, seriously," Amy said. "You weren't doing drugs or something I hope."

"Amy! I wasn't fucking doing drugs! I'm not my mom, OK!" Clare exclaimed. That stopped Amy in her tracks and the room fell silent.

"I'm sorry," Clare said. "I shouldn't have snapped."

"It's OK. I'm just your verbal punching bag," Amy replied. "You went to the airport again, didn't you?"

"Maybe," she said. Amy shook her head sideways.

"Oh, Clare," Amy said.

"What?" she asked. "I like it. It's actually kind of peaceful."

"Uhuh," Amy said.

"How did you know I was at the airport, anyway?" Clare asked.

"Well no offense, but you don't really have anywhere else to go," Amy said.

"Ha! I could have been at the bar with Jenny," Clare said.

"Yeah, right. Because you're the kind of person who spends all day at the bar drinking," Amy retorted. Clare just rolled her eyes.

"Are you OK, Clare?" Amy asked. This time, Clare paused the show.

"No, Amy. I'm not OK. Don't get me wrong, I love you and your family, but I can't keep imposing on your life."

"That's bullshit and you know it. We've been friends since we were little. You are family." Clare could see that her words had upset Amy and now she felt bad.

"I know, I'm sorry. It's just that Steve is the closest I've come to meeting someone who seems like they could eventually be part of my life and it sucks that we didn't exchange numbers or anything." Clare ran her hands through her hair and closed her eyes. "It eats at me, Amy. Seeing my mom didn't help anything either." She felt like she was on the verge of tears and there was no way she was going to start crying in front of Amy.

I need to stay focused. Amy thought. *I'm just going to say it.*

"Why are you here?" Clare asked.

"I talked to this guy at work and I told him about you," Amy said.

"Ugh. Why did you do that, Amy?" Clare said. Having lost her appetite for the show, she let out an exasperated sigh and got off the couch realizing this was going to be a lengthy visit. Amy followed Clare to the kitchen.

"Well, because since we got back from Thanksgiving, you've been sulking," Amy said. Clare turned to her friend and made a rude face.

"Are you kidding me?" she exclaimed. "I have not been sulking."

"You've been sulking," Amy repeated.

"Have not," Clare fired back.

"Have too," Amy said. Clare shook her head defiantly but she knew it was true. Clare wanted to see Steve again, so badly. The holidays were upon them and Steve was the only present she wanted. She didn't want to be alone on Christmas for another year,

Clare R.

and since running in to Steve didn't appear to be happening any time soon, she had taken up refuge at home in her free time.

"OK, fine. Maybe a little," she said, giving in. "But YOU told me not to give up on him!"

"Yes, I know that. But that doesn't mean I want you here all the time," Amy said. Clare busied herself with making another cup of tea and pretended not to hear her.

"Do you want any?" Clare asked.

"No thanks, I'm fine," Amy said. "So...Will you see this guy? His name is Jamie."

"No, Amy I don't want to. I'm busy," Clare said flatly.

"Yeah, you're busy watching hot, medieval dudes ride around on ponies, killing things," Amy said.

"Exactly," Clare replied. "Who wouldn't want to watch that?"

"Come on, Clare. Please. I just don't want you to dwell on this, that's all," Amy said. "What if Steve's forgotten about you anyway?" Amy waited patiently. She knew she could wear her friend down.

"He didn't," Clare said confidently. "But if it will shut you up...I'll do this."

"Really?" Amy said.

"But if it doesn't work out, it doesn't work out," Clare clarified.

"I'm not going to force anything," Amy said. Clare rolled her eyes as she took a seat at the dining table and dunked the tea bag up and down, watching the water turn from clear to minty green. The sweet smell tickled her nose and she smiled.

"What's he like?" Clare asked.

"I don't know," Amy said. "He's tallish, darker hair." Amy

made a gesture with her hand indicating Jamie was about her height. Clare made a note of this but didn't say anything, so Amy continued.

"Um...He doesn't look ripped but he's not scrawny. I don't know...I think he's good looking," she finished.

"Then why don't you go out with him?" Clare said.

"He's not into me," Amy replied. Clare doubted this statement but didn't say anything. Guys always seemed to have a thing for Amy. Instead, she stared at the cup of tea again.

"When is this taking place, anyway?" Clare asked. There was no hiding the nervous expression on Amy's face as she pulled a phone from her jacket pocket.

"In about forty-five minutes," Amy said.

"What!" Clare exclaimed. Amy wasn't about to back down, no matter how angry Clare became.

"I told him tonight because I knew if I gave you any time, you'd figure a way out of it," Amy replied. Clare got up from the table with her tea in hand and gave Amy a mental high five.

"Very clever," she said, walking past Amy to her room. There was a loud, aggravated sigh followed by a slamming door. Clare was not happy about what Amy had done. It was a behind the back maneuver that they'd silently agreed not to do to each other. But Clare knew she'd been sulking and it wasn't logical to shut out other guys forever, especially if she never heard from Steve again. Before changing, she stared longingly at the bookshelf.

I'm not giving up, Steve, she thought. *I'm just doing this to shut Amy up.*

Clare had spent a good deal of time wondering what she might wear if her and Steve ever got to go on another date, and that had been enjoyable because she knew he would appreciate it.

Clare R.

But going on a forced date with some random dude named Jamie didn't sound enjoyable at all. In the end, she decided to wear a plain, semi-formal outfit and of course, Amy made fun of her for it.

"You look like you're going back to work," Amy said as the pair walked down the street to the coffee shop that Amy had designated as the meeting place.

"I do not," Clare said. "I never wear these shoes to work. Or this jacket." Amy laughed and Clare gave her a little shove. A few minutes later, they arrived at the coffee shop. The red and green neon lights looked very inviting in the growing darkness and they eagerly stepped inside to escape the chilly breeze. Normally, Clare would have welcomed the delicious smells of the coffee shop, but tonight she was frustrated and had no appetite for sweets. She just wanted to go home.

Once they were inside, Amy pointed out a dark-haired gentleman who was hunched over the table reading a magazine of some kind. But even if Amy hadn't been there, she could have picked him out. Jamie was the only guy sitting by himself. Clare gave Amy another disapproving look, which Amy ignored. She wrapped an arm around Clare's and dragged her over to Jamie's table. After Amy introduced Clare to Jamie, she bolted, leaving the odd pair alone.

Although Clare knew the difference in her outfits, Jamie did not, and he couldn't help but think he was meeting someone for an interview instead of coffee.

I wonder if I should make an interview joke, he thought. But he decided against it.

"So," Jamie started.

"It's nice to meet you, Jamie," she began.

"You, too," he replied, nodding a bit excessively. Clare

didn't really know what to think. Jamie was cute, but it was more of a funny cute. He was wearing dark blue frames that hung very close to the end of his small, round nose. As she stared at him, she realized Amy was right. He wasn't scrawny but he was nothing like Steve, who had broader shoulders. Jamie was tall and thin and when she allowed herself to briefly imagine them sharing a dramatic "end of a movie hug," she immediately pictured Jamie toppling over backward.

"What's so funny?" he asked.

"Oh, nothin'," she replied. "So, what are you reading?"

"A graphic novel," he replied.

Duh! Clare thought. *I can see all the pretty colors and fast action on the cover.*

"That's cool, dude," she said instead.

"Yeah, so how long have you and Amy known each other?" Jamie assumed this would be an appropriate starting place since Amy was the one who had orchestrated this get together.

"Uh, since we were little," Clare replied. "Unfortunately." She added the last remark partly out of annoyance for the situation, but it did make Jamie chuckle. A waitress appeared and took their orders. Clare got more tea and he got a coffee.

"Why do you say that?" Jamie asked when the waitress left.

"About Amy? Long story," Clare offered. "But most of it centers around tonight." She wasn't sure if Jamie had picked up on the tone of her voice like Steve would have. But the comment did made Jamie chuckle again and Clare came to a swift conclusion that she didn't care for his "chuckle." She much preferred Steve's.

"Oh," he replied.

"Jamie, Amy's awesome and she's my best friend. Amy can just be a little stubborn is all," Clare said, and then thanked the

Clare R.

waitress when she brought them their drinks. "So, do you like your job?" Clare was struggling trying to think of anything to talk about.

"Yeah, it's all right. It's fun most days and the people are nice," Jamie said. "What about you? What do you do exactly?"

"Amy didn't tell you?" Clare said.

"Nope, she didn't tell me much about what was going to happen tonight," he replied.

"Oh. Well, I really like my job," Clare said. "I work for a logistics company that works in conjunction with movie companies to get people moved around to different sets and props shipped and such." Jamie seemed to think this was cool but not for the same reasons she did.

"Does that mean you get to meet a lot of famous people then?" Jamie asked eagerly. Clare nodded but didn't reply. That was typically the first thing people asked her. However, meeting a celebrity or two was not the reason she enjoyed her job. It was the puzzle that came along with mashing everyone's schedules to fit the timeline of the filming schedule. Not to mention getting important props shipped to the sets in a timely fashion. She was very good at her job.

"Clare, you seem really nice, but I have to ask you something," Jamie said.

"Yeah, sure," she replied. Clare was aimlessly stirring her tea after adding a packet of sugar.

"Do you really want to be here?" Jamie asked. "I mean, I don't want to be rude. You just don't seem that excited."

Well, at least he's not a dunce, she thought. But she also couldn't hold the charade any longer and let out another sigh.

"To be perfectly honest, Jamie...Not really," Clare said.

"Amy kind of sprung this on me and I said yes so she would stop badgering me."

"OK, cool," Jamie said. "I mean, no offense." She made a half-smile and shrugged.

"That's fine. You're into Amy, aren't you?" Clare asked. Jamie chuckled again and she still didn't like it.

"Yeah, I am. Amy's great and I've been too chicken to ask her out. But then she came over to talk to me at work today. She asked me to meet you for coffee and I said sure before I really knew what I was getting into," Jamie explained. Clare knew that Amy was just trying to have her back.

"Well, we'll fix this," Clare said and she took a sip of her tea to test the temperature. Jamie chose to hide his excitement by asking another question. With the pressure for this date to work out reduced to nothing, he actually felt like they had reached some sort of common ground, so he made a confident stab in the dark.

"So, who's the guy?" Jamie asked. Clare was surprised at her willingness to even mention anything about Steve to someone she hardly knew.

"He's this really great guy who I met awhile back and I haven't been able to quit thinking about him. The thing is, we met in passing and I'm not sure if I'll ever see him again," Clare confessed.

"Well, you seem pretty cool, so if he's got a brain in his head I'm sure he's thinking about you, too," Jamie offered. "If it's meant to be...It's meant to be."

"Thanks, Jamie," Clare replied. All of a sudden, she had an idea and set some cash on the table. "I vote we move this get-together elsewhere. Did you drive here?"

"Yeah, why?" he replied.

Clare R.

"I'll tell you when we get there. Can I have a ride?" Clare asked. Jamie nodded and after getting their drinks to go, they headed out the door. They drove up the street but turned at Clare's direction and headed toward Amy's house.

"Just park here," Clare said. "Hang on." She got out of Jamie's car and ran up the steps to Amy's house. Clare hadn't said much during their short drive together, so it was no surprise that he sat there feeling a bit confused. At first Jamie thought he'd been giving her a ride home but Clare wasn't going inside...

Unlike Amy, Clare didn't like to burst through the doors of people's homes, no matter how close friends they were. So, while waiting for Amy, Clare stood on the doorstep, shivering in the chilly breeze that had come up again.

"Well, that was quick," Amy said when she opened up the door. "I hope you gave Jamie a chance."

"You're an idiot," Clare said. "He's not even remotely interested." The mild insult didn't even faze Amy.

"Yeah, well if you didn't talk to him...How could he be?" Amy asked defiantly. But Clare just laughed.

"I did, but it didn't matter," Clare said. "You like him too, don't you?"

"Well, yeah," Amy said. Then she nudged Clare's shoulder. "He's kinda my dreamy airport guy."

"Oh my God. Why did you try and set me up with him then?" asked Clare.

"Because I want you to be happy," Amy replied.

"I am happy," she replied and before Amy could protest, Clare turned and waved at the car. Jamie got out and started walking across the street. "Jamie's into you, Amy. So, I'm thinking the date should be going on right here."

"What? Really?" Amy asked surprised. "Wait, you brought

him here?" She brushed her hair back with a hand trying to make herself presentable.

"Yep, and please don't ever do that to me again," Clare mumbled as Jamie came up the steps with a nervous grin on his face.

"I won't," she replied. "Hi Jamie!"

"Hey, Amy," he replied.

"Have fun you two. I'm going home. Talk to you tomorrow!" Clare said. After a quick wave, she backed down the steps and started walking home. With each step, the happy demeanor from setting up her best friend on an unexpected date diminished until all that was left was an unwanted sense of jealousy. When Clare got home, she gladly climbed back into a pair of sweats and resumed watching her medieval show, wishing the entire time that Steve could be there too.

Chapter 18

Meanwhile, Steve's evening was about to become equally interesting. He was just putting the finishing touches on a set of plans when a lady from another department stopped over to see him.

"Hey, Steve, what's up?" she asked. Her name was Lucy and she was about his height with curly, blond hair and her eyes were outlined by thin, brown glasses. After being hired she was one of the first people he talked to on a regular basis, and they had even worked on a couple of projects together.

"Not much. I'm done for the night...finally," Steve replied. He eagerly put on his coat and scanned his desk to make sure he didn't forget anything. "What's up with you?"

"Oh, nothin'," Lucy replied. They walked down the hallway to the exit. "I was just going to see if you had any plans or anything. I'm going to Chuck's for a drink and something to eat if you wanted to come." At the mention of food, Steve's stomach grumbled for the umpteenth time that day but that didn't do much to ease the apprehension he was feeling. That morning, after leaving behind the ice world that was his parking lot, Steve narrowly escaped a car accident, which left him stressed out the rest of the morning. By the time lunch came around, he was gifted with a flat tire in the parking lot and had to spend his lunch hour in the repair shop.

"Hmm. That's tempting," he replied.

"I mean, only if you want to," Lucy said.

"All right," Steve said. "They do make good pizza."

"So, I'll see you there?" she asked.

"Yep," he replied. "I'm going right now." They parted ways at the parking lot, but when Steve sat down in his tan sedan, he felt terrible. The excitement in Lucy's eyes had been so apparent and Steve knew his enthusiasm was not. In fact, he felt like he was sinking into a quagmire of his own guilt and sadness, and that was somewhere he did not want to go again. Yet, Steve also knew that if he returned home, the most exciting part of his evening would be scanning the Internet in search of a woman he might never see again.

What am I doing? he thought. Imaginary Clare immediately appeared in the passenger seat to answer the question in his head.

"It sounds like you're going on a hot date," she said.

"It's not a date and it's definitely not hot," Steve said and he was pleased to see his figment laugh again.

"I'm not sure she knows that then. You better clarify that," imaginary Clare stated.

"Clarify," he repeated. "That was clever." Imaginary Clare grinned at him.

"I thought so," she said. But then her expression changed. "I thought you weren't giving up on me?" Her voice sounded distressed.

"I'm not," Steve replied immediately. "I won't go."

"Well you can't do that," imaginary Clare replied. "You already said you would go and I know you wouldn't stand up a lady. Would you stand me up?"

Clare R.

"Absolutely not," Steve exclaimed. "You really are something else, you know that, right?" Clare kept staring with a pensive expression.

"Then why did you say yes to going?" she asked.

"I'm not sure," Steve said. The figment tilted her head suggesting he should have known better.

"Well, you should figure it out," Clare said. When Steve looked over, she was gone and it left him feeling oddly distressed because he didn't want her to be upset with him. Then Steve shook his head remembering that this phantom Clare was just a figment of his imagination. When he finally made it to the restaurant, Steve met Lucy outside the door and then they went inside. Chuck's wasn't terribly busy but from what Steve could see their main patrons that evening were other couples.

You have got to be kidding me, Steve thought. He already felt uncomfortable but now the feeling was much more noticeable. Lucy and Steve were not in any way a couple and the longer he stood there, the more he realized he didn't want to be. But politeness won out and Steve led her to a nearby table. After they shed their coats and ordered a drink, conversation moved to work.

"How are things going in your division?" Steve asked, trying to keep things neutral even though the last thing either of them wanted to talk about was work.

"Good," Lucy replied. "We were really busy the last couple weeks, but then we slowed down and there wasn't much going on today, so I absolutely couldn't wait to leave tonight."

"Yeah, I hear you there," he replied.

"So, how are you liking the city?" she asked. "You've been here awhile now."

"Yeah," Steve said. "It's not bad. After moving so much

lately, it's nice to be settled down. I'm liking it more I guess." It wasn't exactly a lie, but in truth Steve was indifferent. Nowhere he'd been in the last two years had actually felt like home. Steve often wondered if he would feel more at home if he and Clare were together.

Their forced conversation continued like this for several minutes and the guilt was welling inside Steve like magma inside a volcano.

This isn't right, he thought. Thankfully for Steve, Lucy could tell something was up.

"Are you all right, Steve?" she asked. He shrugged.

"It's been a long day," he said.

"Tell me about it," she said. "You seem preoccupied."

"I am," he said, grinning sheepishly.

"Work stuff? Family stuff? Or another lady perhaps?" she offered.

"I'm not quite sure how I should answer that question," he said and Lucy laughed.

"Honestly would be good," she suggested.

"Well, I did meet someone awhile back," Steve began.

"Ah," Lucy said. "Another lady then." He nodded and shrugged his shoulders.

"Yep, but it's complicated," he added. Steve had always found the phrase *it's complicated* to be incredibly lame but it was legitimate in this scenario.

"How come?" Lucy asked.

"Um, this girl and I met at the airport a couple months ago; when I went for that site visit," he explained. Lucy laughed again.

"So, that's why you were so excited when you got back. I just assumed something good had happened with the project," Lucy said.

Clare R.

"Nope, just the best delayed flight of all time," Steve said. He tried to distract himself from the awkward conversation by mulling over the menu even though he wasn't hungry any more at all.

"What happened, then?" Lucy asked, now slightly curious. "Didn't you get her number or something?"

"No we weren't really paying attention to the time and we had to split before we could exchange anything," he said.

"So, how come you came out with me then?" Lucy asked.

"I think because... I just wanted to make sure about how I felt," Steve said. Lucy was bummed, but at the same time she was relieved that Steve had simply told her the truth.

"I like you, Steve, but if you want to just be friends, that's fine," Lucy said.

"I'm sorry, Lucy," he said. "I don't mean to be a prick or something."

"You're not," she said with a soft smile and then Steve realized it was time to go.

"Lucy, I think I'm gonna head out," Steve said. Again, she just nodded and smiled and Steve felt a surprised expression cross his face. This made her laugh from behind the menu.

"Really, it's fine. There are some other people coming down anyway," Lucy replied. He nodded again and felt his stomach begin to swirl as he stood up. "Have fun on your vacation, Steve, and I hope you find her again."

"Thanks, Lucy," Steve said, trying to smile. "I'll see you in a couple weeks." He made his way to the bar and paid for their drinks and then skirted past the several couples who were enjoying dinner together. Hearing the laughter and happiness gnawed at him like a virus.

Steve diverted his gaze the best he could and walked in the brisk evening air wishing his stomach would settle down. All Steve wanted was to see Clare. Even the ghostly apparition would be a welcome sight. He kept glancing at the passenger seat expecting to see her during his trip home, but she never appeared. For some reason this just stressed him out further.

How could a figment get irritated? Steve wondered. To make matters worse, no good songs came on the radio his entire ride home. He stabbed at the plastic buttons hoping for a soothing melody, but station after station was just depressing music. One in particular that came on almost seemed like it was taunting him.

Say something...I'm giving up on you...

Steve squeezed the steering wheel in frustration, which caused his knuckles to go white.

"I'm not giving up on you, Clare!" Steve said through gritted teeth.

~~~

The afternoon he met Clare, Steve could remember this intensely warm sensation that had spread throughout his entire body and his heart had beat with feverish excitement he couldn't ever remember experiencing. But when Steve got home that night from Chuck's, that feeling was nowhere to be found. Instead, his stomach was a fit of knots, twisting and churning, and it was almost unbearable. Steve wondered if he was going to vomit.

I can't take this, Steve thought. *It's too much!* It had been one of those days. Not only did things seem to be going downhill all day, but he had to endure the sightings of countless romantic couples that evening when he went to Chuck's with Lucy. All Steve wanted was one thing. But she wasn't a thing. She was a person

Clare R.

and her name was Clare and for some reason he couldn't see a way to be with her. He couldn't figure out what to do.

When Steve got home, he immediately changed out of his uncomfortable work clothes. But no amount of warm, comfy clothes could combat the chill that had fallen over Steve and he went back downstairs, seeking a cup of tea. He shoved a cup of water in the microwave and collapsed on the couch trying to combat his ailing stomach. A beautifully sad love sang came on the radio and Steve just let himself sink further into the couch.

Unsettling feelings continued to well up inside of him, but there was something more, something more ominous that he couldn't place. As the timer on the microwave reached its end, Steve reached over on the cushion beside him and picked up his phone. The pale light from the screen lit up his features, accentuating the exhaustion and pain that he was feeling. The microwave beeped again. Steve stared at the phone wishing that Clare could call him or send him a message. But nothing came. The song on the radio reached its climax just as the microwave beeped for a third time, and then Steve caught sight of the date.

Today was the day. Today was the anniversary of his father's death.

The phone slipped from his grasp as Steve buried his face in his hands. In an instant the nauseating feelings collided with ones of extreme sadness and frustration. Steve lashed out at the coffee table in front of him, sending it toppling over with one fearsome kick. Everything that had been resting on top sprawled out across the living room floor. Tears were running down his face and the pain inside him burned like a wildfire as a multitude of memories flooded his head.

So many people crying...his mother shaking him awake...

pictures of the burning house on the news...the funeral...the tombstone that haunted his dreams...

Steve hadn't cried for nearly two years, not since his father had died. He knew that he had left home for a reason. He had left everything behind because it was too hard and painful. When a few months had gone by, the crying stopped, and Steve remembered feeling lonely and empty. Nothing had mattered any more. Nothing was satisfying. He had felt numb.

Then by some miracle, Steve had met Clare and being around her had been like gulping fresh air after nearly drowning. Her personality was charismatic. Her charm was intoxicating, and for the first time since his father had passed away, Steve hadn't felt empty. But just as quickly as they met, they had been separated again.

Steve remained on the couch, reliving the last several weeks over in his head and the more he thought about that time, the more it felt like some perverse form of torture. He had been talking to himself for weeks because he enjoyed imagining conversations with the girl of his dreams and then somehow, she had appeared. A ghost, an apparition, or simply a figment of his imagination.

But as much as he loved it, Steve hated it because he knew she really wasn't there and just when he thought it could last, this imaginary Clare would disappear again. The tears were running faster now.

"Please," Steve said staring up at the dark ceiling. "Just give us a chance." When he could stare at the ceiling no longer, Steve rested his head in his knees, which were now pulled up against his chest. Then he felt her hands on his arm and looked up to see her bright face looking down at him.

"Stevie, what's wrong?" imaginary Clare asked quietly. Her kind eyes were locked onto his and Steve felt like he couldn't have

Clare R.

looked away even if he wanted to. She sat down next to him and wrapped her arm around his. The touch of her free hand on his cheek was soothing but tears continued to roll down his face.

"I'm sorry I went out with Lucy," Steve said.

"I don't care, you dork," imaginary Clare said with a shrug. "Now you really know what you want." Steve nodded and a choked up laugh followed. He loved thinking about Clare calling him a dork.

"The problem is... I don't know what to do," Steve said. "I'm so alone. I hate being alone. I just want to be with you. I've spent so much time looking and I can't find anything." She didn't say anything at first and instead wiped tears from his face. Each time her delicate fingers brushed across his cheek, a very reassuring warmth followed. The glow from the street lights outside his house caught the shine in her eyes and made them look like stars.

"You promised you wouldn't give up on me," she said with a worried expression on her face.

"I know," he said.

"Well, do you want me to go?" she asked, and for the tiniest instant, Steve considered saying yes because it was so difficult to share these heartfelt moments with imaginary Clare and then have her disappear. But deep down he know how important she was to him.

"No, I don't want you to go and I know I promised you that I wouldn't give up on you," Steve said. "I'm not going to. It's just so hard when you go all the time."

"I'm not really leaving, Stevie. I'm still here," she said, and just as she'd done the night she first appeared, imaginary Clare tapped gently on his head and then down on his chest over his heart. For some reason this made him smile.

R. K. Blessing

"You know what I mean, though. I just wish you and I had a chance to really meet again and hang out," Stevie replied. "And my goodness, I'm giving you my number and a kiss!" The last part made her laugh.

"Oh, Stevie," Clare said, leaning in to kiss his cheek. "You worry too much. We will have a chance." It should have made him feel better, but there were so many unsettling thoughts in his head.

"What if you're with someone?" he asked. The thought of Clare being with another guy made his stomach churn even more.

"Do you really think that's the case, Stevie? You know that we have something special and besides, would you really let that stop you?" his figment replied.

"No," he replied. "I don't want to keep giving up. I have to try."

"Good," she said. Then she looked at the mess created by his sudden outburst at the coffee table and smiled again.

"You forgot your belt this morning, you know," she said. "Bet you looked kind of funny without it." A teary chuckle escaped him and he looked at her gratefully.

"Yeah, I realized that when I got to work. I felt sort of goofy," Steve said.

"I guess it's a good thing I like goofy then," imaginary Clare said. A big grin spread across his face and he used his free arm to wipe away the remaining tears. But when he put his arm down, she was gone and he was alone again.

"Ugh, you little turd," he said. However, Steve ended up laughing. Clare was the only one who could make him feel better like that. Steve got off the couch and went to retrieve the cup of tea from the microwave. Then he went upstairs to finish packing. Although it was only Thursday night, it was his unofficial Friday because he was taking the next day off as part of his two week long

Clare R.

vacation for the holidays which would begin in Pittsburgh for the cooking conference.

While Steve packed, he simultaneously cleaned his room, and for the first time in two years, Steve shelved the copy of *Coping with Death*. He stared at the blunt type face of the title, wondering if he'd ever read it again. It was worn out and tired and he didn't want to be stuck in its pages forever. With one final glance, he twisted the switch on the lamp and the room went dark. After getting into bed, Steve stared out the window at the moon. Its pale luminescence was soothing and hauntingly eerie at the same time.

"I miss you, dad. I miss you so much," he whispered. When Steve closed his eyes his thoughts returned to Clare and he felt the cool touch of her finger pressing gently on his cheek, turning him away from the window.

"Everything is going to be all right, Stevie," she whispered before planting a kiss on his cheek. "Go to sleep, OK?" He barely managed a nod before sleep took him away.

~~~

When Clare woke the next morning, a sense of foreboding hovered over the bed like a heavy rain cloud ready to unleash a downpour, and she rolled over trying to induce a good dream about Steve. All she wanted was to stay in bed or go back to the airport. But that wasn't an option since this week had been an action packed cluster fuck of schedule changes, and she knew that today would be no different. It didn't help that anxious feelings were spreading through her and she had no way to quell them.

After leaving the warm sanctuary that was her bed, Clare trudged to the bathroom and got in the shower. Normally, she preferred to shower at night, but after dealing with Amy's stunt the previous evening, Clare had binged on episodes of the *Lunar Chronicles* until she fell asleep on the couch.

Clare took several deep breaths of the steamy air trying to get the strange dreams out of her head. Instead of dreaming about Steve like she hoped for at night, she had dreamed of her, Amy, and Jamie being lost in a fantasy world.

From then on her day started to go downhill. The toaster for some reason didn't kick up her bagel, which caused it to become fatally burned, and when she walked out to the car, Clare took a sip of her tea only to find that she'd forgotten to heat up the water. Traffic was heavy an hour earlier than it normally was and Clare found herself checking the time repeatedly wondering if she'd slept in by accident.

Finally, after a forty-five minute commute, which was nearly triple the time it usually took, Clare made it to work, but the late arrival meant her normal parking spot was taken. As a result, Clare was forced to park in the back of the building where the lot was in terrible shape. The asphalt was cracked and broken everywhere and small craters were slowly becoming sinkholes the more it rained. She took extreme care not to put the heel of her boot in a pothole as she walked up to the door.

"I sure as hell have a topic for the next I & A session," Clare grumbled. In an effort to salvage some sort of breakfast, she went to find something in the kitchen. There was actually a lot of fruit and she was able to grab an apple and a banana. Then she tried to make another cup of tea, but before Clare could escape to her office to start on paperwork, another unfortunate event occurred.

When a coworker came into the kitchen to make some breakfast, Clare mumbled hello from behind a yawn and he replied with

Clare R.

a sleepy nod. Since she was occupied with adding honey to the cup of tea, she wasn't really paying attention as he moved between the microwave and coffee pot. The smell of bacon in his breakfast was making her stomach grumble and her mouth water. For a moment, Clare considered leaving to go find a real breakfast somewhere.

But then all thoughts of food vanished from her mind when her coworker swung his arm down to get the cup of coffee. He unfortunately misjudged the cup's location and knocked it over, sending hot coffee across the counter and down onto her foot.

Her dress pants and socks did nothing to protect against the scalding hot fluid from getting on her skin, so Clare spent much of the morning hunkered in her office with an ice pack on her foot. It was already a cold day and she was infuriated at the fact that there was an ice pack on her foot. By the end of the day Clare had finished all her work, but her mood was beyond foul. She had barricaded herself in her office and skipped lunch. All she wanted was to go back to bed.

~~~~

Steve spent the majority of his trip enjoying the crisp, clear weather of mid December, but as he got closer to Pittsburgh, the weather began to take a turn for the worse. The trees along the highway were starting to twist and turn in the wind and the skies were no longer that beautiful partly cloudy. Instead, they were inky black and menacing and the world had become dramatically darker even though it was only three in the afternoon. When a brilliant bolt of lightning arched across the sky, Steve turned down the radio and violent rumbles of thunder could be heard over the car's engine.

Thank God this isn't a barbeque conference, Steve thought. The sign for the hotel was a welcome sight because the clouds were nearly bursting with rain, and by the time he parked his car and walked up to the hotel entrance, huge fat drops of rain had started to fall from the sky.

"Good afternoon, sir," the clerk said politely. "Hope you didn't get too wet out there." Steve chuckled.

"Nope. Thankfully I made it to the door before it started to come down very hard," Steve replied. The clerk nodded and began typing away on the computer as he processed Steve's reservation.

"Good. Good. Are you here for the cooking expo?" asked the clerk.

"You bet," Steve replied. "I'm pretty excited." The clerk's round features picked up a subtle vibration as he tittered behind the counter.

"It's your first time, then?" he said.

"Yeah," Steve replied. Another speed giggle came from behind the counter.

"Well, you're in for a good show. Be sure to keep an eye out for the regulars. They stick out like flaming fondue stands," said the clerk. An image of an overzealous tourist popped to the front of Steve's brain.

"Thanks. I'll keep that in mind," he replied. After exchanging the necessary information, the desk clerk gave Steve the keys to his room.

"Good day to you, sir! I hope your stay is delectable," said the clerk. Steve nodded and made his way up the beautiful wooden staircase. When the key lock beeped, Steve pushed the door open and felt his jaw drop slightly. The room was spacious with a small loveseat and coffee table in front of a large TV. Off to the right was a doorway that led to a washroom and a bedroom with a very large bed.

Clare R.

"Seriously, Gus? This is swanky," Steve said to no one. He picked up the takeout menu and skimmed through it before tossing it on the bed. Nothing sounded that appetizing because all he wanted was to get cleaned up and sit down for a while. But when Steve got back into the room, freshly showered and dressed, his figment was sitting on the bed flipping through the takeout menu.

"So, Stevie, I really think we should probably go for a walk," imaginary Clare said. Steve tilted his head and glanced out the window.

"What do you mean?" Steve said. "It's raining... It's pouring."

"Yeah, but I know you love being out in the rain," she said with a grin. Steve laughed. There were so many rainy memories... *stomping in the mud puddles when he was younger and hiking around the farm in the spring...*

"Are you serious?" Steve asked.

"Yeah, I'm serious you dork," she said standing up. "And don't forget your raincoat." Steve peered at her with a keen eye.

"Well, you're coming, too, right?" he asked.

"Yeah! Of course I am," she replied.

"All right," he said. The expression on his figment's face revealed nothing, so Steve put on his shoes and raincoat and they headed back downstairs. The lobby wasn't terribly busy and the weather outside looked like it was steadily deteriorating. Water pounded the sidewalk beyond the safety of the door.

"Try not to get too wet, sir!" called the clerk. Steve nodded and laughed to himself. The clerk looked absolutely bewildered that someone would be willing to walk into the downpour that was falling outside. Then Steve glanced at imaginary Clare and she was beaming.

"What? I'm excited, OK?" Then she started laughing. For a split second, she seemed so real that Steve wondered if the clerk had heard her, but he resisted the urge to turn around. They both put up their hoods and walked outside. A round of thunder boomed over the city and the rain continued to fall.

"Which way?" Steve asked when they stopped for a moment in the middle of the sidewalk. The street was vacant of other people and there were hardly any cars driving about. Imaginary Clare looked up at him with water dripping off the brim of her hood.

"That way," was all she said. As they walked down the sidewalk, Steve tried to take note of any appealing restaurants, but it was raining so hard now that he could barely see in front of him, let alone across the street.

"I've never seen it rain this hard. This is nuts!" Steve exclaimed. The phantom at his side just beamed at him.

"I know," she said. "Isn't it beautiful?"

I am going nuts, aren't I? Steve thought as he stared dumbfounded at imaginary Clare. He was about to protest but then she tugged on his arm.

"Come on, Stevie. Let's go," she said. He nodded and they continued down the sidewalk. They hadn't walked a long way before they came upon a couple shops and a grocery store. As they passed by the parking lot, their walk was suddenly interrupted by a loud swear that someone shouted over the rain, one loud curse that echoed like the thunder. Through the pounding rain, Steve could just make out the form of a shopper who appeared to be having a terrible time getting their groceries into the trunk of their car.

"That sucks," imaginary Clare said. Steve couldn't have agreed more.

"I'm going to go help that person real quick, OK?" Steve

Clare R.

said. But when he turned to his figment, she was gone again. Steve shrugged and headed across the parking lot.

Chapter 19

Clare finally reached her breaking point. She slammed the phone back in its cradle after another coworker tried to pawn off their last Friday afternoon task on her. Curse words were exploding violently in her head like huge fireworks and it took everything not to begin shouting them as a stress reliever. There was still a painful red mark on her ankle and with every minute that ticked by, the more defeated she felt.

Clare finally called it quits and walked out of the office, only to find she was standing in a cold drizzle. She berated herself for not grabbing her rain coat earlier that morning, but in her defense it hadn't been raining yet. All she had was a meager overcoat but it did little to shield her from the rain. Along with everything else, Clare had also forgotten the charger that morning, which was why the phone clutched in her hand beeped every few seconds conveniently reminding her it was nearly dead. This left her swearing as she tried to find a radio station that wasn't all commercials.

Big rain drops splattered against the windshield as the precipitation picked up, and she took a few side streets in an effort to avoid the increasing traffic. But when she was about halfway home, Clare remembered she was nearly out of food at home. With another frustrated sigh, she flicked on her turn signal and

Clare R.

turned into a grocery store she liked.

Clare wasn't thrilled about shopping because she knew it was just another opportunity for something else to go wrong, so as she milled through the aisles, she tried to grab only the bare essentials. But the bare essentials ended up being several bags worth of groceries and it was a lot to try and carry out to the car.

It was raining even harder when she stepped out of the grocery store, and with a glum expression, she watched rivers of water running across the pavement into drains near the entryway. Clare ran across the parking lot as fast as she dared with all her groceries, and tried her hardest to get the trunk open as quickly as possible to avoid getting terribly wet. But the plastic bags were getting slippery and as she fumbled for the car keys, one slipped free.

Of all the bags that could fall it was that one. The sound of eggs cracking was still very audible over the rain, and it was no surprise when another swear escaped her lips. At once, her emotional thread came undone and she nearly dropped the rest of the bags as tears started to run down her face. Clare didn't want to cry but she didn't know what else to do. It wasn't like anyone would have noticed because the rain was pouring so hard you couldn't tell the difference between tears and raindrops.

"Excuse me, miss," said a voice from behind her.

Great! she thought. *The last thing I need is to talk to someone when I look and feel like absolute shit!*

Clare turned, ready to tell the person to buzz off, but the words caught in her throat. A handsome guy, who of course had a rain coat on with the hood up, was standing a few feet away, and when he stepped closer, Clare realized it was the only guy she'd wanted to see for the last two months. Her breath caught in her chest, but for some reason he didn't seem to recognize her.

"Please let me help you," Steve said, holding out his hand to take a couple of the bags. A very grateful grin crossed her lips and she nodded but didn't say anything. Steve took several of the bags and Clare finally got the trunk open. Once the bags were put away, they both took a moment to look down at the bag of cracked eggs. Shell fragments and streams of yolk were pooling out of the carton as the bag filled with water. If anyone had been passing by, it would have looked like the odd pair was saying a silent prayer for a dozen fallen heroes.

Then Steve looked up with a half-smile and Clare put her hands over her face. She was slightly embarrassed and frustrated because she certainly hadn't expected that the next time she saw Steve, she would be soaking wet and crying.

Steve watched the rain run down her nose when she pulled her hands away, and his smile broadened. Her jacket was completely soaked and her damp hair clung to her face under her very wet hood. Streaks of makeup were running down the sides of her face as well. Despite all that though, he couldn't help but notice how beautiful she was even though she looked so sad. Steve did the only sensible thing he could think of.

He took off his raincoat and draped it around her shoulders.

"What are you doing?" she asked in disbelief as Steve bent over to salvage the yolky mess on the pavement.

"Wait a minute, please?" he replied after straightening up. His smile was making her legs get wobbly. "I'll be right back." Clare watched Steve take the crumpled grocery bag to a nearby trash can. It looked like he was heading into the store but then he stopped and stood in the downpour getting soaking wet himself. Clare couldn't help but smile. She was no longer getting wet, so

Clare R.

she stood watching, hoping that he had finally recognized her.

It was the one time in Steve's life he could truly say he had an epiphany. In the short time it took Steve to walk across the parking lot with this woman's carton of gooey, broken eggs, the rain seemed to increase and all of a sudden he remembered the fortune from several weeks before that came with his takeout— *Even on the rainiest of days, love and happiness will find you.*

Steve felt his hands start to shake and each heartbeat felt more powerful than the last. Every rain drop that hit the top of his head felt like an explosion, as if the rain itself was trying to help him realize that Clare was standing right behind him.

Eggs can wait, he thought. Steve turned and ran back across the parking lot. Rain was pelting his face but he didn't care. Clare was still standing there, now smiling and laughing, and she spread her arms wide when he neared. But Steve didn't slow down much. In one swift motion, he wrapped her in a hug and picked her right off the ground, which caused her to laugh even more.

"Took you long enough, you nerd!" she exclaimed.

"I know, I'm sorry!" he replied, as their foreheads touched. Clare didn't care though, and just kept beaming. After two months of promising himself that he wouldn't squander a chance, Steve gently planted a kiss on her lips. The sound of the rain faded away and Clare giggled. She wrapped her arms around his neck and hugged Steve as tightly as she could. Then after what felt like several minutes, he set her down.

"All right, wait a minute again. Please?" Steve said. Clare nodded. She was dizzy and deliriously happy. Her lips were tingling so much from their romantic kiss that Clare wondered if there was actually electricity humming across them. When Steve disappeared into the store, Clare waved her arms in excitement and even jumped up and down a few times. Then she climbed back in the car to get the heat going.

A few minutes later, Steve was back and knocking softly on the passenger window. Clare broke out laughing because she was singing along to an awesome love song that was playing on the radio. She gladly rolled down the window and he held up a bag with a fresh carton of eggs inside as well as two cups of steaming hot tea from the cafe inside the grocery store.

"Will you come in for a second?" she asked.

"I hope you don't mind...I got you some more eggs," Steve started. His heart was still racing and it was difficult to form words.

"I don't mind at all, but you didn't have to," Clare said. Steve shrugged and handed her a cup of tea. He was pleased to see that she was still beaming.

"I wanted to," he continued. "You uh... You looked kinda bummed." Clare laughed.

"You have no idea," she replied, glancing over at him again. "Thank you so much." Clare could tell he was a bit nervous because he kept averting his eyes to look down at the carton of eggs. She hoped he would say something else because she wanted to keep talking.

"You're welcome," Steve said. Then he grinned and reached over with his free hand. "I'm Steve, by the way."

"Clare," she said. It was difficult to keep a stoic expression on her face because Clare felt like she was bouncing in her seat. Then she tilted her head. "I knew you looked familiar. We've met before!" Steve laughed.

Only two awesome people would take the time to do this, he mused.

"Yeah, yeah. You're right! We met at the airport a couple

Clare R.

months ago... When our flights got delayed," he said.

"Yep! You really made me laugh that day with that, uh...dirty joke and you bought me a cup of tea," Clare said. "You know, Steve, I haven't looked at polka dot socks the same since." Steve laughed again.

"I think we should toast to airport delays," he said. Clare beamed and they gladly bumped their foam cups together.

"What are you doing here, Steve?" she asked.

"I'm here for a conference," he replied. "What are you doing here?"

"I live here!" she said. "What kind of conference? Some engineering thing?" His cheeks reddened slightly.

"Actually, no. It's, um, a cooking one," he said. "I've been in these cooking classes for the last six weeks."

"Stevie! That's awesome!" Clare exclaimed. "Wait, you like to cook? You never mentioned that?"

"Yeah, I love cooking," Steve said. "Hopefully sometime I could make you something."

"Oh my God. That would be amazing," she said. But even before the words left her mouth, her mind was spinning. Opening her own bakery suddenly didn't seem so daunting. Especially, if Steve loved cooking.

Maybe he would be interested, Clare thought. But before she could ask him more about cooking, Steve continued.

"I can't believe this Clare. I haven't stopped thinking about you. You look amazing!" Steve said, and Clare's cheeks reddened because she knew she looked terrible.

"Thanks," she replied. "I haven't stopped thinking about you, either," she replied, and they both fell silent while taking drinks from their tea.

"I tried to find you," Steve said.

"Yeah?" replied Clare. He turned in the passenger seat and nodded.

"Yeah, I searched through a bunch of social media sites but I didn't know your last name," Steve confessed.

"Well I don't know if you would have found me anyway. "I got rid of my one account a few years ago," she laughed. "But my last name is Reilly. What's yours?"

"Brooks. It's very nice to meet you, Clare Reilly," he said. "You should totally take this by the way. I'm not forgetting this again." Steve dug a pen and paper from his jacket pocket and wrote down his number for her.

"Yeah! Perfect!" Clare said. "Here's mine." Clare tore a sheet from the notepad that was shoved between her seat and the console.

"Thanks," Steve said. His hand was shaking as he reread the phone number enough times to memorize it. When he finally looked up at Clare, her eyes had a delightfully seductive look about them and she still had that notepad in her hands.

"What's up?" he asked.

"Well, I thought about you a *few* times while I was working and this..." Clare said, "...is my list of questions for you." She flipped the notepad open and ran her finger down the page looking for a suitable first question.

"Oh my goodness," Steve said.

"Would you care if I asked you some? Or do you have to go soon?" she asked.

"Definitely not busy right now. I would love to hear your questions," Steve replied. The rain continued to pelt her car but neither of them paid any attention.

Clare R.

"Did you tell anyone about the dirty joke?" Clare asked. "Like your mom?"

"No," Steve replied while shaking his head. "I don't, uh, typically share dirty jokes with my mom." Clare started laughing again.

"Did you tell Amy?" Steve asked. Clare nodded. At the mention of her best friend's name, all of the other awkward things she had said to Clare during recent conversations came to mind.

"Yeah, I told her," Clare said. Steve found it very amusing watching her try to maintain her composure.

"Why all the laughing?" Steve asked.

"I hope you don't mind, but I'm not going to say right now. You'll understand when you get to know Amy," Clare said, and the red tinge in her cheeks spread even more. Steve was happy to know that Clare wanted him to meet her friends, and by the look on her face, he was sure that Amy was probably quite a handful.

"All right then," Clare said. She straightened in her seat and put on a serious expression. "Don't laugh at me." Her pursed lips quickly faded into a grin when Steve mocked her by putting on a serious expression as well.

"OK, go ahead," Steve said.

"Mmk, something simple. Do you prefer dogs or cats?" Clare asked. Steve mulled over the pros and cons for a bit before answering.

"I like both, but I would definitely pick dogs over cats," Steve replied. "Do you like dogs?" Clare nodded vigorously.

"Love them," she said. "What about... Favorite food?" Steve laughed.

"Right now it's pancakes," he said. "I eat a lot of pancakes!" Clare had no idea what to say.

Please don't be bullshitting me, Stevie Brooks. Because this could possibly be the best night ever, Clare thought. After a few more entry level questions, she shifted in her seat again.

"How about we continue with... First kiss?" Clare said. Before he could stop himself, Steve said the first thing that came to mind.

"I think you're making me melt." Clare's laughter filled the car.

"Stevie!" she exclaimed.

"Does that mean first real kiss or first illegitimate kiss?" he continued. Clare loved how technical and serious Steve was taking her game and she played right along.

"To be fair with this, we should cover all aspects...so both," she replied.

"Well the first, illegitimate kiss would have been in kindergarten," Steve said. Clare feigned a look of surprise.

"Wow, somebody started young," she replied, prodding his shoulder.

"No, no, no. I was cornered. Coerced against my will," Steve exclaimed. "I was terrified of girls at the time. You remember how it was." Clare moved her head up and down in agreement. The rambunctious sounds of kids chanting about cooties suddenly played in her head.

"Where did it happen?" Clare asked. Although the juicy details were nice, she didn't really care who he had kissed or where it had happened. This was more about seeing how comfortable Steve really was with her.

"You are enjoying this so much, aren't you?" Steve replied. Clare's eyes were dancing with delight. "If you must know, I was cornered in the cubby room." When Steve pretended to put on a

Clare R.

stressed expression, Clare burst out laughing yet again.

"OK, OK," Clare said. "Real one?"

"The first real one would have been after a basketball game in middle school," Steve replied. "I hope you know I'm going to come up with my own list, too."

"I hope you do," she replied. "All right, this is a little more straightforward. What's your family like? You mentioned your mom earlier," Clare said.

"Um, it's small, but they are pretty cool, I guess. My mom's name is Patty. She was a nurse for a long time, but a few years ago she took over more of an administrative position at the hospital back home. She got a new dog last year, too. His name is Toby. I bet you'd like him."

"I bet. What kinda dog is he?" Clare asked.

"A German shepherd with a basset hound. Kind of a different mix," Steve replied.

"Aren't those two dogs really different in size?" she asked.

"Yeah, either way you swing it, it's goofy," Steve said, and he watched Clare shake with silent laughter. "Anyway, my brother, Matt, is an engineer like me. He's married now and he and his wife just had their first kid last year, which is pretty cool. I suppose that means I get to be the cool uncle now. His wife's name is Katy, by the way." Clare smiled as well, even though she would never know what it would feel like to have a true niece or nephew since she had no siblings. When Steve gave a sheepish grin and turned his attention back to the carton of eggs, Clare realized that he hadn't mentioned his father.

"What about your dad?" she asked. Steve swallowed and his throat felt hard. His stomach started to swim as well. Steve thought that the brief talks with Gus and imaginary Clare had helped him, but the rotten feeling still presented itself. Steve looked up at Clare but didn't say anything.

How am I supposed to answer that? Steve wondered.

"My dad passed away a couple years ago," Steve said slowly. "Actually it was two years ago yesterday." The lump in his throat felt like it was growing and he had no desire to breakdown in front of Clare. But then she put a hand on his arm.

"Steve, I'm so sorry," she whispered, and before she could stop herself, the next words flew from her mouth. "Can I ask what happened?" Steve's expression didn't change much and he didn't seem mad, but that didn't stop her from feeling awful about asking. Clare didn't want to make him upset.

"My God, I'm sorry," she said with a nervous laugh. "I shouldn't pry." Clare reached for the cup of tea wishing she hadn't asked because the longer Steve went without saying anything the more nervous she became. But then Steve shook his head and nudged her knee with his hand.

"No, you're fine," Steve said, trying to gain his composure. "It's just... I haven't talked to people about it much..."

"If you don't want to, that's fine," Clare said. "The last thing I want to do is ruin this..." Her own doubts started percolating in the depths of her brain.

"You didn't ruin anything," Steve said, and then he started. Clare felt her heartbeat start to race. "My dad and uncle ran a farm together up north, where I'm from. They have farmed for as long as I can remember. It was so beautiful up there and I worked there for a long time. But my dad was also a volunteer fireman. My hometown isn't that big so we didn't have a full-time crew of firefighters. He always used to tell my brother and I that he felt obligated to help people..." Clare felt her chest tighten when Steve

Clare R.

paused. He nodded his head trying to stop himself from getting too choked up. Then he continued.

"We'd been at the farm all day snowshoeing and practice shooting. We even cooked out for lunch. It was such a fun day. Then when we got home, he got a call. My dad had been called before, so we didn't think much of it. My brother and I just hung out at home, waiting for mom to get off work. But that night he never came home." Steve had to stop again because he could feel his insides aching. More painful memories flashed in his mind... *Blue and red lights flashing outside the house. His distraught mother waking them up...*

"Apparently, it was a really bad fire. I think they said it was because a Christmas tree caught on fire and because of all the snow on the roof, the house had collapsed while he was still inside." A silence filled the car like a heavy cloud of smoke. Tears welled in her eyes as she thought about the sadness Steve had to endure. When she ran a hand along his back, the tenseness in his body made her think of a coiled mousetrap.

I know it still eats at you, she thought. *But I wanna be there for you...*

"Hey," she said, and ruffled his hair playfully. He looked at her with a wry smile and she promptly kissed his cheek. When she pulled away, Clare found herself contemplating whether or not she should tell him about her own past. Then, as if he was reading her mind, Steve broke the silence with a deep winded sigh.

"So, what about your family?" he asked. "Hopefully it's a little less glum." For some reason, Clare laughed. Maybe it was because of the half-smile on Steve's face or the fact that she had actually found someone she could relate to. Steve tilted his head, wondering what was so funny, but as he continued to stare at the love of his life, the humor faded from Clare's face while she picked at the Styrofoam cup with her fingernail.

"No, actually. It's pretty glum, too, Stevie," she said. Her hands were starting to move erratically as her nerves kicked in. "Good word choice by the way. Glum... Great way to describe it."

"Clare," he mumbled. Steve had no intention of upsetting her or prying at uncomfortable memories. When she looked at him, the half-smile on her face quavered. He reached out his hand and Clare took it gratefully.

"I don't have anyone, Stevie," she said. "It's just me. The girl you met at the airport. I mean, I've got Amy. But I don't have any family. No parents. No siblings. My mom left my dad and me when I was only a couple years old." She paused and stared at the rain drops rolling down the windshield. "My dad hated nights like these because she left one night when it was pouring like this. I don't think he ever really recovered and after she left it made things really hard for him." When Clare grew silent, Steve squeezed her hand affectionately.

"We were really poor," she continued. "But my dad and I made the best of it and he took good care of me. Then, about a month after I graduated high school, my dad got really sick. I guess he'd been sick for a long time, but he just toughed it out and never told me. I watched him die right in front of me..." Clare's face scrunched up and she looked away not wanting to cry in front of him again.

"I'm so sorry," he said.

"Thanks," she said, wiping away a few of the tears. "What makes it even worse was that my mom actually showed up out of nowhere this Thanksgiving."

"Wait! What? You're kidding?" Steve exclaimed.

Clare R.

"Nope. I'm not. It was awful. She showed up after we finished eating and she was a wreck. It was kind of pathetic," Clare said. More tears rolled down her cheeks and a silence filled the car that was only disrupted by the pouring rain.

Oh God. Why did I tell him that? she thought.

"I'm really sorry, Stevie. This got a lot more emotional than I expected," Clare finally said. "I'm sorry I brought all this up."

"Are you kidding me? Don't worry about it," he replied. She looked away but Steve continued to stare. Clare was more amazing than he could have ever imagined and he certainly didn't care about the tears when he leaned in to plant a soft kiss on her cheek. It wasn't long before their lips were touching again.

...I belong with you, you belong with me, you're my sweetheart... They stopped kissing and listened to the song playing on the radio.

"You like this song?" she asked.

"Yeah, you?" he replied. When she moved her head up and down, her nose brushed against his cheek and the resulting tingles made them both giggle.

"You know Clare, if we were somewhere we could dance right now, I would totally woo you with my awesome dance moves."

"Awesome dance moves, huh?" she said.

"Yeah. Totally kick-ass!" he said. Clare let out a choked up sob and smiled gratefully at Steve. Then he did something that took her completely by surprise. She could remember talking and joking with Amy about guys who tried to serenade girls with a pretty song. But when Steve started to hum in her ear, Clare's whole body shivered in the most pleasant way. His voice resonated inside her and it left her feeling cared for and safe. The gloom from a rather depressing conversation no longer hung over them.

Instead there was a warmth and a strong sense of understanding.

"Do you think it would be a stretch to ask you out for another cup of tea?" Steve asked.

"I would love to, but I should probably take these groceries home first," Clare said.

"Yeah, sure. I mean, it doesn't have to be right now," he said. Steve hoped he didn't sound pushy. "If you have other plans—"

"No, I want to. That sounds great," she said, cutting him off slightly. "Actually, wait, what time is it? We've been here a while."

"Almost seven," Steve said. "Why? What's up?"

"I'm supposed to meet Amy for dinner tonight at seven thirty," Clare explained.

"Oh, well you should probably get going then. I don't want to keep you. I mean, yeah I do. I would love to keep talking, but..." Steve said. Clare giggled and moved her head from side to side.

"No... You should come. I don't want to stop hanging out either," Clare said. "My friends could meet you! It would be awesome."

"That would be sweet," Steve said.

"Well, would you want to just come with me?" Clare asked. "Then we could drive over there together."

"Yeah, that would be great," he said. "To go with you, I mean."

"Yeah?" she said.

"Yeah," Steve said again. In one quick motion they both turned to put their seat belts on and then Clare started the car.

"Oh, hey. There's something I wanted to tell you," Steve said.

"What's that?" she asked.

Clare R.

"That raincoat looks great on you," he said. Clare felt herself blush in the darkness as she maneuvered the car into the street.

"Thanks. It's a little big on me," she replied.

"That's all right," he said. "You should keep it." Her heart was racing and she didn't stop smiling the entire way back to her house, because finally Steve was here, making her happy again.

Chapter 20

After a quick pit stop at Clare's house to change into dry clothes and put away groceries, the pair zoomed back downtown to meet Amy at the bar.

"Are you sure this is OK?" Clare asked, after pulling into a parking spot. "I mean, they have really good food here." Steve responded by continuing to stare. When they got to Clare's house, she had showered and put on dry clothes before they left for dinner. The outfit she chose was simple and beautiful; jeans and a colorful flannel shirt. Locks of her reddish-brown hair hung loosely on her shoulders and a thin necklace could be seen, glinting around her neck.

"You OK, Stevie?" she asked. Her finger was pressed gently under his chin and he loved it. He was in a daze, trying to commit the day to memory.

"You are so beautiful," he managed. The butterflies that erupted in her stomach made her feel lightheaded.

"Stevie," she whispered. He grinned and kissed her cheek.

"Of course it's OK. I'm just glad to be spending time with you," he answered.

"Me too," she said. Clare felt like she was getting to experience something she'd missed out on for so many years. Their blos-

Clare R.

soming relationship was cheesy and romantic like a corny movie, but she loved it because being with Steve was right. She took his outstretched hand and led him to the door.

~~~

Jenny's night was moving slower than molasses and she was fairly certain it was because of a concert up in the city. Her clientele had thinned out significantly which was fine, but it would have been nice to have a few more patrons to keep things moving along. She was also anxious to see her two girlfriends who both had been M.I.A for a while. Just when she reached under the counter for her phone, Jenny caught sight of Clare walking in the door. Her eyes widened when she saw she wasn't alone.

"Well, well, well. If it isn't Clare Reilly and something tells me that this must be...Steve," Jenny said.

"Um, did the huge smile on my face give it away?" Clare asked. Jenny laughed and turned to Steve.

"I'm Jenny. It's nice to meet you," she said.

"Steve," he replied, and they shook hands.

"You're gonna have to fill me in on what happened," Jenny said.

"Oh, I will," Clare replied before Jenny left to get their drinks. But the surprises weren't over yet. Neither Clare nor Amy had talked to each other that day, so when Amy walked in with Jamie by her side, Clare just about lost it. She stood up excitedly and frantically waved them over.

"Do you mind?" Clare asked, looking at Steve as the other pair wandered through the tables towards them.

"No way," Steve replied. He got up and pushed another table

up next to theirs so there was room for more people. Amy pointed at Steve before they all sat down.

"Who the hell is this?" Amy asked. Clare exchanged glances with Steve and they both smiled.

"It's nice to meet you, Amy, I'm Steve," he said holding out a hand. The look of surprise on Amy's face was indescribable and they both wondered if the gum in her mouth was going to fall on the floor.

"Wait! What is going on?" Amy said. "Steve, Steve. Like, Steve from the airport, Steve?"

"Yeah, Steve from the airport," Clare said.

"How much did you tell her about me?" Steve asked. Clare shrugged.

"Clare wouldn't quit talking about you," Amy said. "She was insufferable. At one point, I tried to get her to go on a date but she bailed because she's so into you."

"Oh my God," Clare said, putting a hand on her face.

Leave it to Amy to try and embarrass me, Clare thought, and then she jumped when Steve poked her side.

"Really?" Steve said. "With who?"

"Me," Jamie said, raising a timid hand. "Amy tried to set us up but I've actually been into Amy for a long time, so...it was sorta bound to crash and burn anyway. I'm Jamie."

"Nice to meet you, too," he replied. With the introductions behind them, the expanding group of friends took their seats and within seconds, animated conversation blossomed between everyone at the table. After ordering some appetizers and more drinks, Jenny came to join them.

They were talking about nerdy action movies when the strange, twist of fate occurred. Jamie was going on a rant about

Clare R.

how awesome the *Marvel* universe was, and Clare and Steve were having thumb wars under the table while they pretended to listen.

"Oh, my friend Suzy had her baby!" Amy interjected. "I knew there was something else I wanted to tell you two."

"That's awesome," Jenny said.

"What did she name her?" Clare asked.

"They named her Anna," Amy replied. "Suzy said she's adorable. You know, those cute, round, baby cheeks and big round eyes..." At the mention of the baby's name, the gears in Steve's head started clunking and he straightened in his seat. Clare tilted her head because he'd stopped playing thumb war.

"Hey, are you OK?" Clare asked.

"Yeah, I'm good," Steve said. Everyone's eyes were locked on Steve like they thought he might keel over, and it didn't help that there was a strange expression on his face. His gaze shifted to Amy. "You said your friend Suzy had a baby named Anna?"

"Yeah," Amy said. "Why?" Clare was also curious about Steve's sudden interest.

"Yeah, why?" Clare asked. Steve didn't answer and instead gave her the quickest wink, which she found oddly reassuring.

"Is her husband's name, John, by any chance?" Steve asked.

"Yeah. It is! What the hell?" Amy said. "How did you know that? You're not a spy or something are you? I swear I pay my taxes." Everyone at the table laughed hysterically at Amy's startled expression.

"No," he said. "That's agent Clare over here."

"What's going on?" Clare asked when she got control of her laughter. She kept exchanging glances between Amy and Steve hoping for an answer, but Amy just shrugged her shoulders and waited for Steve to continue.

"I grew up with John. I went to school with John. He was my neighbor," Steve began. He turned to Clare. "I just saw their new baby when I was up visiting my mom last month... Right after we met."

"Wait... Wait!" Amy said, holding up her phone. "I just talked to Suzy before coming over here. She was about to tell me about one of John's friends who was having girl troubles or something." Clare was shaking her head in amazement.

"What did she say?" Steve asked. Amy shrugged again.

"I don't know," she said, raising her eyebrows. "Something about Anna burping, or farting, or pooping. I don't know. Suzy had to go and said she would call me back."

"Stevie? What is going on?" Clare exclaimed. When Steve turned to stare at her, the smile on his face made her feel like she was melting.

My goodness, I love the way you look at me, she thought.

"I saw John and Suzy when I was up visiting my mom," he repeated. "Suzy left to take the baby inside but John and I kept talking. He asked me if I was seeing anyone and I said 'no' but I had met this really amazing lady the week before. When I told him I wasn't sure if I would get to see her again, John told me that Suzy had lots of friends from her time at college. I guess John mentioned our conversation to Suzy." Clare was grinning wildly and Amy looked absolutely awestruck.

"We went to college with Suzy," Clare said, motioning between her, Amy, and Jenny.

"Yeah, Suzy and I did a lot of sports stuff together in high school," Jenny said. "And even though we went to different schools, we ended up going to the same college."

"And Clare and I met Jenny and Suzy in the back of this re-

Clare R.

ally lame biology course," Amy finished.

"It was not lame!" Clare exclaimed. "Our professor talked like *Kermit the Frog*." Everyone laughed again.

"Well that's pretty, damn sweet. That will make this next phone call a lot more interesting," Amy said. She still sounded shocked. "I think we need more drinks." Clare and Steve both nodded and Jenny grinned as she left for the bar.

"Can you believe this?" Steve asked Jamie. Amy's new beau had been shaking his head sideways for the past five minutes straight.

"No. This is some goofy shit. I'm just the boring local guy from Pittsburgh," Jamie said.

When there were only crumbs and empty dipping sauce containers left of their appetizers, Steve excused himself to use the restroom. Clare had a dreamy look on her face as she watched him walk away, and then her eyes fell once again upon the pool table. A wonderful idea came to mind and she turned to Jenny, who was still sitting and chatting with them.

"Hey," she said. "Do you have any change?"

"Yeah, sure," Jenny said. Her hand moved to the cloth pouch that hung from her waist. "Why?" Clare tilted her head toward the pool table.

"It's pool time, I think," Clare said. Jenny chuckled and gave Clare enough quarters for a couple games. However, when Clare moved to get up, Jenny stopped her. There was a mischievous look on her face and Clare knew she was going to say something funny.

"Clare," she said. "I don't think this one needs any ice cubes." Clare shook her head in agreement and let her smile widen. The pool area was vacant when she started pushing quarters into the coin slot. A clatter arose as the balls fell onto the track and rolled into the opening at the end of the table. Clare grabbed the triangle off the wall, set it on the table, and started setting up for a game.

When Steve came out of the bathroom he'd been anxious to get back to their table, but the sight of Clare bending over the table was enough to stop him in his tracks. Her beautiful hair was dangling in front of her face as she filled the triangle and her head was moving about as she hummed to the tune playing on the radio.

He shook his head and smiled. Steve loved everything about her and he loved playing pool. In just a few strides he was at her side, and when he put his hand on her waist, Clare looked up in surprise. Steve gently pulled her close to give her a kiss. Amy's voice could be heard as she gave them a sarcastic hoot and they broke apart, laughing.

"I don't know if you like to play," Clare said. "But I thought it might be kind of fun."

"I love playing pool," Steve replied, grabbing a couple of sticks off the wall. "It's been awhile though." Clare beamed and took a stick that he handed her.

"Hopefully you're not too rusty," she said. "I don't want to embarrass you if I kick your ass."

"Uh, huh. Do you play a lot then?" Steve asked. A funny noise escaped her lips.

"No," she said, but her break was perfect and several balls found their places in pockets around the table. Several shots later, Clare sunk the eight ball in the corner pocket and she beamed at Steve with a very triumphant expression.

"That was a nice shot," Steve said, raising his glass to his lips. But before he could take a drink, Clare took the glass from his hand.

"I win," she said sweetly. Even as Clare took a drink, she

Clare R.

continued to smile and he could feel his face reddening.

"You're amazing," he said.

The second game reached another level of intensity. Jamie and Amy decided to team up against Clare and Steve and the battle began. Jenny continued to hang out with them as well and she did her best to cheer for each team equally.

While they waited for their turn, Clare leaned gently into Steve and grinned happily when he kissed the top of her head. It was a simple and endearing gesture that she loved very much. They watched as Amy put a striped ball in a side pocket. Her next shot, however, was a miss.

"Go on, Clare," Steve said. He poked her playfully in her side. "We need this." Clare winked at Steve, lined up her stick with the cue ball, and expertly sunk a ball in the side pocket. Her confidence exploded when she heard Steve hoot and holler for her.

Patience is key though, she mused, and began surveying the table for the next shot. Steve continued to watch but his thoughts drifted elsewhere. After being gone and alone for so long, he was astonished by the fact his life suddenly felt normal again. It was as if the universe had finally pressed play again.

Never could he remember feeling so grateful for someone. She had let him into her life and now he was surrounded by new friends. Jenny was busy talking to Clare about her next shot and Jamie had moved off to make a phone call and Amy was standing a short distance away, fiddling with a pack of gum.

It was a true double take and his mind was reeling as he watched Amy continue to fiddle with the pack of gum. Amy was a bit startled when she noticed Steve staring at her, shaking his head.

"What?" Amy said loudly. "You want a piece?"

"No thanks," he said.

"Then why are you staring at me?" she asked.

"We've met before," Steve said. "Well, sort of..." Jenny was now paying attention, and Jamie had got off the phone as well. Amy shook her head stubbornly.

"No, we haven't," she replied. "Believe me, if we'd met already, I'd remember. You and Clare would have been together a lot sooner, watching your medieval shows or whatever!" Clare chortled at the comment and came to stand next to Steve. He grinned at her and then looked back to Amy.

"I was in the gas station traveling for Thanksgiving. I held the door for you because you were fiddling with your pack of gum," Steve said. The pack of gum fell to the floor.

"Say what?" Amy replied, but she knew it was true. Recollections of that day flashed in her head and she could clearly remember a quick thanks to some guy who had held the door for her. Steve was startled to his senses by a hard prod in his side. Clare was looking at him with an even more astonished expression.

"Are you kidding me right now?" she asked. Steve smiled and shook his head sideways again.

"Stevie!" Clare exclaimed. "I was there! I was in Amy's car!" The notion of Clare being that close to him hit Steve like a freight train. "Amy and I were going back to her parents' for Thanksgiving."

"Seriously?" he asked. Clare nodded and ran her hands through her hair. "Oh my goodness! What is going on?" Steve reached out and grabbed her shirt, pulling her into a huge hug. Jenny, Jamie, and Amy all shared shocked expressions.

"And I thought last night was weird," Amy said.

"Tell me about it. I had two dates in one night," Jamie said. Amy swatted him playfully in the stomach.

Clare R.

"Well, I'm getting more drinks... For everybody," Jenny said, and wandered back to the bar.

"I can't believe you were right there," Clare said quietly.

"Me either," Steve said. They embraced once more and then Clare let out a resounding groan.

"All right lovebirds," Amy said. The gum in her mouth was smacking loudly and she was holding her pool stick at arm's length threatening to poke Clare again. "Let's get back to the game." They both laughed and she turned to give Steve another quick kiss before returning to the table.

It didn't take long for Clare to find her groove again and with an extreme sense of patience and finesse, Clare systematically buried their last three balls in pockets around the table.

"Unbelievable," Amy exclaimed and turned to Jamie. "Seriously. What the hell! All she does is read, think about Steve, and watch that medieval hub bub on TV. I never knew she was this good." Jamie just laughed. Steve spread his arms wide and wrapped Clare in a celebratory, game winning hug.

"Do you play all the time, or what?" Steve asked. "Because we should definitely play again." Clare just kept laughing.

"I would love to!" Clare said. "I have no idea where that came from, Stevie. I don't ever remember playing that good."

"Well, it was awesome to watch!" Steve said. Jenny congratulated them all and then bid her farewell.

"It was great to meet you guys. I should get back to work," Jenny said. Steve and Jamie both nodded and shook her hand. Then she looked at Clare.

"Next time, you're going to take me on," Jenny said, looking at Clare.

"Pshhh, bring it on," Clare said, embracing her newfound

confidence. Jenny laughed and gave them all one last goodbye before returning to the bar. Not long after, the two couples decided to call it a night.

Frigid, winter air engulfed the new group of friends as they stepped out of the restaurant that evening. The rain stopped, and to their delight, delicate snowflakes were falling down all around them. They exchanged goodbyes and then Clare leaned into Steve's shoulder as she watched Amy and Jamie walk off across the parking lot hand in hand. It made her happy to know that her best friend had found a good guy.

Then she turned to stare at her own good guy and Steve's green eyes looked back at her, full of love and compassion. There were no words exchanged when they leaned in to kiss each other.

"You ready for that movie?" Steve asked. Clare moved her head up and down. It had been a long time since she'd seen a movie with someone and she was very much looking forward to curling up on the couch with Steve.

"Awesome!" he said. Steve's footsteps patted against the pavement as he walked off toward the car. It only took a moment, however, for Steve to notice that Clare wasn't at his side, and he turned to look back for her. Clare was still standing under the awning with a grin on her face. All Steve did was smile and give her a subtle nod. Then he turned and kept walking.

Without any further hesitation, Clare slung the strap of her purse across her body and started running. Each time her foot hit the pavement, it was as if one bad memory dropped away, never to bother her again. It was exhilarating in a way Clare never knew to be possible and at the last second, she jumped. She was free.

Their laughter rang out across the parking lot when Clare landed squarely on his back and wrapped her arms securely around

Clare R.

his neck. Steve caught her legs and they finished making their way to the car.

"You know, Clare. I'm still kind of hungry. All that excitement from pool worked up an appetite," Steve said.

"Hmm," she replied. "I could think of something we could make."

"Is it a breakfast food?" he asked.

"Yes," she said.

"Pancakes? Scrambled eggs? Bacon?" Steve offered. Clare grinned and buried her face in the warmth of his hoodie.

"Yes," she laughed.

"Good," he replied. "Would you care if we stopped by the hotel real quick? I have a couple books that you would like to see."

"A couple? What's the other one?" she asked. They had reached the car and Steve let her slide off his back.

"It's this cool cookbook I picked up. It's about baking cupcakes... Like an anthology of recipes," he explained. "Maybe we could bake some this weekend. I haven't had one in forever." Clare was awestruck.

"You've got to be kidding me," she said.

"No, why?" he asked. Her dreams of opening a bakery filled her up like delicious crème pastry.

"I wanna open a bakery," she finally blurted out. There was no scoff or a look of derision from Steve, just another wide grin.

"Well, let's go get that cookbook then," he said. Clare beamed at Steve and they got in the car. "Oh, by the way. Merry Christmas, Clare."

"Merry Christmas, Stevie."

Epilogue

"Are you two sure you can handle being alone for an hour," Amy said. Her dark hair was pulled back in an official looking ponytail and as usual, the gum was smacking loudly in her mouth. She had a meeting with her old marketing team to make up posters for the new bakery. Her tone was serious yet playful as she stared intently at the two individuals in front of her.

Clare and Steve were standing side by side in front of their beautiful new woodblock countertop. Cooling in front of them were three dozen, freshly baked cupcakes, several stainless steel bowls filled with rich, creamy frosting, and an assortment of food coloring containers for adding color to the frosting. On one side of the kitchen was a floor to ceiling bookshelf that was chock full of spiral bound notebooks, extra sheets of paper that were clamped together with binder clips, and stacks of dessert cookbooks. On the other side of the kitchen rested brand new stainless steel appliances, which were gleaming in the morning sunlight.

They both nodded, almost obediently, even though it was painfully obvious the pair was holding in a great deal of laughter. Clare's pursed lips were curving into a smile as she saluted her best friend. Amy nearly lost it herself and turned away shaking her head.

Clare R.

"I'll see you guys later," she replied. A moment later they heard the jingle of the front door opening and closing and then the kitchen was a zoo of raucous laughter.

"Clare, you saluted her," Steve said.

"Well, I mean, she was acting very boss-like," she said with a shrug. "It seemed like the right thing to do." Steve shook his head and laughed even more. He pulled gently on her apron and she gladly stepped forward. Clare's hair was twisted in a simple bun behind her head while a few of her bangs dangled in front of her face. When her brilliant blue eyes locked onto Steve's, he could feel his legs getting rubbery just like they had the day they met.

"You ready to frost our first batch of cupcakes?" he asked. Clare nodded eagerly and after a wonderful embrace, she turned to the counter with flushed cheeks. She placed a few drops of red and blue food coloring into a bowl. Steve grinned as he watched the white frosting change into a pale purple hue.

"What do you think?" Clare asked.

"Looks good to me," he said.

"Me too," she replied. With years of practice behind her, Clare expertly frosted the first cupcake of their bakery business.

"Sprinkles or no sprinkles?" Steve asked.

"Definitely need some sprinkles," she said. Steve gently tapped the jar in his hand and a tiny waterfall of colorful sugar fell onto the frosting. He was thrilled. It literally was the icing on the cake to a whole new life and it was amazing. Yet, when he looked up to see Clare's reaction, her head was tilted with a sheepish grin.

"Is that OK? Are you OK?" he asked.

"Yeah." Her response was quiet and soft and she leaned into

his shoulder. "I just wish my dad could see this. I know he secretly loved when I brought sweets home from Amy's."

"Well you know, we could eat one for him," Steve said, after kissing the top of her head. Clare giggled and picked up another cupcake. After smearing it with frosting, Clare held it up to Steve's mouth.

"What do you think?" he asked.

"Dad would approve," she replied with a mouthful of cupcake. Steve took the opportunity to change tactics and picked up one of the bags of frosting that they had set up earlier that morning. It already had a special extruding tip attached.

"Have you ever used one of those?" Clare asked.

"Nope," he replied with a grin. Clare put a hand on her hip, waiting to see what happened. Then she realized that it was time to tell him something important and couldn't resist the opportunity to phrase it a certain way.

Steve lowered the tip of the frosting bag to just above the cupcake, and began applying pressure to the bag. He felt Clare lean in close to him and the smell of her wonderful perfume tickled his nose in the most pleasing way.

"Stevie," Clare said softly. Her mischievous grin was unmistakable.

"Hmm," he said.

"There's something I've been meaning to tell you," she said.

"Hmm," he replied.

"I've got a bun in the oven," she whispered. Clare couldn't remember a time when she laughed so hard. Steve's reaction was priceless. His cheeks flushed and he squeezed the bag way too hard, which caused frosting to splooge all over the cupcake. Clare

Clare R.

was doubled over, nearly in tears, and Steve pressed a hand to his face in embarrassment.

"Aw, Stevie," she said. "That looks so good." Her voice was ripe with sarcasm as she leaned closer to mock his frosting job. Steve smeared a fingerful of frosting across her cheek. Clare knew she'd asked for it and simply kept laughing. There was nowhere she would have rather been and she was with the one person she wanted to be with forever. Steve knew it too, and once again he pulled gently on her apron. Her words repeated themselves in his head.

"You know, Clare, you're the funniest person I know," he said.

"Really? Thanks," she replied.

"You joke a lot," he said, and she nodded.

"A lot," she repeated, and Steve started laughing.

"Was that a joke?" he asked. She opened her mouth to speak but nothing came out. She just laughed and shook her head sideways. Steve beamed and picked her up off the ground.

"I love you, Clare," he said. When she put her hands around his neck, he could feel the cool touch of the ring on her finger along with the soothing warmth of her skin.

"I love you, too, Stevie," she replied. Then she bit her lip and leaned back slightly.

"What?" Steve asked. Clare grabbed the overly frosted cupcake and pressed it right into Steve's face.

The End

About The Author

R.K. Blessing

R.K. Blessing loves the outdoors. He also enjoys writing, cooking, drawing, and binging on a good television series when one presents itself. He lives and works near Columbus, Ohio.

CPSIA information can be obtained at www.ICGtesting.com
Printed in the USA
LVOW08s2340131114

413608LV00003B/126/P